DARK LIAISON
A CHRISTIAN SUSPENSE NOVEL

Other Books by D.I. Telbat

Dark Edge, COIL Prequel (free)
The COIL Series, Two – Five
~

Distant Boundary, Legacy Prequel (free)
COIL Legacy Series, One – Three
The COIL Legacy Collection
~

The ELM Series, One – Four
~

The RESOLUTION Series, One – Four
Resolution Collection: Books 1 - 4
~

The STEADFAST Series, One – Six
Steadfast Collection: Books 1 - 6
~

Last Dawn Series, One – Four
~

The Leeward Set
Fury in the Storm
Tears in the Wind
Leeward Collection: Books 1 & 2
~

Standalones
Arabian Variable
Called To Gobi
God's Colonel
Soldier of Hope
~

Short Story Collections

DARK LIAISON

A CHRISTIAN SUSPENSE NOVEL

Book One in The COIL Series

D.I. Telbat

In Season Publications

USA

Publisher's Note: This is a work of fiction. Names, characters, places, and incidents are a product of the author's imagination. Locales and public names are sometimes used for atmospheric purposes. Any resemblance to actual people, living or dead, or to businesses, companies, events, institutions, or locales is completely coincidental.

Book Layout ©2013 BookDesignTemplates.com
Cover Design by Streetlight Graphics

Dark Liaison: A Christian Suspense Novel/
D.I. Telbat. -- 1st ed.
ISBN 978-0-9864103-1-4

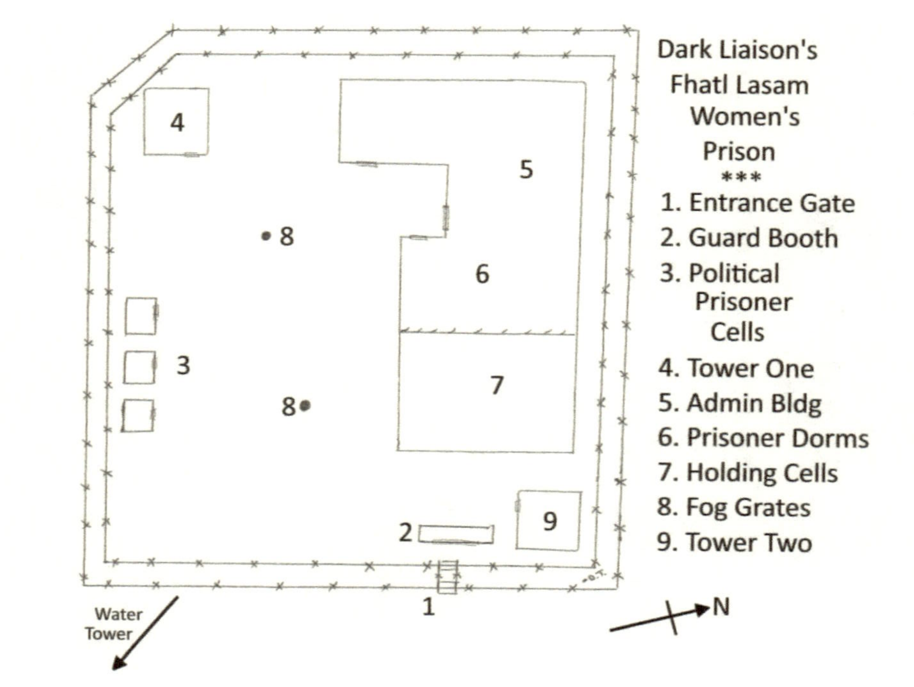

Dark Liaison's
Fhatl Lasam
Women's
Prison
***
1. Entrance Gate
2. Guard Booth
3. Political
Prisoner
Cells
4. Tower One
5. Admin Bldg
6. Prisoner Dorms
7. Holding Cells
8. Fog Grates
9. Tower Two
1
2
3
4
5
6
7
8
8
9
N
Water
Tower

✝

Fred "Memphis" Nelson's eyes fluttered open. A naked light bulb swung in front of his face. He felt its heat and sensed the eerie shadows it cast in the otherwise dark room. There was so much burning in his shoulders. But where were his arms, his hands?

Memphis' mind swam as he tried to focus through the poison they'd pumped into his veins. His head rolled to one side, his eyes on the ceiling. There were his arms, his wrists bound by rope from a ceiling rafter. That was why he felt like he was floating; it wasn't only the drugs. Inches from the ground, his body hung on display before his captors killed him. Except for a pair of boxer shorts, he was naked.

Shaking his head, his vision cleared a little. Boxes and crates were stacked around the room. Two men stood facing him on the far side, whispering in hushed tones. They were both larger than Memphis, but one had shoulders like a gorilla. Memphis strained to catch a few words that he didn't understand.

He thought they were speaking Russian. *Russian?* That didn't make sense. Oh, yes, he was in Russia. This was his first assignment, but everything had gone horribly wrong. It was supposed to have been a simple job, something an ex-high school math and P.E. teacher could handle. But his

1

inexperience had surfaced, though he had followed instructions perfectly. Moscow Canal had been on his right. The warehouse had been on his left. That was when they'd ambushed him.

On his flight over the Atlantic, he'd studied just enough to be able to read the Russian street signs in order to find the warehouse. He was certain he'd found the right place. The military chopper was supposed to have been in the warehouse. Everything was for sale in Russia, he'd been told. And Memphis knew choppers. Even though he'd never been in the armed forces, he qualified as an Air Force mechanic. He wasn't a bad pilot either.

Memphis closed his eyes at the memory of his own pursuits, trying to block out the agony of the past. But it didn't help.

The Apache he'd rebuilt back home had been his baby. He still remembered the first time he'd flown it—cruising at a hundred seventy-five knots, the twin engines purring. Memphis always wore a fire-control helmet even though he would never mount the bird with Hellfire missiles. The freedom of flight—it had been his passion.

Opening his eyes, Memphis blew his blond bangs from his view, then clenched his teeth in memory. That was the day she'd died—his Sammie—while he'd been out playing with his helicopter. He'd been giving their house a fly-over, shaking the windows and startling the neighbors. Later, he found out she'd not been home. She'd been driving out to his shop with a cake to celebrate the day. Then some drunk driver . . . It was too horrible to think about.

"Sammie," Memphis mumbled.

"Da?"

Memphis peered across the room. The two men had heard him and were walking toward him. His heart thudded against his rib cage. This was it. This was what he'd been warned of. He prayed that he had the strength to endure to the end.

"You avake, da?" the smaller of the two big men asked with a rich Russian accent.

At thirty-two years old, Memphis was six-two and weighed two hundred pounds. He thought he might be able to take the gray-haired one—if his hands were free. The guy was older, somewhere in his fifties, and a little overweight. Probably too much vodka, Memphis mused. But the bigger Russian . . . no way could he take him. He was muscled, probably fifty pounds heavier, and moved like a cat on his feet.

"You American, da?" the gray-haired one said, taking his time pulling out a cheap cigar. The gorilla-sized Russian lit the cigar for his partner, but never took his eyes off Memphis. The older one puffed twice, yellow teeth biting down, and blew smoke into Memphis' face. "You na speak? Blowtorch I have somevhere. Maybe you speak den, da?"

Memphis kept his mouth closed, his lips tight. Regardless of what he'd told his new employer, he realized he wasn't trained for this, though he'd been warned of the possibility.

"Vhere you come from?"

The gorilla-sized one cracked his neck twice and flexed fists with gnarled knuckles, like he was used to beating on people.

"America," Memphis blurted. When he'd parked in front of the warehouse, they had come out of nowhere. Their ambush had been perfect. They'd gotten everything he had in the car, including his passport. "I'm from the United States. I'm a US citizen."

"Good, good." The man waved his cigar. "Speak more like dis or my friend here will . . . Ah, you na vant dat."

"My name's Jack O'Connor. What's this all about? I want to talk to the American ambassador."

The older one laughed. From a pocket, he tugged out Memphis' passport. He studied the photograph and legend information, all of which Memphis had memorized for his cover.

"Jack. You na look like a Jack." He turned to the giant. "Vycke?"

Without warning, the gorilla's left fist snapped out like a rattler and connected with Memphis' abdomen. It took his breath away. He'd been only half-tensed, but he would know better now. Ready for anything. Memphis had wrestled in college; he'd been hit before.

"Jack eez not your real name, na?" He blew into Memphis' face again. Memphis caught his breath only to suck in a lungful of nasty tar-smelling smoke. "Vhere you from in America?"

Memphis tensed. The tough guy looked anxious for more. He'd surely been holding back on the first blow.

"Buffalo, New York. That's where I live."

"Who send you?"

He thought back two days when he'd been in the man's

office, the man with no name. Memphis was sure the office had been a front—maybe just for him.

"So, you want to be a spy, huh?" the no-name had asked. He had studied Memphis with expressionless eyes. Memphis hadn't been able to read him, only stare back at his brown eyes, brown hair, average size, fifty-something face. "Think you can handle it?"

"I think so. I believe in this cause, you know," Memphis had answered. "And I'm not coming to you empty handed. I can fly anything with a wing or rotor."

"Well, you're not really the agent type, Mr. Nelson. You don't even have an FBI file. No combat experience. You speak Spanish, I see, but everyone does anymore. You know what I see when I look at you? I see a gym coach. Not much more. That's what you are, right? A gym coach?"

"Physical education," Memphis had confirmed with a nod.

"And what's with the name? Memphis. Says you're from Arizona on your app."

"Memphis, Arizona." Memphis had known the man was testing him, that the two wouldn't be meeting if his application hadn't already caught someone's eye. "I play the blues harmonica. The kids at school started it, you know? Coach Memphis. It stuck."

"So, you're not a wanna-be gunner pilot with a gunner's handle already picked out?"

Memphis had chuckled.

"No, sir. Nothing like that. It's just a nickname."

"Maybe coming to us . . . you have a death wish, Mr. Nelson." The man drummed his fingers on his desk. "Hmm?

Something to do with your wife's recent death?"

Memphis hadn't liked the implication. He'd felt a heated flush crawl up his neck while No-name watched him, read him, sorted him out. His wife's death hadn't been mentioned anywhere on the application.

"My wife died, that's true. I'm trying to move on." Memphis had sat up straighter. "But every part of me wants to live for Sammie, not die. She always thought I should use my flying skills somewhere in the field. Part of me is doing this for her."

"What's the other part doing this for?"

"For God, first and foremost. And for the people in the field. I know I can help them."

"We're not like other spy agencies, Mr. Nelson. If you're interested in killing for God and country, you can apply elsewhere. Our agents don't even carry guns—not conventional ones, anyway."

"I have no interest in killing, sir. Like I said in my application, I just want to help Christians in the field, especially the ones in danger. They're in the real battle zone. Whatever you have for me—supply drops, transport, recon—I can handle it."

"The places we would send you, if we decide to bring you on board, will be dangerous. You'll be flying low and unarmed, maybe doing extractions while getting a little surface-to-air action."

"I can stay focused. My flight log speaks for itself."

"And we'd want your Apache, too, if we want you. It's a nice bird."

Memphis smiled.

"I was about to volunteer it myself, sir."

"But we may not want you at all. You're an unknown without a file. There's no way to know your loyalties for sure. We have a lot of enemies. Some don't want the gospel preached, and they don't want us protecting those who preach it. Maybe you're one of them, an imposter, or infiltrator."

"You can't really believe that," Memphis had scoffed. "My faith in God is my foundation. We're on the same side."

"You really built your Apache?"

"Rebuilt, yes. It was an old trainer, a castaway."

"Our organization recently acquired another chopper, something for transporting gear and supplies, maybe a few passengers. I think it's a BellJet Ranger. It's in Russia, though, so I don't know its condition. If you had, say, an hour to look her over, would you be able to tell if it's something for us? Something that maybe you could fly?"

Memphis had shrugged, struggling to contain his excitement.

"Sure, but . . . I'd have to ask why the Russians would be selling a Ranger, especially if she still runs."

The man with no name had laughed, his first sign of emotion or any kind of personality.

"That's good. Your instincts are worthy." But then his face darkened and he suddenly seemed intimidating. "Go to Russia, and remember that anything is for sale there, especially in Moscow."

…✝…

The gorilla-sized Russian slugged Memphis in his right

kidney, snapping him back to the present. The young pilot's eyes bulged. Such pain!

"I say, who send you?"

A gnarled fist clubbed Memphis' brow. The world spun.

"No one sent me. My wife died. I'm here on vacation."

"Vacation in Moskva? Hah!"

A blow to the cheekbone followed.

"Lies! Vhat you vant vit varehouse?"

Memphis chuckled to himself. Maybe he was losing his mind, but he thought it was funny. The older Russian had no idea how to pronounce a *w*, no matter how hard he tried. That was funny. If they were going to kill him anyway, Memphis figured he may as well die laughing.

"Vhy you laugh?" the older man asked. He turned to the gorilla and spoke in Russian. The giant nodded, admiring freshly broken skin on his knuckles, and wandered into the shadows, out of sight for a moment. "He find blowtorch. You talk den."

"Look, I was just turning my car around at that warehouse," Memphis claimed, drooling blood onto his chest. "If you're going to kill me, I might as well know what this is about!"

"You know already, sneaky American! You come to steal!"

"Steal what?"

"Da missiles!" the man shouted. He held his lit cigar up to Memphis' torso. Memphis quivered at the heat. "Who tell you about da varehouse? Hmm? Who?"

Memphis choked back a scream as the cigar seared through the flesh below his ribs. Squeezing his eyes shut, he prayed for strength—or total weakness. Was it wrong to hope for a quick death at this point? He would see Sammie again soon.

The burning stopped, but the pain did not. The man's cigar had gone out. Panting, Memphis opened his eyes to find that the giant had returned, a propane-fed blowtorch in his hand. Expertly, he used it to relight the older man's cigar, then waved the torch's flame near Memphis' head, close enough for a few strands of hair to shrivel in a wisp of acrid smoke.

"No, please . . ."

"Last chance, Jack O'Connor. Who send you? Who you vork for? Vhy you come to varehouse? You not Jack, da?"

"God, please make it quick."

"Vhat? God? You pray? No God here. Pray not help you, Jack O'Connor. Vhat you say to dat?"

Memphis swallowed hard. He tried not to look at the blue flame inches from his scalp.

"I'm a Christian." He licked his lips, his courage building. If he was about to die, he would say his piece. "I don't hate you. We both have our jobs, our master. Whatever you do to me, just know that I'm going to a better place because I serve Jesus Christ."

The man spat Russian at his comrade. The giant nodded with an evil look and stepped closer to Memphis—close enough to breathe the same breath. Memphis closed his eyes. *Sammie, I'm coming a little sooner than expected. Lord, take me home.*

He heard the blowtorch click off, and its gaseous hissing quieted. Maybe they would simply shoot him, Memphis hoped. That was less messy for them and less painful for him.

Slowly, Memphis opened his eyes, but the two men didn't move; they only watched his face. The giant finally stepped back and discussed something with the older man. The man dropped his half-smoked cigar and crushed it under his shoe. The giant set the blowtorch down and reached up to the rafter that held Memphis' wrists. With a tug, the rope came free. He caught Memphis' limp arms as they fell.

"What's happening?" Memphis mumbled.

The giant gradually lowered his arms and cut his wrist binds with a dagger. Memphis' knees buckled, but the giant held him close and eased him to the cement floor. Stabbing pain pierced Memphis' arms as the blood began to flow again. He wiggled his fingers, then looked up at the two men standing over him.

"He's Johnny Vycke," the older man said, his hard exterior melting away. "And I am Fost Ivanovich."

"What? You believe me?"

"Believe you?" the giant asked in perfect English. He smiled and shook his head. "No, you can't lie to save your skin, but that's okay. The boss just wanted to see what you were made of. Welcome to COIL, Memphis. You're hired."

PART I

*"May darkness and the shadow of death
claim it; may a cloud settle on it; may
the blackness of the day terrify it."*
Job 3:5

$$\dagger$$

<u>*CHAPTER ONE*</u>

Corban James Dowler had been shot before. This time was no different; the pain was no less. He stood in the shadow of a residential portico in Rome, Italy, gathering his senses before checking his wound. There was a dim streetlamp on the far corner but the light didn't reveal where he was hiding. The mass of moving water to his left was the Tiber River. Because of darkness, it was out of sight now, but he knew where he was. Of Rome's seven hills, the peak of Palatine was a stone's throw away. His rental car was ten blocks up the street to the north, his destination four blocks to the south.

Taking stock of the wound in his left side, Corban found blood streaming down his leg. Though it felt like a million needles, it didn't seem to be too serious. That love handle would never be the same, but he was thankful the bullet had missed his kidney and ribs.

He eased farther back into the shadows as a lean man crept into the street and then paused. The man still held the silenced pistol he'd used to shoot Corban. There was only one reason the assassin was standing in the street: he wanted to finish Corban off. The man waited, listening, twenty yards away.

Corban took off his glasses. His eyes were fine, but the glasses were part of his costume, so he blamed his current wound on his disguise. Tonight he was Muhammad ibn Affal, an alias from his past that opened more doors in the Middle East than anywhere, but resulted in misfortune in places like Rome. It was his most accessible alias, requiring little prep-time. He'd had little choice but to use it on this emergency visit to Italy.

His foe still stood in the street, listening to the night. The slightest whisper of clothing would alert this predator. Nevertheless, Corban was calm as he disassembled his eyewear. Pulling off both earpieces, he was left with two stubby, straight lengths still connected to the frame. No one ever noticed that the frame itself was unusually thick and round as a pencil.

The man in the street seemed to look right at him, but Corban knew the darkness hid him. Corban also knew his foe was debating if he should venture into that darkness to investigate.

The assassin slinked toward the portico's shadow, his pistol leveled and sweeping.

Pressing both frame lengths toward the lenses, Corban aimed each end at his foe. Since he knew the armed delay of his miniature weapon, he counted the seconds. It was calibrated for ten yards, but this was a little close to use on a man with a drawn pistol.

A tiny red laser beam shot out. When Corban saw the red dot on the man's chest, he instantly crouched low against the building in anticipation. The sharp pop of a CO_2 cartridge sent a tranquilizer dart tipped with falaco into the man's chest, right where Corban's laser sight had beamed. In return, two silenced rounds from the pistol slammed into the wall over Corban's head and peppered him with white dust. Like ricin, falaco required two beats of the heart to reach the vital organs. It was a powerful narcotic that would've killed the man if the dart had been dipped in more than a tiny drop of the toxin upon preparation.

The killer shuddered on his feet, then crumbled in place.

Reassembling his glasses, Corban put them back on his face. If his foe wasn't alone, Corban would be in trouble. Though he had other non-lethal weapons at headquarters in New York City, he'd brought only the glasses on this trip.

Corban smoothed down his fake beard and mustache, both trimmed and styled in the most loyal Islamic fashion. Ignoring his trickling wound, he stepped out of the shadows and into the quiet street. Kneeling next to the killer, he checked the man's weapon: a 9-millimeter, custom-made, machine pistol with a French label. Corban had never seen one like it, which meant the man was a professional, a hunter-tracer of some type.

Rolling the man over, he dragged him out of the street. Falaco's effects would last for an hour, but no more. Though Corban was in a hurry, he was curious, as well. He checked the man's pockets. Two packs of chewing gum and a pack of cigarettes, but no matches or lighter. Corban was tempted to keep the cigarettes, but he decided against it. One never knew what the new generation of spies and assassins carried. It could be a transponder or even a bomb that would explode two steps away from its recognized body heat signature.

Studying the assassin's face up close, Corban engraved his features into his mind. The man was not over forty. His face was lean, cold, and clean-shaven, and he had black hair and bushy eyebrows. He appeared to be Italian. The Italian government wasn't hunting Muhammad ibn Affal, but he was on more than a few countries' watchdog lists. To them, he was an arms thief and smuggler—a terrorist. Such an alias was generally safe to use, even near Western countries that knew him well. But they were only supposed to watch him, not kill him. If someone wanted his identity gone, something in the world of terror had shifted.

Finished with his examination, Corban left the killer and jogged across the street. He slowed to a walk and entered a vine-crowded alley. Pausing every twenty paces, he listened to the night: the city traffic in the distance, a dog yelping, but no trailing footsteps.

A few blocks later, Corban put his back to a telephone pole and watched his target house and the surrounding neighborhood for several minutes. The Italian assassin, even if he woke early, wouldn't know Corban was coming here. Or would he? Every stage was a potential ambush. The Italian could have followed him from the airport, or perhaps he began to tail him later. If his rental car was marked with a transponder, it didn't matter. He wasn't going back for it.

Corban kept a watchful eye on the house. It had a short, stone wall around its front courtyard. An ornate fountain sat dry and littered, molding from whatever last rains had graced its bowl. An old Audi was parked in the driveway. There were no lights on in the house. He knew it was a four-bedroom residence with a pool in the rear. The whole place reeked of neglect, but Corban expected no less. With the death threats that Tye and Sarah Mentolla had been receiving from extremists, he didn't blame. them for remaining in the safety of their home and calling for help.

It was an age-old struggle that had started in the 1500s—apostate teaching versus the biblical teaching that came out of the Protestant Reformation. The Mentollas had been Christian missionaries in Rome for nine years, trained to reach apostates specifically. But the superstitions of the people had won over the washing of Christ's redemptive blood this day.

The Mentollas' dog had been killed a week ago, and the phone calls were becoming more threatening by the day. Just sixteen hours ago, their house had been stoned. Normally, other field agents would've handled this volatile situation, but they were in demand elsewhere. It was up to Corban to get them out this time.

He saw headlights far up the street. Climbing over the Mentollas' stone wall, Corban pushed through the bushes that choked a brick walkway until he reached the back door of the house. As suspected, the backyard pool was filthy, but drained. He was about to knock on the door when he heard breaking glass and shouts from the street. Jogging back to the walkway, he saw a car stopped in front of the house. A half dozen youths were throwing rocks at the windows as another lit a Molotov cocktail.

Returning to the back door, Corban kicked it in. Wood splintered before him as he barged through the frame and into the house. From there, he could see through the dining and living rooms to the front window. As he watched, the cocktail crashed through broken glass. Flames engulfed the floor and furniture.

A child cried, and Corban heard voices from down the hallway to his right. The thugs in front were lucky Corban wasn't the man he'd once been—a man who went heavily armed on every mission. He would've had no qualms about dashing into the street with his Beretta and . . .

But Corban was no longer that man. God had changed him six years before. Since then, he couldn't bring himself to kill. He had to retire from the CIA early, his pension only a few years away, yet his convictions intact. In many ways, though, he was still that old spy tracker. Even though he was fifty-six and not in the best physical condition, he still felt like a man of twenty. After years of honing his skills, he could move like a panther and think like a computer. He was the last of the old-school spies, and although he no longer used his craft for the government, he still used it— to preserve the defenseless.

Fire reflected off his forehead and glasses as he stared at the growing flames. A man shouted at him in Italian. Corban recognized Tye Mentolla right away. He'd never met his family, but Corban knew them well. In the man's arms was his four-year-old daughter, Lacy. Six-year-old Forest was behind his father, clinging to his panic-stricken mother, Sarah. Corban couldn't speak much Italian, but he didn't need to—the Mentollas were Americans.

"I'm here to help you," Corban said over the roar of the fire. The father didn't move. "Sixteen hours ago, you called your mission board in the States. You requested emergency leave. I'm here to get you out. Carry what you can. The fire's still low, but we don't have much time. Quick! We'll leave out the back."

"They said no one would be here for another week," Tye insisted. "They said the threat level wasn't high enough."

"Fine. You want to stay here?"

Coughing at the smoking flames, Tye set his daughter down on the floor.

"Quick!" he urged his family. "Go get dressed!"

His children scampered down the hallway.

"I'll get the albums." Sarah hurried to a display cabinet against a wall. A stone thrown from outside bounced off the floor and hit her leg. She screamed and dropped a handful of photos. "Tye, help me!"

"Sarah, go get your clothes and help the kids!" Tye said as he knelt to gather the pictures from the floor. He muttered a prayer for safety and kept a wary eye on the encroaching flames. "I never thought it would come to this. After all our work."

Corban spotted movement from the corner of his eye. He pivoted to face a tall form in a hooded sweatshirt looming in the back doorway. It was one of the thugs he'd seen in the street. The chiseled shape of a machete rose to strike down at Corban. Shifting his feet, Corban heel-kicked the youth in the solar plexus, sending him skidding across the patio and into the empty pool. Corban heard the thug gasping for air and knew the hooded figure would be fine once he caught his breath.

". . . and so that's when I called the board," Tye was

saying. He turned to Corban, oblivious of Corban's confrontation with the youth. "What'd you say your name was?"

"I didn't say. Maybe you should get dressed, too, Mr. Mentolla."

Tye nodded and jogged down the hallway. Corban spied the growing flames while keeping an eye on the back door. Sarah soon emerged, pinning her hair up and helping Lacy into a sweatshirt, then Tye and Forest came from the hallway together, both carrying their Bibles. Sarah picked up her purse and a small bag.

"Do you have a plan?" Tye asked, gathering the stack of folders and albums. "We'll never get our car out with them blocking the way."

These were good, caring people, Corban thought as he watched Forest tug a baseball cap down over his brow. He hated to see the darkness overwhelm the light so horribly.

He turned toward the pool and the shadows.

"Follow me."

†

uigi Putelli regained consciousness and sat upright. If his memory served him, he'd been on the street when he and Muhammad ibn Affal had exchanged fire. Since Muhammad was gone now, Luigi was no longer in a hurry.

Feeling a twinge of pain in his left pectoral muscle, Luigi smoothed down his dark blazer and plucked the dart out of his chest, studying it in the hazy glow from a nearby streetlight. It was an inch and a quarter long, with tiny spines for stability rather than feathers or fins. Something potent, but apparently nothing deadly, had been on its tip. He didn't seem to have any side effects from the toxin. Surely the drug from the dart would've lasted longer if Luigi hadn't been a perfectly fit and healthy man.

For years, Luigi had been tracking Muhammad's movement around the world. He'd known the conspirator to be in Italy a half dozen times in the last twenty years, but Luigi had never caught him—until this night. As a French DGSE agent, he was only to observe terrorist operatives such as Muhammad, but Luigi had been tipped off and the tip had come with a bank account full of euros. Someone wanted Muhammad dead, and Luigi didn't care who had put up the money. He had freelanced before, and he would freelance again—if he survived this job.

Luigi stood and eased the dart into his pocket. He wanted it analyzed. After everything he'd read and studied about Muhammad, Luigi knew it was out of character for the infamous Egyptian arms dealer to let an enemy live. It made no sense. When two killers met, one died and the other lived, or sometimes both died. Those were the rules. But Muhammad hadn't killed Luigi, even though he'd had the chance.

Digging into his pocket for his gum, Luigi instead found his pack of cigarettes. His gum was in his other pocket—the wrong pocket. Luigi smiled. Small gestures went a long way. Muhammad had swapped the contents of his pockets to let Luigi know he'd been searched. Interesting, but what else could it mean? Sometimes Luigi overanalyzed situations, but he couldn't help it. He fingered two sticks of gum into his mouth. It was his new vice. He tapped the cigarettes to count each one. None were missing, which was also interesting. Muhammad was not a smoker. Luigi would add that information to the man's datasheet, his collective profile.

Luigi grinned at Muhammad's craftiness. If Muhammad had taken one of Luigi's cigarettes to smoke, he would've been dead in a week. A year prior, Luigi had smoked one of the cigarettes only to find that someone had laced his filters with a deadly strain of pneumonia. But the pneumonia was in place to mask the anthrax spores as they did their dirty work. As Luigi had lain on his deathbed, the doctors had been stumped as to why the pneumonia was not responding to medication. Meanwhile, Luigi had the filters analyzed, and the results were rushed to him from DGSE headquarters. The strain and the anthrax had shown up in the culture. He had started Cipro-floxacin in time to live, but it took him a month to recover. Later, he'd retrieved the cigarettes from the lab and kept them as a reminder of his brush with death. Thus, Luigi no longer smoked cigarettes. He chewed gum.

Of course, Luigi wouldn't have been disappointed if Muhammad had taken a cigarette. It would've made his job much easier.

At that hour of the morning, Luigi couldn't help but be drawn to the ruckus a few blocks away. As he approached a burning house, he could sense Muhammad's presence. This was no coincidence. He was sure the Egyptian had been there.

The fire engines honked their horns, but such a crowd of hooded youths had gathered and blocked the road that no water had touched the blaze yet. It was an odd sight, Luigi decided from a distance. The youths encouraged the blaze. Had they started it and not Muhammad? He was sure Muhammad had been headed that direction, but none of it made any sense to Luigi.

Walking through a neighbor's yard, Luigi hopped the wall and landed next to an unfilled pool. The pool was not completely empty, though; a young man stood in the bottom, shielding his face from the fire's tremendous heat. Luigi ignored the heat. He was a man accustomed to the harshest of elements.

"Hey, mister! Give me a lift out of here, yeah?"

Kneeling, Luigi offered his hand. He yanked the young man out and nearly all the way to his feet. Dressed like those in front of the house, the hooded figure's face contorted in agony as he held his chest and struggled to breathe.

"What's wrong with you?" Luigi questioned.

"The devil kicked me. It's nothing."

Without asking, Luigi lifted the youth's sweatshirt to see a clear heel print on his upper torso from a perfect solar plexus kick.

"Where's the man who did this to you?"

"Um . . . I never seen him before. He was in the house. I saw him light the fire. Honest! I was trying to put it out."

Luigi's eyes narrowed. The youth was lying. Luigi prided himself in the detection of such things.

"He had a beard, black hair, thick glasses?"

"Yeah, that's him."

"Who lived here?"

"Filthy pagans. I hope they burned to death."

"Of course you do." Luigi scoffed. *Ignorant hooligan.* He reached into his pocket and drew out his pack. "Cigarette?"

"Sure. Thanks. Um, I don't have to go down to the station or anything, do I?"

Luigi forced a smile. He really hated smiling, unless it was to himself. But sometimes smiling was part of his cover. In this case, his grin put this worm at ease. Luigi hated worms, maybe because he was a worm himself. Other worms presented competition, but few were as smart as he was. Worms fed off death and disease and profited from each. He decided the young thug deserved that cigarette. Maybe he would go share it with his friends who were still in front of the house.

"No, I've got your statement. Get out of here."

The youth ran away with his cigarette, and Luigi turned his back to the house as it crumbled. He stared out across the Tiber River. Rome's lights blinked. A barge drifted. Muhammad was out there. He would surface again. Luigi knew this because he knew Muhammad was a worm as well. They both fed off others. It was their way.

However, Luigi was troubled. It was not worm-like for Muhammad to save people from religious hoodlums, if that was indeed what Muhammad had done.

Feeling uneasy, Luigi realized he now had more questions about Muhammad than when the night had begun. The unknown was not predictable. He'd been so close to Muhammad, yet he'd failed. Muhammad was good, very good. But apparently, he wasn't as deadly as his reputation led others to believe.

Luigi licked his lips. Now he would hunt Muhammad not only for the money, but also out of sheer curiosity.

†

CHAPTER THREE

Chloe Azmaveth was a beautiful, forty-four-year-old Syrian-born Jewess. She knew she was beautiful, too, with her curly, black hair and daring brown eyes, a distinct nose and a ready smile. As COIL's primary attorney and public relations liaison, she used her God-given assets to make things happen.

But that day, events around the world weren't to Chloe's liking. She traced her finger along her plasma screen in COIL's headquarters as she read a number of field reports from that weekend. Strife against Christians was escalating around the world. On the surface, Chloe worked the diplomatic front. But behind the scene, she organized covert teams who infiltrated troubled countries and extracted persecuted believers. COIL denied personal involvement, but they were everywhere they were needed.

Looking up from her screen, Chloe glanced at the closed office door to her left. Corban was in there now. She'd debriefed him herself as he nursed a bullet wound on his left side. Another team in China had been injured as well, but the missionaries were safe. That was all that mattered in this battle against the devil himself.

Normally, Chloe didn't debrief field operatives. She

preferred reading their lengthy reports while Corban, COIL's founder and director, debriefed the agents. Chloe had pulled a dozen years as a Mossad agent, working alongside the Israeli Defense Forces. But the terrorism she'd witnessed in the IDF didn't disturb her as much as the brutality she saw everyday against the servants that COIL supported. Such a wholesale effort by adversaries to rid the world of missionaries—and all Christians—was nearly over-whelming the agency. COIL was bringing in new agents all the time, and perhaps too quickly, with less screening and training than Corban preferred. Even though they were technically an intelligence agency, their foes weren't other international agencies. Their primary adversary was fought at the spiritual level. The field operatives were often reminded they weren't to fear the one who could kill the body, but to fear the One who could destroy both body and soul.

Chloe had been with COIL since its birth two years ago. It had existed prior to that time, but not in name or any official capacity. Corban, since he'd become a Christian, had used his every resource to ensure the safety of like-minded believers abroad—with minimal aggression. He had drawn assistance and manpower from a number of global contacts until he'd quit the CIA altogether and created the official COIL agency.

C.O.I.L., Commission of International Laborers, was an agency with which to be reckoned, though few understood the true power of this organization built by Christ.

Next to Corban, Chloe knew the most about COIL, but that didn't mean she knew everything, especially when it came to Corban. There were gaps in Corban's file—seventeen unaccountable years, to be exact—which were not detailed in even the Mossad's databases. Chloe had checked out her boss in depth, but she'd found little. He'd gone to college at sixteen, but no one knew where. Certainly, he had not enrolled under his own name, or if he had, no one knew his real name. At age nineteen, the CIA had come to him, desiring his expertise in Modern Standard Arabic and Russian. That had been at the latter end of the Cold War.

After that, Corban's file remained vague. For eighteen years, he "pursued compromised intelligence," which was an indistinct way of saying he hunted spies within the US as well as abroad.

Chloe knew Corban had designed one of the most utilized misinformation networks within Langley, because he often used the network even now. Langley pretended not to notice that their databases were being sifted through and information was being copied and extracted by other agencies and countries. The foes of the US analyzed the data that was filled with just enough truth to make them bite, but the data was, in fact, polluted with half-truths and misconceptions.

For instance, Corban's alias, Muhammad ibn Affal, had been a real man, an Egyptian arms dealer—a ghost in many respects. Corban had caught the man years ago and then had taken his identity to open doors Corban couldn't otherwise open. Using the "reliable" misinformation network in Langley, Corban could paste his own bearded face above Muhammad's name. He had the real

Muhammad's bank accounts, his estates, and his relative physique. It was an easy swap since Muhammad had rarely met with contacts face-to-face, and Corban knew his tactics well, having hunted him for over ten years.

Thus, Corban had kept the smuggler's legend alive. Those who believed they were extracting sensitive data from Langley sold it to the highest bidders. Those buyers sold it again and again. Eventually, the CIA, with its own lust for intelligence, happened across this same data and paid an impressive sum for it. Without knowing otherwise, they accepted the information as truth—as did the rest of the world—and the lies came to life. Covers were turned from fiction to fact. Lives were saved. Because this system of misinformation worked so well, Muhammad was hunted by the same government—the US—that had spawned him. On the other hand, he was welcomed with open arms into pro-terrorist countries, his name and face purchased and confirmed to be the evil arms baron that Langley itself sought to apprehend.

At age thirty-seven, Corban's file, and his known past, went blank. For the next seventeen years, he'd stayed underground. Surprisingly, he'd maintained a marriage to his first and only wife, Janice, for twenty-three years, but whatever operations he was involved in were non-existent, at least on paper.

Chloe could count on one hand the old-school agents who'd been known to last that long. Twenty-five years? Not as a sleeper, but as an active agent, too! She'd spoken to England's MI6 and the French Industrial Espionage Agency, the DGSE, and had even checked with Beijing,

Moscow, and Berlin. The Mossad was not the only agency that thought of Corban as a legend, though not all of them knew his real name—if Corban Dowler was his real name. But Chloe had connected the dots, not because she was still a spy tracker, but because now working in the private sector had made her no less cautious.

Seventeen unknown years or not, Chloe was sure Corban was legit and genuine. She often wondered about his ties to the CIA, if he still worked for them. There were a few signs that suggested he did. He met once a month with the Agency's deputy director, William Buchanen, a super-spy in his own day, nearly a generation before Corban.

That brought her back to COIL. In its two official years, it had grown and woven itself into a powerful force, mostly because of Corban. And like any real force, there was a serious financial burden. Again, to make sure her employer was legit, she'd done her homework. Donations and contributions supported fourteen percent of COIL's expenses. That wasn't much. Most of those contributors were private entities, not churches, since COIL was essentially underground as an agency, but not as a "mission liaison."

After that, eleven percent of support came from a best selling author known as A.B. Leever, who Chloe suspected to be Corban himself, or maybe his wife, Janice.

That left a hefty seventy-five percent—a monumental amount in the eight-digit-figure annual budget—from an unknown source. Maybe another agency covered the bill. Possibly, the CIA was still funding Corban for intel he gathered along the way or covering the cost for maintaining covers he'd established years before. It was said that one never truly left the Agency. Or maybe it was dead money—money that floated unclaimed in numbered accounts when a terrorist cell or warlord network was toppled. All one had to do was know where to look for those accounts, and Corban would know where to look.

Corban was no longer an "enforcer," but he still had his sources and resources, his secrets and disguises. COIL had always made payroll, the funds allocated to the penny every two weeks from an outside party. The pay was good, but one never got to enjoy it. COIL employees received salaries, then bonuses for voluntary overtime. Like all services in high demand, however, voluntary overtime was not so voluntary. The world was at war. The Lord's laborers were needed.

Zvi Azmaveth, Chloe's husband, hardly saw her anymore. More often than not, she was on a conference call begging a country's ambassador to arrange the release of certain Christians from their prison.

But Zvi had his own hectic schedule—a precious metals market that demanded his attention, often overseas. Micron Incorporated was his brainchild. While many Brooklyn Jews handled diamonds or gems, Zvi dealt in the forever AU. Gold—micron gold, specifically—was usually shunned by large mining operations, but Zvi collected and purified it. It was a stressful job that had cost him most of his hair and an inch in height. But Zvi was no less gentle and loving, and the two short nights he spent with Chloe every week made them feel like there was nothing else in the whole world. But the weekends always ended, and they were left with their wearisome tasks. Since they were both believers in Christ, they understood that their expertise in their fields was to be used to help others. In this way, they independently served God.

Chloe's eyes settled on an empty desk outside Corban's office door. That was his wife's station, but Janice only worked part-time. The couple had adopted a blind girl two years ago, and much of Janice's time was spent with the six-year-old child, Jenna. But Corban kept his private life private, including his marriage. The COIL headquarters occupied two huge suites in an apartment building that overlooked Times Square in Manhattan. Of the fifty employees and volunteers within the headquarters, with shifts that worked around the clock, only a few knew Corban was married to the bright-eyed woman of fifty-seven who sat at the desk a few hours a week. Now that Chloe thought of it, few of those people even knew Corban's full name. He was "the boss" to many and "Mr. Dowler" to the rest. Only those who were close to him called him by his first name. But whether they knew him by name or not, everyone had heard that the average looking, aging man, was something of a legendary hero. The rumors and gossip—they were impossible to suppress entirely.

The office door opened suddenly and Chloe snapped from her reflections. As always, everyone in the suite looked up to see what the secretive man would say or do. He pointed to Chloe and motioned for her to enter his office. She clicked off her computer screen and walked into his office. Corban closed the soundproofed door behind her. The windows overlooking the Square were double-plated and bulletproofed, providing both surveillance security and protection. The two suites were swept for listening devices every morning, with an extra random sweep weekly. Corban had brought more than a few of the Agency's skills to COIL.

Corban sat in a worn, leather chair behind his desk. Chloe, with notepad and PDA in her lap, took a straight-backed chair facing Corban. Four phones were placed on his desk. They were labeled with numbers, each with a dedicated line coordinating with a primary alias that Corban maintained. One phone, routed through Cyprus, was for Muhammad ibn Affal, which he answered in Arabic. Another phone was for Christopher Cagon, a Red Cross ambassador. There were two other phones, but even Chloe was not sure of the identities to which they belonged. And no doubt he switched his aliases from time to time.

"I found the Italian," he started without introduction. She knew he meant the assassin he'd crossed in Rome two nights ago during a missionary family's extraction. "I had to pull a few favors to track him down, but I had his face to start with, so that was half the job. I've sent his file to your inbox."

"Okay. What would you like me to do?"

"His name is Luigi Putelli, age thirty-nine. Italian, though he works for the French—an industrial branch. Work your magic. I don't think he was sanctioned by the DGSE to take me out. He's been hired by an outside source to take out Muhammad. Find out who hired him."

"I'll get our Berlin office on it." Chloe was thankful that

COIL had offices in Moscow, Berlin, Guatemala City, and a dedicated office in China's Nanjing.

"Thank you."

"Anything else?"

"What does today's report look like? I haven't had a chance to check it out."

"Problems in the Philippines. I'm watching the islands closely. Sudan is getting ugly again. And two in Saudi Arabia were caught with Bibles—our favorite two."

"The Craigens again?" He frowned. "Can we do anything?"

"No . . ." Chloe looked at her hands. "They're . . . gone. According to *Al Jazeera*, two Western radicals were executed this morning. I saw the footage. I won't watch it again."

"How?"

"Stoning. They died on their knees praying."

Corban hammered the desk with his fist, then stood abruptly and walked to the window. The honking, swerving traffic four floors below was muted through the glass layers. They often commented that it was like watching a busy ant farm.

"Could we have done anything different for them? If we could've gotten to them in time?"

"No, Corban. They were warned, and we offered to pull them out. After their public scourging last time, they knew the risks of staying to work in the country. A second Bible smuggling offense is unforgivable in Saudi Arabia. They knew that. Some feel they should leave when danger is near. The Craigens chose to stay. It's not your fault."

"How many underground Christians did they leave behind?"

"The numbers I've received suggest there are between fifteen to twenty believers, all nationals."

"Have Johnny smuggle them whatever they need—Bibles, hymnals, anything we can do." Corban faced her. He took a deep breath and sighed slowly. "It's sad, but, praise God, martyrs draw converts. Let's make sure those believers can handle the pressure of greater numbers. Let them know we're here for them. And maybe see if those people we pulled out of Iran last year—"

"The Penningtons?"

"Right. See if they can go to Arabia to take up the Craigens' ministry. We can't leave that church without a shepherd. Are the Penningtons free?"

"I think they're still in London, looking for a new ministry. This will be perfect for them. Dangerous, but if they could handle Iran . . . I'll look into it, Corban."

"Good. Thank you."

"Oh, about Malaysia—all dead ends with Helena Rauch."

"The German girl?"

"Right."

"Brief me, Chloe. It's been a while."

"Nurse, single, German-sponsored. Converted an official's daughter to Christianity from Islam. The official had her arrested three months ago. I've been monitoring her, since no one else seems to be. Her health is suffering. She's only twenty-four, Corban. She must be terrified."

"What in the world is the German ambassador doing?"

"Nothing. He says the charges are legitimate, technically."

"Then get with our own ambassador and—"

"I already have. He's met with Helena, though she doesn't speak English, and he doesn't speak Malay because he's fresh out of the States. He told me she looks abused, but she's a German citizen in a Malaysian prison. His hands are tied. I thanked him for looking in on her, but he can do nothing for us or Helena."

"Who do we have that speaks Malay or German?"

"We have a couple missionaries in the region down there."

"No, don't bring them into this. They don't know we exist, and we don't want their ministry to suffer. Who else?"

"No Malays. Um . . . Nathan speaks German."

"Our Nathan?" Corban rubbed his chin. Nathan "Eagle Eyes" Isaacson was COIL's primary operations field agent. He handled the heavy jobs, like extractions. "Where is he now?"

"Guatemala, handling a kidnapping."

"Who else could we send?"

"Besides yourself?" She tapped into her PDA. It had been well worth the time to digitize COIL's assets months ago. "Everyone who knows German is tied up, but, you know, I was in Germany for over a year. I've studied the language and I'm fluent."

Considering this, Corban paced in front of the window.

"We should've taken care of this girl a long time ago, Chloe."

"I know, but it's our policy—'diplomatic measures exhausted first, when possible.'"

"What are you telling me? We're done with diplomacy?"

"Yes, Corban, that's what I'm telling you. We're dead in the water."

"If you go down there yourself, you need to understand we don't have time to set up diplomatic immunity for you through the Pentagon. You know what that means."

"So what if I don't have diplomatic premise? I'll visit her as a friend. And if they arrest me?" She dismissed the thought with a smile. "I won't break, you know. I was in ops for more than a little while."

"It's risky, you going in. I don't like it. It jeopardizes us all. You know and handle so much. Too much."

"No more dangerous than your stunt in Italy," she said, glancing at his injured side.

"Chloe, I hate arguing with you." Corban stared at her intently, his hands on his hips. "Do you want to go?"

"I do. I've been worried about this girl for three months. Everyone else has abandoned her. There seems to be no other hope, and you know I'd be better than Nathan."

"There may still be a place for Nathan," he argued.

"Not to visit Helena, though. Two seconds and they'd spot him for the commando he is."

"But you said it yourself: diplomacy is a dead issue. That means we bring in Nathan. I'm not saying we should lay siege to the prison she's in. I'm just saying it wouldn't hurt to begin collecting intel. Start with a map of the prison. I can get one for a fee, but I don't want to raise any alarms.

If you're going in, see what you see."

"Okay. I can do that."

She nodded as he contemplated the mission. He said the phrase "See what you see" to someone almost daily. He meant to really, truly, see and memorize what could be noticed through those two orbs in the skull; be super observant.

"And shoot Nathan a memo about all this. We'll want him when he's done in Guatemala. Then tell Johnny to finish up with that new pilot in Moscow—"

"Memphis."

"Right, and start prepping for Malaysia."

Chloe's heart fluttered. Action was what she loved most. She missed the old days of fieldwork.

"So, we're really going to get her out?"

"One step at a time," he urged. "Maybe Helena is where God wants her to be. Talk to her. Only she can know God's will in her life. As strange as it sounds, she may want to stay where she is if she feels God is using her there. And Chloe?"

"What? Don't tell my husband?" She smiled.

"Well, I'm not telling Zvi." He chuckled. "Just be careful."

"You, too."

"Me?" He followed her eyes to a plane ticket on his desk. It wasn't like him to leave such things lying around. He swept it into a drawer. "It's nothing."

"It's never 'nothing' with you, Corban. Something I should know about?"

"Just a thing in the Middle East I need to check out. You

handle the Malaysian situation. Keep me posted. I don't want another Craigen incident."

Of the many Christian servants they warned of danger or rescued from it, there was still a percentage that ignored COIL's advice or helpful hand. But every death pierced Corban's heart just the same. Regardless of his usual expressionless face, he had a big heart.

"I'm on it," Chloe assured him.

A phone rang, its light beckoning for attention. It was the first phone on the right. Corban let it ring, gazing at Chloe expectantly.

"Oh." She gathered herself and blushed. "I'll let you get that."

"Thank you, Chloe. And tell Zvi I said hello. Maybe we can have dinner in a week or so."

Chloe walked out of the office and closed the door as Corban reached for his phone. She was still a spy at heart herself. Corban had so many secrets; she couldn't help her agitated curiosity. But she checked herself. Whatever Corban was up to in the Middle East, it didn't concern her right now. She had her own op to coordinate in Malaysia.

$$\dagger$$

Luigi Putelli let the line ring and ring. He had his headset and recorder on as he walked around his expensive Naples office with nothing better to do but to call his newfound enemy. Muhammad ibn Affal didn't know Luigi was his ultimate foe, but Luigi knew. He was obsessive like that. Normally, he would never call a rival or a target. It just wasn't proper. But there was so much about Muhammad that Luigi found uncharacteristic for a Muslim extremist; Luigi simply had to call him. He'd tracked down a man who worked for the Prince of Jordan. The kindly servant had given Luigi Muhammad's contact information for ten thousand euros. _Extortionist!_

Why didn't Muhammad pick up his phone? Luigi cursed. He could leave him a digital message through the Internet. That was the most covert method for operatives to make contact, but Luigi had reasoned against it. Speaking was better at this point—and certainly more exciting.

By now, he was sure Muhammad had identified him as a French secret agent in Italy's industrial sector. That worried Luigi just a little. He'd blown his cover by underestimating Muhammad in Rome. But chances were that a man who hadn't killed him when he had the chance wasn't going to kill him by exposing him as a double agent to the Italian authorities. Unless his identity was to be traded for something of value. Luigi considered this prospect. He had a few enemies, most of whom didn't know he was working for the French DGSE. They would pay Muhammad nicely for that bit of information. But did Muhammad really need the money? Luigi thought not and dismissed any immediate danger. He couldn't worry about everything, but he did a good job at it, anyway.

Someone picked up the receiver.

"*Salam Alaykum*." A man greeted in Arabic.

Luigi smiled. Thanks to previously recorded intercepted calls, his computer verified the man's voice pattern to be that of his namesis.

"Muhammad, we both speak English." Luigi muffled a knowing snicker. "Please, my Fusha is limited."

"Who is this, and how did you get this number?"

Forever compiling enemy profiles, Luigi made a mental note of the rich accent and word usage.

"A mutual associate gave me your number. You know me perhaps better than I know you."

"Is that so?"

Flipping a key on his keyboard, Luigi turned off his voice pattern application. He now viewed an experimental program that measured tone, frequency, and pitch, and then produced an equivalency summary that made sense. Emotion indicators showed Muhammad's voice had no stress peaks, with the current summary registered on "indifferent." Muhammad was bored.

"We met two days ago, but I've been an admirer of yours for quite some time."

"Remind me. I have so many," Muhammad claimed.

"Rome."

"Ah, I do miss the Tiber. I have not been there in years. Have you?"

Again, Luigi smiled. He loved this game—show me more than I show you. But the game was won only by the one who anticipated what the other knew, though not even Luigi knew who was paying him so handsomely to kill the mysterious Arab.

"I have a vacation cottage on the Tiber, not so far as the Puteoli Harbor, though." Luigi fumbled with a chewing gum wrapper. He really wanted a smoke, but the last one hadn't gone so well. "We really should meet sometime, Muhammad, visit face-to-face."

"Since we both have very busy schedules, I don't see how that is possible, my friend."

"My calendar is open."

"It will soon be very busy, I believe."

Luigi froze. His eyes narrowed. What did he mean by that? Friendly banter or a threat? What did Muhammad know? From his desk, Luigi picked up a plastic baggie that contained the dart he'd plucked from his chest.

"I have something that belongs to you."

"My second wife? I knew she ran off with someone!" Muhammad joked. "You can keep her. I have four others."

"I had the dart analyzed. I analyze everything. But this, I've . . . not seen before."

"It's something special."

"And quite exotic. A plant from Belize, among other things." Luigi waited for a response, but got nothing. That's how the entire conversation was going. He baited the man for information, but received nothing! "I must ask you a question. It's rather frank, as the Americans say."

"The name is not familiar to me."

"It's an expression. It means—" Luigi stopped. He realized Muhammad was playing him, but Luigi had to stay in control! "Anyway, on the street, I was unconscious, and yet you didn't live up to your reputation."

"I am not a barbarian, though I do have wives who claim otherwise."

"What does that mean?" Luigi frowned. It was another riddle that may have meant nothing at all, but Luigi wasn't certain.

"Only a barbarian would take a man's gum while he takes a nap on the street."

Luigi hit the mute button as he laughed. He checked his monitor. Muhammad still registered as bored, even unresponsive. The man's voice was without emotion, flat. The software, Luigi decided, was written for detecting lying housewives, not Egyptian arms dealers.

"Do you not find me a threat?" Luigi asked.

"No, I do not. Perhaps you do not know me as well as you think you do, my French friend."

"Perhaps."

Grimacing at the mention of his French connection, Luigi feared someone could be listening, but Muhammad didn't seem to care. Luigi had five pages of data on Muhammad, information he'd bought a piece at a time from scores of sources, some by way of specialists who'd hacked into the CIA's own databases.

"If you were a threat to me, then you must be measured equally with my other dangerous enemies, yes?"

Luigi licked his lips. Muhammad was talking about America, England, and Israel, no doubt. They were always hunting men like Muhammad.

"I feel that I—"

"Let me say this," Muhammad interrupted. "Do you feel confident in your abilities as you are used by others to be my enemy?"

Luigi's eyes darted about his office. He wanted to get off the phone now.

"What are you asking?"

"I'm asking you," Muhammad continued, "why I would take gum from you when I can just as readily receive it freely from the gum machine?"

With lean fingers, Luigi traced across his cheek. He triggered the headset button and ended the call, suddenly feeling sick. Luigi noticed his reflection in the window. It took a lot for his Sicilian blood to drain from his face. He felt insulted, but it was his own fault. Calling the man was a mistake, and Luigi hated feeling guilty. Muhammad had given him only riddles. What was that last bit about being used by others? Muhammad obviously knew Luigi was being paid to hunt and kill him. Luigi wondered if he knew which "gum machine" was really footing the bill, because Luigi certainly didn't know. A gum machine like the Mossad could do its own dirty work. What did Muhammad know?

Luigi felt a rush of excitement. He'd wounded Muhammad, and Muhammad still hadn't killed Luigi as he'd lain in the gutter. That was unheard of!

It didn't matter, Luigi decided. He would still finish the job. Half the money had been paid already, but he wanted the rest. Luigi was certain he had the advantage since he didn't have to worry about dying while pursuing this target. What more could an assassin ask for?

Pulling up the Italian International Airlines on the computer, Luigi booked a flight to Lebanon. He was going to meet with Muhammad whether he liked it or not. The top buyers and sellers in the jihadist movement were to be in war-torn Tripoli in two days. It was that time of the year again. The Muslims were buying and trading toys to kill each other and everyone else. Luigi was sure he still had a *bisht* in his wardrobe. He would fit right in at the mosque in the black, silk robe. And it wouldn't be the first time he'd disguised himself to find a foe.

He mindlessly balled up a gum wrapper. Perhaps Muhammad was expecting him in Lebanon. Maybe that was what he'd meant by his schedule getting busy soon—busy hunting Muhammad. Luigi swore to himself. Muhammad was a step ahead of him all the way. And Luigi didn't like second place.

...✝...

Two days later, Luigi flew into Tripoli. He checked into a five-star hotel, which had been rebuilt since the last Israeli bombing. The rest of Lebanon was just as scarred from conflict brought on by Lebanese-born militias, such as the infamous Hezbollah fighters. Though there was disarray around him, Luigi didn't care. No matter which country he was in, he had a way of locating each society's base pleasures, and Tripoli was no different. Thus, Luigi found the underground pleasures of the city to tend to his flesh as the sun set over the Mediterranean.

Early the next morning, Luigi paid a taxi driver to take him to Aholibama Mosque. The taxi was a sore sight on the dusty parking lot filled with limousines and bulletproofed SUVs, but it was of no consequence to Luigi. He dismissed his taxi and scoffed at the bodyguards crowded around the sunbaked vehicles. They all held Kalashnikov rifles, which reminded Luigi of the greatest rule on the premises: no guns allowed inside the mosque, not even through the front door. Everyone in the prayer auditorium would be unarmed. Luigi couldn't think of a safer place for one killer to meet another.

Luigi straightened his *ghutra* headdress and tightened his *agal* headband as he stepped toward Allah's servants who guarded the door against infidels, crusaders, and *kuffar*. The universal Islamic flag—the crescent moon and star against a field of forest green—hung over the central doorway. They would never let him enter if they knew he was an Italian atheist assassin and corporate spy for France. Luigi didn't even know Fusha, only enough to grunt in agreement.

He handed the doorkeepers his dagger as he passed through a metal detector. They were taking no chances on this day. No doubt, the Mossad and Americans were nearby taking pictures. Only the daring few would try to get inside.

The dagger was given back to him once he was cleared, and he slipped it inside a fold in his robe for easy access. Twelve steps later, he was inside the prayer auditorium.

Looking up at the decorated dome ceiling, the balcony caught his scheming eye. Luigi found the staircase and ascended. He sat at the balcony rail along the west wall and surveyed the mosque floor below.

Over a hundred men gathered in the first room. They were friendly, though brief, in their greetings. Each man had oil money or other such resources to spend and hurried into the two adjoining rooms that were full of tables burdened with photographs of the merchandise. Again, no risks were taken by the sellers or buyers. The sheik who sponsored the event every year strictly enforced all transactions. The arms themselves were stored in a warehouse guarded by the sheik's private army.

In the next room, the brief and friendly atmosphere disappeared. The men bartered and argued prices with more passion than they had applied when arranging dowries for their wives and daughters.

Searching for the average-height, bearded man he knew so well, Luigi laughed to himself. They were all of average stature and bearded. He would need to mingle with them on the floor if he intended to find Muhammad. Reaching into his pocket for his gum, Luigi popped two sticks into his mouth to calm his nerves.

Supposedly, no one had any real weapons in the mosque, and supposedly, Muhammad hadn't had any on him three nights ago in Rome, either. Luigi had followed him all the way from the airport that night. The man had met no one nor picked up any packages. Yet, Luigi could not deny the laser-sighted weapon that had beamed on his chest an instant before the dart had knocked him out. If

Muhammad had been armed in Rome, he would be armed here. Airports had metal detectors, too. That hadn't stopped Muhammad.

Touching his chest, Luigi felt the slight bruise he still had from that dart. After having it analyzed, Luigi knew the toxin slowed the heart rate to nearly a third. That was slow enough for someone to check his pulse and presume him dead. If he was pricked with a dart with the same toxin in this crowd, they wouldn't think twice about burying him in an unmarked grave—though he'd still be alive. He shivered at the thought. Swimming with the sharks in Greece, where he'd learned to scuba dive, sounded more appealing now.

Luigi left the balcony and began to mingle downstairs. Muhammad had glasses, he remembered, which few others wore. He paused just inside the second room and nearly snorted his disdain at the wares on display in the photographs. There was an outdated BRDM Soviet reconnaissance vehicle, Mikoyan spare parts from the company that had produced fighter jets since before World War II, and plenty of SAMs, all portable and primed to take down the next civilian airliner. He even saw a T-62 Soviet tank—very extinct in that day. It had to be a collector's item, Luigi surmised. These men had money to play with.

Besides old Soviet arms, there were scores of Iranian-made missiles for sale, particularly the unpredictable Fajr rocket with its short-but-deadly forty-five mile range. Kassam rockets, a specialty of the Gaza terrorists, were plentiful as well.

Someone bumped into Luigi from behind. It was crowded, so he thought little of it. Turning to step aside, he locked eyes with Muhammad. Luigi's jaw went lax, his wad of gum half protruding from his mouth. He'd always been the predator, yet here was Muhammad surprising him yet again. Luigi hadn't realized how old and short the man was. Muhammad appeared to be in his late fifties, and he was well under six feet. Standing so close to Muhammad, Luigi had to peer down at him. And Muhammad's eyes were livelier than what his airport footage had revealed.

While Muhammad's eyes remained on Luigi's face, Luigi glanced the Arab up and down. The man had to be armed, probably under his robe. Luigi wondered if he could draw his own dagger from beneath his own robe before anyone could stop him, but even if he killed Muhammad where he stood, Luigi would never get out of the mosque alive. Once they started questioning him in Fusha, he would be discovered as the infidel he was. He couldn't remember what they did to infidels who were found in Lebanese mosques, but he was not anxious to find out.

"Putelli." Muhammad spoke first, identifying him by name. It was something he'd not done during the phone call. "Seems you are lost. Or are you a follower of Allah?"

Several men nearby cast scowls at them for speaking English. This was no place for such defiling language. A true follower spoke Fusha!

"The balcony, hmm?" Luigi offered.

He didn't wait for an answer. The sooner he was off this floor of sharks, the better. Luigi walked away and climbed the stairs to the balcony where he sat in the dimly-lit back row. He cautiously eased the end of his dagger from beneath his robe.

Muhammad sat two seats away, facing him. Luigi felt Muhammad's eyes measuring every twitch, every chomp of his teeth on his gum.

"It's good, us meeting like this," Luigi began. "After Rome, I've been looking forward to it." Muhammad said nothing. "I've thought about our phone conversation and about the people who want you dead. Maybe we could help one another."

"I do not think so. Besides, you do not know who is using you."

Luigi struggled to remain as calm as the man facing him. Sharks. He remembered the sharks in Greece.

"How do you know?"

"Those who hire men such as you to kill men such as myself do so anonymously. Do you know why?"

"Why do you think?"

"It is not a thought. It is a fact," Muhammad stated. "They know that men such as you often fail in the hunt for men such as me. And they certainly know that if you did know, I would make you tell me who they are."

"I could find out."

"How?"

"Demand a meeting."

"Then what? Have me pay you for a name I already do not care about? I think not. You—and what you know—have no value to me."

Luigi felt small, so very small, in this man's presence. It was supposed to be Luigi who intimidated people, not the other way around! He reached his hand into his pocket.

"Cigarette?" Luigi held the pack out. He had nothing to

lose by offering. He'd even dared to bring a lighter.

Muhammad hesitated an instant, then reached out, drew a cigarette from the corner and put it to his lips. Slipping the pack back into his pocket, Luigi fingered the lighter. He couldn't take his eyes off the cigarette, nor could he believe the wily Arab had taken it. Maybe he wasn't so crafty after all. As his other hand eased toward his dagger, Luigi was left with a dilemma: should he let the anthrax do the job or use the dagger to finish him off here and now? He could be off the balcony and hailing a cab outside before anyone ever found the body.

"You do not need the knife, Luigi," Muhammad voiced. With his cigarette lit and barely dangling between his lips, he sat back. He held his hands open. "See? We are just talking."

Though Luigi heard him, he didn't move his hand away from his dagger for nearly a minute.

Finally, he stretched and flexed his fingers casually, then rested his hand on the back of the seat.

He watched Muhammad's cigarette burn. But that's all it was doing—burning. Muhammad was not inhaling, nor had he inhaled to light it. Taking the cigarette from his lips, Muhammad held it with two fingers. He pretended to exhale smoke, but Luigi could see the masterful acting as Muhammad obviously suspected the cigarette.

"You are not going to smoke?" Muhammad asked him. "It is not allowed, but no one will know."

"I quit, actually." Luigi palmed a new pack of gum from his other pocket. "Just this now."

Luigi peeled the wrapper from the new pack and chose

two sticks. He tried not to fumble as he moved. Muhammad was watching him so closely. Still he didn't smoke that cursed cigarette! Spitting his old wad of gum onto the floor, Luigi started chewing the new.

"Tell me about this bounty hunter." Muhammad pressed on. "Who could it be? You are a French agent, so we know it is not them. The English, perhaps? Or other Westerners? Hmm?"

"There is an American flavor to the deal."

Flavor. Luigi suddenly realized that his gum had a strange flavor. But it had been a new pack. *Odd.* He kept chewing.

"If it is the Americans, why do they not do it themselves?" Muhammad asked.

"You know Americans. They hate to be implicated unless they can wage all-out war." Luigi wiped his hairline. Why was it so hot on that balcony? "The payment is a large amount, but it could've come from a private, non-governmental source. It's not always government, you know. Individuals can have vendettas as well."

"Of course." Muhammad shifted the cigarette to his other hand. "What do you propose?"

"Excuse me?"

"Propose. What do you propose? Something between you and me, perhaps? I have money."

Luigi blinked rapidly several times; he was having trouble focusing. The gum—it had tasted different. The new pack . . . He patted his pocket. Three packs. But he had carried only two, and neither of them was new. Realization washed over him—he'd been poisoned.

Flashbacks of the year before flooded Luigi's mind: the hospital stay, the brush with death from the cigarettes. Cigarette . . .

Leaning forward, Muhammad put the burning cigarette between Luigi's lips. Luigi reached for his dagger, but his movements were sluggish. Muhammad had no problem stopping him. Luigi's tongue fumbled as he tried to push both gum and cigarette from his mouth and breathe at the same time.

Muhammad gripped Luigi's jaw and cheeks with one hand, forcing him to inhale the cigarette smoke. He questioned Luigi, but Luigi couldn't concentrate. His senses blurred; sound and light became one. The cigarette tumbled onto his lap. Releasing Luigi, Muhammad picked up the smoldering butt, crushed it and removed the filter.

Luigi knew he'd been a fool to think Muhammad wouldn't see through the trick. As his eyes closed, Luigi saw Muhammad pocket the filter and walk away.

†

CHAPTER FIVE

Chloe Azmaveth sat like a stone in the tiny visiting booth designated for prisoners and their attorneys. Though she hadn't been in the field for a few years, her mind was on automatic, soaking up everything, seeing what she saw, storing it all to use later.

A minute earlier, she'd been frisked by a male guard who had granted her a visitation pass. It was the first time she'd been groped by a Malaysian correctional officer, but it was part of the role she had to endure.

The Fhatl Lasam Women's Prison outside Kuala Lampur had been built fifty years earlier. She noted the cement cracks and bacteria on every wall and corner. The stench of human strife and filth barely masked the acrid smell of industrial pollution that drifted on the breeze from the nearby city of over one million. Environmentalists were worried about a few trees being logged in Idaho, as exhaust spilled from every available orifice along the Asian Pacific Rim.

For the first time in five minutes, Chloe moved, brushing aside a bead of sweat from her brow. She knew it would be humid, so she'd dressed in her lightest business suit. But still, it was worse here than in the Everglades. Even worse than Guatemala or Brazil. The old prison smell didn't help either. Fhatl Lasam had once been a men's prison, but currently it was primarily used for women and the occasional high profile or political male prisoner. Men now had a new prison farther outside the city.

As terrifying as the situation was, Chloe was calm. Her God was mightier than these diseased walls. Besides, no matter what happened, her husband, Zvi, would contact Corban. Between God, Zvi, and Corban, she figured her back was covered. If she was somehow delayed or held in the prison, Chloe had instructed her Malaysian driver and interpreter, Fuzzi, to call both men. She imagined Zvi hearing news of her arrest or abduction or injury. He would call Tel Aviv and talk to every old Mossad contact with whom she still communicated. Yes, Zvi would get to the bottom of any dilemma within twenty-four hours. Until she was found, or rescued and back in his arms, she knew he wouldn't sleep a wink.

Corban, however, would be much less emotional, though Chloe knew he cared deeply for all his employees and team members. She imagined the aging spy would first pray for direction, remaining ever-expressionless about her status, then he would be like a general, calling out the cavalry to tear down the walls of Jericho, if need be. Corban wouldn't kill to get her back. He wasn't that man any longer, but he was still aggressive. The weapons the ops teams carried were non-lethal guns that looked like paintball guns and were just as silent. Nathan "Eagle Eyes" Isaacson would rally his team at night outside in the street and storm the prison fence with such—

Shaking her head, Chloe stopped herself. Hopefully it wouldn't come to that. She was in no danger yet. Nothing immediate. Soon, Helena Rauch would show up in the other side of the booth, they would visit, and everything would be fine.

After a sweltering two-hour wait, a guard opened the door at her back.

"Visit over! You go!"

"But—"

"You go!"

The wiry man grabbed her by the wrist and dragged her from the booth. On the ride back to the hotel in the city, her driver, Fuzzi, tried to encourage her to visit again the next day, but she was too furious to listen.

Chloe was old enough to be Helena's mother, and she knew the young woman didn't have one back in Germany. Helena was all alone. That broke Chloe's heart. There wasn't even a safe way to let Helena know that people were trying to help her.

Arriving at the hotel, Chloe dismissed Fuzzi. She pronounced his name "Fuzzy" because it made the twenty-year-old laugh, but she knew it was really "foo-zee." The boy had learned English as a technical support operator for a US-based software company.

"I am market laborer. Cheap, but I smart. I get English, and English more value than cheap 'puter talk on telly!" Fuzzi had explained. "I help now all rich Americans and very exciting girls from American college. I smart!"

Sitting beside the hotel courtyard pool, Chloe wrote a full report on her day at the prison. She sent it off to COIL's headquarters via her compact laptop's satellite uplink. Corban knew how to outfit his people—but not needlessly. They always had the best of the basics, just what was needed to get the job done.

She took a swim to cool off before bed, then found a response from Corban in her inbox.

"It's a blessing in disguise, Chloe. You're getting extra opportunities traveling in and out to see more of the prison. God knows His children. Helena is in His hands. He's the Jailer, not the guard you mentioned. Stay focused. Rest up. Patience. Try again. And don't forget to pray. —C P.S. Call Zvi. He's driving me mad asking about you."

Chloe laughed aloud. That was Zvi. He could simply go into the den and e-mail her, but he would not relax until he heard her voice. Corban's message had given her encouraging insight and optimism about the next day, so when she dialed her husband a few minutes later, she was cheery. She rarely spoke about cases with Zvi, so she merely relayed that she had run into a couple snags. He encouraged her to remember the persistent widow that Matthew wrote about in his gospel.

The next morning, Fuzzi was waiting by his taxi for her.

"Ah!" he exclaimed as she walked from the front lobby. She wore the same suit, since it was the only one she'd brought, but he admired her footwear. "New shoes!"

"Yes, new shoes, Fuzzi," Chloe affirmed, as she climbed into the cab.

"Back to prison?"

"Back to prison."

"Okay!"

As Fuzzi drove, Chloe studied her shoes. They were men's shoes, actually, and too wide for her feet, but they would do. She'd worn lace-up sandals the day before, which were more comfortable and cooler, but these shoes were special. It took practice to walk without pressing her toes on the liner ends where there was a slightly indented plastic tab. If pressed in her right shoe, a quarter-inch needle sprung out and locked into place from the toe of the shoe. The needle was no thicker than a paperclip and as sharp as a bee's stinger.

On the left shoe, the needle sprung out from the heel. Whether in front or behind, anyone who assaulted her was at risk of a pinprick of falaco toxin. Then it was naptime.

While walking in her hotel room that morning, Chloe had accidently sprung both needles into place. To retract the needles back into the shoes, she had to press the button with her toe and use the other shoe to snap each needle back into hiding. Falaco had a long shelf life and required only two spore-sized microns in the bloodstream to work its magic. And after experiencing how the guard had searched and yanked her about, she knew her shoes wouldn't be checked. Their eyes and hands had been focused elsewhere.

She'd been aware the day before, though still too nervous to see everything about the prison that the ops team would need her to see. This time, on the walk to the visiting booth after a brief frisking, she used her eyes to measure the distances between buildings, fences, and yard lights. She eyed the two prison towers, counted personnel and the weapons they carried—or didn't carry.

And this time when she entered the booth, a frail, child-like, young lady huddled in the opposite chair. This was a shadow of the Helena Chloe had seen in a smiling passport photograph. Helena's once long, silky-blond hair was now dirty brown, cropped short as if it had been hacked off with a jagged piece of glass. Her blue eyes were yellow and partially blood-shot, and her slouch made her five-four frame seem even more diminutive. She was obviously not eating well.

Chloe didn't wait for an introduction. She knelt in front of the girl and wrapped her arms around her.

"Oh, that they would take me and let you go," Chloe murmured in German.

After a full minute, she released Helena and held her at arm's length. Tears ran down Helena's cheeks. Chloe wiped them away with gentle fingers.

"Forgive my memory," Helena said in a weak, old woman's voice. "Did I know you before? In Germany?"

Pulling her chair closer to Helena's, Chloe held her hands.

"We've never met, sweetie. My name is Chloe Azmaveth. I'm from America. I work as an attorney for an organization called COIL. We monitor hundreds of Christian missionaries in many countries. I've been following your case very closely since you were arrested three months ago. I'm so, so sorry nothing has been done for you yet."

"I remember the ambassador said an American woman had been bothering him." Helena tried to smile, but it was more of a grimace. "Are you her?"

"Yes, I am. Are you injured?" Chloe turned the girl's arm

over. She saw bug bites and bruises. The sackcloth gown she wore was dusty and, no doubt, mite infested. "They've hurt you?"

"It's not a friendly place, Chloe. Are you in Malaysia for long?"

"I'm going to try to stay in the country until your release."

Helena's hand went to her mouth in a new flood of tears.

"For me?"

"We're going to get you out, sweetie."

"But how? I'm condemned. And I'm a foreigner, which is even worse."

Chloe brushed the girl's thinning hair with her fingers.

"I don't want you to fret any longer. If you want out, we'll get you out."

"If?"

"Someone thought you might have found a ministry in here. No? I know God can use . . ."

Helena looked appalled.

"God has taught me a lot in here, it is true, and I have spoken to other inmates on occasion, but I am primarily in solitary confinement. And I will be until the guards have—" She choked on her words. "When they tire of me, they will put me out with the others."

Closing her eyes, Chloe drew the girl into an embrace. It was worse than she'd imagined. No more diplomacy. They had to get her out now. Or there would be nothing left of her to save.

It was time to call in Eagle Eyes.

†

CHAPTER SIX

Corban wiped his nose and coughed into his handkerchief as the speaker introduced him. He'd developed pneumonia from barely inhaling the cigarette smoke while with Luigi Putelli in Lebanon, but he'd detected the anthrax in time to combat that. The pneumonia strain could've been deadly if gone untreated, but when Luigi had stared so intently at the lit cigarette, Corban became suspicious. Naturally, Corban had sent the filter to the lab in care of William Buchanen, Deputy Director of the Agency in Virginia.

For today, Corban had shed the Muhammad guise. He didn't miss the robes or the company in Tripoli. Everyone had been there: Freedom Fighters of Palestine, Al-Aqsa Martyrs Brigades, Hezbollah, Hamas, Islamic Jihad, and even some Al Qaeda faces.

There were two reasons that Corban had attended the arms show. First, he had a legend to maintain, which required certain appearances from time to time. Second, he needed to meet with South Beirut's new imam, Omar al-Halil.

Corban couldn't, in good conscience, deal arms or string along contacts by giving them apprehended mortar rockets in order to maintain his cover, as he may have done as a government operative. Now, Corban made simple, though no less expensive, gestures to get what he wanted. He put off requests for arms by claiming he had unmentioned, dedicated clients with whom he couldn't break contracts.

"However," Corban often offered, "I have a Rolls Royce in which you may be interested, as a gift, perhaps, to symbolize the future relationship between Egypt and yourself."

And when the automobile, which was most often used to buy off targets, was delivered, it was really anything but a gift. Shipped through Cairo, the Rolls would be outfitted with the most advanced tracking and monitoring technology available. The $200,000 vehicle appeased the would-be client, awarded Corban with his request with legend intact, and satisfied the CIA with eyes and ears into the heart of the country. For this type of partnership, the CIA tolerated Corban's minor spy agency.

Omar al-Halil had accepted his newly polished car that day at the mosque and had simultaneously given Corban what he'd desired—protection for an American couple in a South Beirut neighborhood. The American missionary couple would be safe for now, protected until they were discovered to have Bibles or seen leading a Lebanese Muslim family to Christ. Or until Omar was assassinated by the Israelis or the Syrians. Those were the risks, and the missionaries knew them all too well. But they didn't know that someone from a Christian spy agency had bought their temporary safety with an automobile for a well-known, aggressive Muslim who hated "Western crusaders."

Crossing Luigi Putelli in the mosque had come after his deal with al-Halil. Corban knew that the Italian-French agent was a dangerous killer. The Rome incident and the cigarettes spoke for themselves. But someone was paying Luigi to kill the Egyptian legend, and that had peaked Corban's curiosity. Corban had his bellyful of killing. God had saved him from that darkness, but he still saw their faces in the deep of night—innocent and guilty alike. Thus, with Luigi, Corban was like a leopard whose stomach was already full and was content with only watching his prey, though ever warily.

"And here he is, Andrew Bartholomew Leever!"

Rising from his seat, Corban approached the podium. Author A.B. Leever was a best-selling author of juvenile fiction, enjoyed by both youth and adults. His protagonist was an adventurous, orphaned youth who traveled the world in search of treasure and a family of his own.

Corban took a sip of water, wiped his nose, and gazed out at a half-full auditorium of advanced composition students, most of them English majors. A.B. Leever, like his other legends, had a reputation to bolster, and public speaking, book signings, or readings were part of the maintenance.

To the forty or so students who peered up at the stage, he portrayed himself as a middle-aged man with curly red hair, a large crooked nose, and a cleft chin. He was an unattractive man in this costume, but he hoped all that was forgotten when he spoke.

"In 1526, a man completed a manuscript that sent him scrambling for his life. The king at that time deployed agents throughout the country to collect all the copies of that manuscript as fast as they were being produced. But the people were hungry, hungry for the written Word in their own language. This man who completed the manuscript was William Tyndale, and the king's country was England. And while you sit in your comfortable seats and believe you are so distanced from such persecution for what seems to be a simple manuscript, you should realize that this monumental man in history lived less than twelve generations ago."

Corban paused to let that sink in. These weren't Christian students, nor was the college anything of the sort, but Corban would be a wasted servant of Christ, a useless branch blowing in the wind, if he didn't take advantage of every opportunity to impact and challenge men and women to acknowledge their place before their Creator. He used no notes as he spoke and had considered what he would speak about only on the drive over from the airport.

"William Tyndale fled England with thousands in pursuit. But in 1536, he was captured and condemned as a heretic. He was executed for the same passion you have—the written word. He translated the Bible's New Testament into printed English. Each of you here today could be so blessed if you were to use your knowledge of the English language to impact the world, as did William Tyndale."

Unlike Corban, A.B. Leever spoke emphatically, though only rarely used hand gestures.

"When I began writing, I wrote for me. As time passed, I realized that my writing couldn't grow and mature if I wrote only for myself, nor could I grow as a human being. It was a cycle with no momentum, a cat chasing his tail. God opened my eyes and broke the mold I seemed to have made for myself. Others were the answer. I had to reach others through my writing. And in writing for others, I could benefit from their interests, their passions, and, yes, even their criticisms. My book sales exploded as I determined to give through my writing, instead of selfishly writing for merely my own entertainment.

"Could you be like Tyndale, who was engulfed in a world of strife toward what he believed should be printed in English? Therein lies my challenge to you this afternoon. We lounge here on this fine campus while others, even today, labor over parchments, on manual typewriters, on the internet, some in attics, some in prisons, some in offices, some in Mongolia, some in Peru, some down the street. They have one thing in common: language. Communication.

"And while you could be out there blazing a new literary trail, you waste your time here, listening to an ugly author who scribbles children's novels!" He shook his head and drew a few chuckles. "But while you are here, there are three lessons every writer, no matter the content or audience, should never forget . . ."

Corban talked on, never straying from the podium or using a diagram or projector, but he held their attention for an hour, and then sat on the edge of the stage to answer questions and sign a few books.

On the flight back to New York, Corban checked his inbox and was pleased to see a fresh report from Chloe. She'd made contact with Helena in Malaysia, but Helena was sickly and abused. Chloe was so upset that some of the words in her report were misspelled. That was uncharacteristic of Chloe. It was a small indicator that her emotions were getting the best of her. He hoped she continued to care about Helena's suffering, but that she also kept her wits throughout the ordeal. Zvi and Chloe had tried to have children, but to no avail. Perhaps her maternal instincts were on overdrive, but not without cause.

Praying for strength and safety for both women, Corban then considered the situation. It was quickly escalating with Chloe now on the scene—to the point of possibly creating an international incident. COIL didn't need that type of attention, and Malaysia certainly wouldn't want it. He would need to assess the situation himself, though he still trusted his people's abilities. If Helena had to be forcibly extracted, Corban had to sign off on the op.

He arrived in La Guardia late and had to drive straight to Reggie's, a new steakhouse midtown. Discarding the red hair, bulbous nose, and cleft chin, he was back to average Corban: expressionless, though thoughtful, self-controlled, and ever secretive.

"Hello, Corban. You on Central time?"

Deputy Director of the CIA William Buchanen rose from his seat and shook Corban's hand. Corban took in the man's chipped front tooth, steely gray eyes, and feather-white hair. Because of the tooth, people called him Chip. Years ago, it had been an insult, but now it was the sixty-two-year-old's name. Though older than Corban by several years, Chip appeared to be in better shape, yet both knew that Corban had been more dangerous in his prime.

"Sorry I'm late. I was mugged," Corban claimed as they sat down together. "They stole my watch and apparently my honesty."

"Sounds tragic." Chip chuckled.

"Flight was slow. Headwind or something." Corban pointed at Chip's plate. "Is that blood?"

Chip grinned and peered down at his half-eaten steak.

"Oh, you know I like 'em rare. How are you, Corban? Why do I always feel like I'm more stressed than you look?"

It was true. Chip was a man who stressed over every detail, and it had cost him two marriages and families. He now lived alone in a grand estate surrounded by expensive security.

"A prayer a day keeps the ulcer away," Corban recited.

The waiter approached and took his order.

"Been busy? You're favoring your left side."

"Tore a muscle."

"You used my name to have a cigarette butt analyzed." Chip leaned forward and lowered his voice. "Now, I'm not accusing, even if you have left the Agency. I know you have your reasons, but you know I'm naturally paranoid when a report that mentions anthrax hits my desk. Took me a day to track down where it came from, and even then, you sign my name too well anymore."

"Someone was trying to show me that smoking kills."

"I guess so. It had your DNA on it. Were you contaminated?"

"I'm on Cipro as a precaution."

The two old spies enjoyed impressing one another with

intelligence tidbits only they could access. As they chatted casually through their dinner, Corban knew that Chip, in a vague way, was debriefing him, but not so that the table nearby would be alarmed by their speech. They met once a month in person, always two days later than the previous monthly meeting, to disrupt routine. Corban shared what his COIL organization needed, and Chip conveyed his concerns over the power that COIL was gaining, with influence and authority in some international circles.

It still saddened Corban to remember what had distanced the men in the first place, but he held firm to his convictions. Two years prior, Corban officially resigned from the Agency because he refused to hunt and kill for the government any longer. He simply couldn't kill, not even his enemies, not if he took the Bible for what it said. Chip had been drunk and called Corban a traitor to his country. Corban had told him, "I'd rather be a traitor to a country than an outcast before God Almighty."

Two weeks after that, the two had reconciled, though Corban knew the real truth was that Chip and the Agency still needed him. They wouldn't kill him—he knew too much. But it would be a difficult task, even if Chip was able to convince the hunter-tracer squad in New York to sanction his assassination. The few who knew Corban, the legend, wouldn't want to cross him or volunteer for the job, even if they knew how to handle an experienced agent. Thus, Corban was thankful the two had made peace.

Toward the end of the meal, a blond, blue-eyed man stepped up to the table.

"Deputy Director Buchanen, great to see you!"

Chip remained seated to shake the man's hand.

"Mr. Fairchild, fancy meeting you here." It was obvious to Corban that the meeting had been previously arranged. "Branden Fairchild, Corban Dowler. Please, pull up a chair."

"Ah, the famous Corban." Branden seated himself.

"That's Mr. Dowler to you," Chip corrected.

The handsome Branden Fairchild looked to be in his early thirties, with a tall, one–hundred-ninety-pound frame. Corban surmised that this man's warm smile and too-white teeth more often drew friends than foes. Anyone so impressive by looks alone made Corban instantly cautious of underlying intentions.

"Branden ran C.A.P. missions all over the Middle East for the Air Force." Corban was surprised at Chip's bragging. "That Combat Air Patrol unit saw as much action as anyone. How many kills you have, Branden?"

"Ah, sir . . ." The man grinned. "It was a squad effort." He turned to Corban. "You're with the COIL operation, right?"

Corban didn't get a chance to answer for himself.

"Branden here has heard of—more than seen—COIL," Chip said. "I guess that's how it is for most of us. Anyway, Branden was assigned as your liaison with the Agency two weeks ago. Under me, of course."

"Of course." Corban nodded with a forced, rare smile. "On behalf of my staff, we look forward to working with you."

"I trust the Rolls Royce was to your client's liking?" Branden inquired as he sipped ice water. "I had the garage put their very best into it."

A questioning look passed from Corban to Chip. Chip raised his hands defensively.

"Hey, you can't expect me to handle all your little designer orders personally. Branden did a good job, right? The Rolls is in place?"

"The car was perfect," Corban replied courteously to Branden. "I'm glad to put a face to someone who can get something done for me on time, besides Chip."

"Well, whatever else you need, just let me know. I'm told you have a green light."

"That's appreciated."

"Is it true your little field agents don't carry weapons?"

"I wouldn't put that rumor to the test!" Chip laughed. "If they're anything like their boss, they have no use for guns, huh, Corban? Prayer and a little Bible reading gets you by now, huh?"

Corban smiled politely and shrugged under Branden's careful eyes—the type of eyes that elicited trust. The type of eyes that gave Corban chills.

✝

CHAPTER SEVEN

Lying on his belly, Nathan Isaacson watched the smoke and ash boil from the active volcano. It would be night soon, and complete darkness would envelop the jungle. He wouldn't be alone, though; he would have about five hundred mosquitoes to keep him company. The Guatemalan rain forest was alive.

Nathan slapped a mosquito on his neck. The nicotine in his system must have dropped too low since he hadn't smoked a cigarette all day. He hated smoking, but the nicotine and smoke helped keep many of the bugs off. It was too late to light up now. A glowing spot of ash could give away his position, so Nathan tried to ignore the bugs as he touched his earpiece comm system.

"Scooter, report."

"Scooter here, amigo. I see one bug in the nest, four on the perimeter, and six in the hut. Over."

As his man listed them, Nathan made a mental count. Eleven guerrillas held the hostages that Nathan was in charge of rescuing. A month prior, three Christian missionaries had been dragged through the streets and beheaded. Then four more were taken captive from a clinic near the coast, along with a few other foreigners. As

Nathan's team tracked them, they learned that the hostages had been trucked and force-marched inland through native lands where board and bush huts had to be rebuilt every time it rained. The captives were being held in the mountains now under a foggy mist that crept in as often as the nearby volcano belched.

Twisting his handlebar mustache, Nathan admired the red sunset through the smoky sky. The mustache was not the most unique hair on his face, though. The bushy eyebrows that capped his chestnut-colored eyes angled sharply down toward his nose. Hence, the name Eagle Eyes, which was given to him in the Marines wherein he'd served for six years.

When Nathan let it be known he was a Christian, his government had stationed him in the Treasury Department, punishing him with a mountain of paperwork on fraud cases. That was where Corban had found him—and stole him away. Now, at thirty-two, he was deeply thankful that the boss had rescued him from that desk job.

"Hey, man!" His earpiece chirped. "I'm being eaten alive!"

"Radio silence, Scooter!" Nathan hushed sharply. "Quit messin' around."

Nathan's team was five strong, all ex-military, all dependable, each with his own skills and personality. He and Scooter were the only ex-Marines and the only two who had known one another in the years before COIL.

Scooter was a little Mexican who was the team's comic relief. He resorted to horseplay so much that it made Nathan nervous sometimes, but the man was top-notch.

Scooter had been a sniper in the Marines, with more time spent in Iran than any other Marine Nathan knew. And, though small, Scooter could still wrestle any of the others into the dirt.

Bruno was as big as a bear and just as black. He kept his head shaved and had a habit of chewing on his lower lip whenever he was nervous.

Milk was a quiet boy from Ohio. He was as white as his nickname indicated, and equally intolerant of its lactose. His real name was Jesse Patters, and his father was a well-known preacher back home.

Toad was the last of the five. He was an ex-soldier in the Chinese paramilitary. He and Nathan were the only ones on the team not married. However, Toad and a pretty Chinese interpreter who also worked for COIL were something of an item.

All the men had their weaknesses and strengths, Nathan mused, but their most outstanding quality was their faith. It always came first. When his COIL men took a knee to pray before they broke camp every morning for a dangerous mission, it nearly melted his heart. Some thought being a Christian was for sissies. Tell that to Bruno, Nathan thought to himself. The man would put someone in a headlock and give a tour of David's mighty men of the Old Testament, then tell stories about John the Baptist, then Paul and John, who both did serious prison time, not to mention the beatings. *Sissies?* Nathan had seen a lot while serving in the Marines, but the toughest, most heroic men he knew were the four he commanded.

Whatever bloodlust the men may have had in their

former lives was non-existent now. They were armed with non-lethal weapons that got the job done, and not one of them complained about the lack of blood during a mission. In fact, the team members had bled more than their foes had, but each did so without complaint. Every scar they gained from live ammo represented a hostage saved or a prisoner rescued without the cost of a life.

Darkness closed in, and Nathan slipped his infrared night vision goggles over his camouflage hat. A monkey screeched nearby and argued with a banana. A parrot swooped down, almost landed on Nathan's stationary head, then flew away when it saw him blink.

"This is Eagle Eyes. Tell me when they're sleeping, Scooter. We'll catch 'em snoozin', boys. Over."

"Roger that."

Scooter had spent much of the previous night getting settled in an evergreen tree near the guerrillas' encampment. Now, nearly eye-level with the camp's only crow's nest, he was about thirty yards away from their perimeter shacks. With leaf and camo netting, Scooter had spent the day in the tree, fighting cramps, flicking at bugs, and watching the camp's every move. He had identified every hut's purpose, where the hostages were kept, and even a couple of the guerrillas' names.

Pulling back a palm leaf, Nathan exposed his satellite phone so he could check his text messages. It looked like the mission was still a go. No headway with the negotiators in Belmopan. Just as well, Nathan thought. The team was ready and prepared to move in. It had taken them two weeks to locate the camp. The captives were surely as anxious to leave the jungle as the team was.

There was a message on the sat-phone from the boss.

"Malaysia welcomes you."

Nathan chuckled and shook his head. That one scared him a little. He'd already read the initial summary of the Malaysian mission, prepared by Johnny Wycke. Johnny did the field prep and recon before the ops team showed up. Malaysia could get messy, no doubt about it. It was an actual prison extraction and evacuation. When it was time to tell the guys about their next mission, he imagined that Scooter would be in a panic. Bruno would chew on his lip while Toad paced the floor, mumbling prayers in Chinese. And Milk would sigh, shake his head, then say, "Why? What's the problem, guys? Maybe we're part angel. Let's get this girl out!"

That was Milk, always reminding the team they had a special place under God to protect His children. He knew they were not real angels, but it was an uplifting thought.

Then they would get her out—this Helena Rauch. They would find a way into the prison, after they tore the heart out of the electrical system and found her cell. Nathan knew her name was Helena, but afterward he wouldn't remember that tidbit of information. He wondered why he always forgot the victims' names, though he could never forget their abused bodies.

The other teams that worked for COIL saw just as much suffering, but they worked more covert, blue-collar missions, smuggling aid workers and Bibles in and aid workers out.

Nathan's team was called the Flash and Bang Team.

Bruno claimed he was Bang, and Toad said he was Flash. Then they would mock-argue about something or other until the others were in tears from laughter, because Toad would lapse into his native tongue and would seem to be winning the argument, though big Bruno only spoke a little Fusha from his days in Iraq.

"Team Leader, this is Milk."

"Go, Milk."

"Two westbound on the east trail. Over."

Nathan twisted his mustache until it hurt. Two more entering the camp made a total of thirteen guerrillas now.

"Roger," he whispered.

He barely breathed as the two arriving guerrillas passed within ten yards of where he lay.

Few guerrillas were militarily trained, but Nathan acknowledged their 7.62mm rifles slung casually over their shoulders. Most were peasants and rebels drawn by the promise of wealth by ransom and a heartfelt cause, whatever that meant in Guatemala.

They moved out of sight and Nathan breathed easier. It was almost time. He settled his pack into the bushes nearby, but within reach from the trail when they retreated in a hurry.

"Bruno, report."

"All quiet, Eagle Eyes."

"Toad?"

"Nothing. Over."

Toad and Bruno were covering the west trail, Milk and Nathan were on the east. Scooter had the center and was in place in his tree.

Nathan checked his rifle. From a distance, it appeared as any other assault weapon, except for the oblong CO2 canister on top. It was lightweight plastic, with a shorter magazine on the underside than an AK's thirty-round magazine. The NL-3, on fully automatic firing, cycled at the rate of six hundred rounds per minute. The magazine itself held five hundred rounds, each round a compact capsule of liquid gas with effects not unlike chloroform, but not as fast-acting as Corban's falaco. When the pellet rounds burst upon impact, the capsule's water-soluble shell turned to vapor with the toxin. Two inhales of the toxin took out a target for twenty minutes. There was little margin for error. The rounds had to be placed on the chest, neck, or face since the gas was lighter than air.

The NL-3 selector switches were set for five-round bursts that night, as the men most often preferred. Each man had target actuators plugged into their infrared night vision goggles. No lasers. Lasers were too visible for a pitched battle. And not one of them would be carrying their gear since their body armor weighed twenty pounds altogether. The plating wouldn't stop a point-blank round, but a hollow-point from over fifty yards away might deflect, if not mushroom, against the plating.

The team was aware of the only restriction with the NL-3 assault rifle: it had a maximum accuracy range of only one hundred yards. It was a fine line between offense and defense, pellet range and armor vulnerability. Thus, they depended on prayer.

Pausing, Nathan looked to the north. Millions of safe Americans were a short plane ride away in that direction.

Most of them probably never thought of the suffering so near. Many forced themselves not to think about it, not because they cared, but because they didn't. As long as they were safe, that was all that mattered to most, he figured. But this was the team's life. They sacrificed their own blood, their relationships, their friendships, and their comfort, all to save others. It was a sobering and humbling thought, but Nathan knew in his heart that this was God's purpose for his life.

"This is Eagle Eyes. Lock and load, Flash and Bang. Gear check. Two minutes to go-time."

Nathan went over his fatigues one more time. He had his canteen on his belt next to two XT95 stun grenades: non-lethal, non-fragmentation, flash-n-bang—just like the unit. Everyone had two. On his leg in a deep pocket, he had two flares, one green, one red. They were for their ride out. Green was to announce the L-Z pick-up site, and the red was to signal the chopper not to land, that it was too hot—if the bird was close enough to see the signal.

"Memphis, this is Eagle Eyes. Do you copy?"

"Roger, Eagle. I copy. Been listening all afternoon. Just tell me when to jump. Over."

"Roger and out."

He already liked their new pilot, and he hadn't even met him in the flesh. Nathan and his boys were long in the bush when Memphis had arrived straight from Moscow. When Johnny had said this guy could fly, Nathan hadn't asked what he'd been doing in Moscow. It didn't matter.

Memphis and the bird were on the other side of the belching volcano. ETA: five minutes.

"Eagle here. Heads up. Rock and roll. Move in. Scooter, take out the nest. Confirm. Over."

They were up and moving at a crouched run, Milk and Nathan from the east, Bruno and Toad from the west.

"Wait one!" It was Bruno. "Three eastbound on the west trail. Snuck up on us. Over."

"Stay put," Nathan ordered, then kneeled with Milk in the east trail. Milk faced their six o'clock angle. "Scooter?"

"The nest is down for the count. Over."

Nathan checked his watch. If the guerrilla in the crow's nest had just been taken out, that left the team twenty minutes until the bad guys started waking up again.

"Roger that. Bruno? Talk to me. Over."

"They're in the camp, Eagle. That's sixteen now. Over."

"Fifteen," Scooter corrected. "Nest is down. Over."

"Scooter," Nathan called, "where are the three new arrivals going? Over."

"Barracks. Second hut. Wait. One's hailing the nest. Move now or we're a bust. Over."

"Move!" Nathan commanded.

They rushed forward, their boots making soft thumps on the worn paths. They were ghosts—or rather angels, as Milk would say—drifting into the compound from the darkness. Above and to Nathan's right, he could imagine Scooter clicking bursts of pellets into the camp, but in reality, the NL-3s couldn't be heard over the jungle's screeching and crying.

Once inside the compound, Nathan moved right in cover formation. Milk moved left to the first hut. Bruno and Toad spread out, and with Scooter's help, they took down the three recent arrivals before they could disappear into a shelter. The three had over twenty rounds pumped into their necks and chest, each round leaving a small welt, but a welt was better than the alternative.

A man emerged from the mess hall tent on Nathan's right. He turned. *Pa-pa-pa-pa-pa*. The middle-aged guerrilla drew a sidearm and fired it into the ground as he collapsed. The gunshot woke the camp and terrified the jungle critters even more. They could hear the men inside the barracks scrambling for their weapons. There was only one door, one exit. Bruno and Toad aimed intently at the door. Waiting, they stood like statues, feet apart, braced. Nathan covered them as Milk assaulted the first hut where the prisoners were held. And Scooter covered them all.

The barracks door burst open in a hail of live gunfire as men poured out, moving left and right. Nathan focused on the group of men to the east. He shot five bursts of pellets, then moved to the next, whether that man fell right away or not. There was no time to count or confirm. They had to trust instincts. Muzzles flashed in response. Toad fell.

"Toad's down," Scooter announced from his perch.

But the Chinese man jumped back up.

"Prisoners located!" Milk yelled from within the first hut. "Three walkers, two carries! I'm gonna need a hand in here!"

"Roger that," Scooter answered for Nathan. "Hold up, Milk."

"Holding . . ."

Nathan moved right and reloaded. A round slammed into his right shoulder and spun him in a 180, but he kept his footing. He refocused and fired from his fresh magazine. Five in the chest. That one went down. Four in the neck, one in the ear. *Sorry.* The next man took three in the throat.

Suddenly, it was quiet except for the sound of running feet and movement in the bushes. Five or six had fled into the jungle behind the compound. Nathan kept his weapon ready.

"Memphis, this is Eagle Eyes. Come in."

"Go, Eagle Eyes."

"Get those rotors spinning. See you at the L-Z in ten. Repeat: ten minutes to L-Z. Over."

"Roger. Ten minutes. Out."

"Toad, how bad are you?" Nathan asked as they all aimed at the ten men lying on the ground. "Can you walk?"

"Just a scratch. Upper thigh. Don't ask me to carry you, though."

"Scooter, eyes and ears. They might come back."

"Roger. Eyes and ears."

"Bruno, help Milk. Milk, bring 'em out. Over."

"Comin' out."

"Eagle, here they come!" Scooter warned. "I'm picking up heat. They must've hid some artillery out there in the bush! Over."

"Get outta the tree, Scooter! Toad, move your skin! Take point if you're not hurt bad. Scooter, you and me, peel and cover! Milk, report!"

"We're coming!"

Toad limped past them as Milk and Bruno emerged from the first shack, each carrying a hostage, three others in tow. They headed east behind Toad down the brush-crowded trail.

"Incoming!" Nathan yelled as an RPG screamed past his head into the crow's nest foundation. Nathan was blown in a twist and landed on his side. He rolled over and found his rifle. Scooter was pumping pellets into the bushes behind the huts, but he couldn't see anyone. The crow's nest creaked, then toppled over. Nathan dodged it by two feet. In unison, he and Scooter lobbed two flash-n-bang grenades into the bushes, then ran like jackrabbits after the others.

An instant before their grenades exploded, another RPG whistled by and exploded. Scooter was knocked off the trail. The flash-n-bang grenades blew, and two men screamed as they went temporarily blind and deaf.

Nathan stopped and pulled Scooter to his feet. Scooter's rifle was in splinters, as was his night vision headgear.

"You all right?"

Scooter fell over. Nathan slapped him. Nothing. Turning, he shot at two approaching guerrillas. They fired back blindly into the dark jungle since Nathan didn't have a telltale muzzle flash to alert them of his position. He pulled Scooter's left arm over his back and lifted him over his shoulder.

"I'm lucky you're light," Nathan mumbled.

With his rifle in his fist, he took off after the others. He could hear the chopper now. Stopping on the trail, he scooped up his pack with the barrel of his gun. The others were retrieving their packs along the way as well. He had no idea where Scooter's pack was, but there was nothing personal or pertinent in it that he couldn't do without.

Blind firing continued behind them. The guerrillas yelled and cursed at one another. Bullets flew over Nathan's head. He tripped over a root, sending the two of them sprawling into a bush. It took him ten seconds to collect himself and Scooter. The guerrillas were coming, chasing them in the direction of the approaching chopper. Nathan dropped his pack and fired down the trail with one hand. A man shrieked, certain he was dying, but he only passed out from the toxin. Picking up his pack, Nathan kept running with Scooter over his shoulder.

Green flares fizzed ahead. His men were already in the clearing. The chopper was coming in too fast! No, Memphis knew what he was doing. He knew they were in a hurry from all the gunfire below. It was a perfect landing.

Nathan staggered from a stand of trees and choking greens. Bruno took Scooter as Nathan crawled into the chopper bay.

"Go! Go!" Toad yelled from the copilot's seat.

Cradling Scooter's head in his lap, Nathan pushed aside the man's bandana and felt his friend's neck for a pulse. *C'mon, Scooter!* There it was. He was alive.

No one on the chopper was without injury except Memphis, but it was too dark to dress their wounds. The way Memphis flew, they'd be on the beach in ten minutes.

"Who are you guys?" a voice asked weakly.

It was one of the nurses from the clinic. From the cockpit's green glow, they could see her arm had an old bandage on it.

"Just friends, ma'am," Bruno answered. "Just friends."

Nathan checked his watch. Twenty minutes ago, they'd been rushing into the encampment. The first guerrillas would be waking up about now. He hoped they had a good headache.

PART II

"And the light shines in the darkness,
And the darkness did not comprehend it."
John 1:5

†

In the Forest Hills neighborhood in Queens, New York, Velt Plavanko sat in a chair gazing through the lace-curtained window. He wouldn't think of drawing back the curtain, not with the man he was watching so near. The elements were set at that moment, just the way he preferred: dark sky, dark room, drawn curtains, and the unsuspecting man with his family across the street.

Velt Plavanko was a man without conscience. Over the years, he'd killed many who'd stood between himself and what the one called Abaddon wanted of him. For the last month, he'd been assigned to watch the man across the street, spy on his wife, and take pictures of his blind adopted daughter. But under no circumstances was he to approach the house or those in it. Not until the given time, anyway. If he got too close, he could be discovered.

Maybe he'd already been discovered by the ordinary-looking man across the street in his ordinary-looking house. One never knew for certain with the old spies—how much they knew or didn't know, how much they were letting their enemy get away with before pouncing suddenly and unexpectedly.

It wasn't just the old spies, either. The new spies—those

who'd been trained by the old veterans—had built-in radars, too. Velt had to be extremely careful in how he dealt with the man, Corban Dowler. But when the man was away from his home, Velt was left to stalk the wife and daughter. He'd become more relaxed around his prey, maybe even a little careless, but Abaddon would never know. Velt would be ready when the call came to take life. He could hardly wait.

Born in Poland, Velt knew, even as a child, that he was special. He obeyed the voice from the darkest corner of his closet, a voice no one else ever heard. Velt did what the voice told him to do. He hated. The voice said it wanted Velt to hate his parents, his classmates, and all authority everywhere. The voice loved hatred.

At nine years old, Velt stole a bicycle. It was easy because he hated the previous owner. Next, he stole fruit from the market and money from his parents. He expressed his hatred by hurting others and taking what they loved or owned. Hating and hurting others pleased the voice, and this pleased Velt.

When Velt hated someone he couldn't hurt, he became frustrated. As he anticipated how he would exact his hatred upon someone, Velt would often scratch his arms until they bled. By the age of sixteen, he had long, white scars that covered his arms. Most of the time, he wore long-sleeved black shirts to hide the scars.

Velt used any reason he could find to hate others. Any careless glance by another youth would send Velt into a rage. He was arrested many times before the age of twenty for beating up both acquaintances and strangers. After one such occasion, when Velt had put three young men into the hospital, Velt was arrested and put into prison for a time. In confinement, Velt didn't hide the fact that he obeyed a voice that told him what to do, whom to hate, and how to hurt those he hated. The authorities in Warsaw sent him to a psychiatric ward immediately. There, he met others who heard voices, but only one of them heard the same voice that Velt did.

For the first time, Velt had a friend, and the two conspired to please the voice. Velt told his new friend, Ryan, of his past deeds against innocent people. Ryan told Velt they would soon escape the ward and begin serving the voice to such a degree that they would usher in the end of the age.

Velt worshipped his new friend. He was an American boy with blond hair and blue eyes, and he spoke fluent Polish and other Slavic languages, some of them extinct. He taught Velt English since he was from the United States, though his parents were Polish ambassadors. The young man hated his parents, so Velt hated them, too. However, Ryan assured Velt that the voice had much more for them to do than to hate and rebel against the authorities.

Everyone, including the orderlies in the ward, loved Ryan because he was smart and handsome with trusting eyes. Velt learned more from his friend every day and obeyed him as well as the voice. He learned to stand quietly in Ryan's shadow, a move which soon won him favor with the orderlies. Ryan heard the voice more clearly than Velt did, it seemed, but Velt didn't care. He was more excited to see what would happen next than to care who heard the voice the clearest or the most.

One day, there was a great explosion in the ward, and many patients escaped. The two friends fled the city of Warsaw and lived in the countryside. They stole from farmers and travelers alike. No one resisted them since they were both so vicious.

Eventually, the two friends left Europe and sailed to America on a barge. They changed their names and began new and separate lives in Philadelphia. Velt prowled the streets every night until a number of mobsters took him to use as their own weapon against their enemies or the government. Since Velt had no conscience, he would do anything he was told, as long as it was evil and hurt others. All the while, the voice assured Velt that he was being prepared for something grand in the near future.

While Velt became a feared thug on the streets of Philadelphia, the voice instructed his friend to join the military. With a quick smile and a strong mind, Ryan rose in rank, status, and popularity. He became a pilot and made powerful friends in the government. Though Velt and Ryan were on different ends of society, they stayed in touch and became the best at what the voice gave them to achieve.

That was when the voice stopped, and they met Abaddon. The man named Abaddon said he was the voice that had comforted them through childhood. Now the voice had taken human form, and he would comfort them as adults—from a distance, for safety's sake. They would communicate through technology.

Abaddon wanted the world prepared for his master's rule, and that meant both Velt and Ryan were going to be even busier. The two obeyed whatever Abaddon told them to do.

That brought Velt to the neighborhood in Queens, though many years of evil had passed since he'd met Abaddon. It had also been many years since Velt had seen his friend from the psychiatric ward in Poland, but he often admired Ryan's success and achievements from afar. Velt knew they were still friends, that they were connected forever by the voice from the past.

At forty-six, Velt was still strong, but he'd gotten bulky because he ate so poorly, and his job allowed him very little exercise. His once jet-black hair had turned salt and peppery, but he kept it trimmed and combed in the latest style. He was not handsome or successful by society's standards, not like his friend, but Abaddon told him to be proud of himself nonetheless.

Across the street, one of the house lights went out. Picking up a notepad, Velt made a note: *Jenna to bed – 8:00*. Abaddon wanted him to take detailed notes. He would use them against Corban Dowler someday, but not until the time was right. And Velt often reminded himself that Abaddon was very wise and would know what to do and when that time would be.

Velt sighed and stretched. He hated it when Jenna, the adopted blind girl, went to bed. He enjoyed watching her through their floor-to-ceiling front windows as she stumbled and touched objects when she walked through the house. And no matter how much attention he paid the Dowler family, Velt still hated them—because Abaddon hated them.

Using a spotting scope, Velt peered through his see-through curtains at Corban and his wife in their living room. Corban was reading the Bible with Janice. Velt noted it on his pad. He knew it was the Bible because Abaddon had told him. The family read from the Bible every night and every morning, but Velt often wondered what they found so interesting about the Book. Velt had not read it himself, since Abaddon had ordered him to avoid the Bible's pages at all cost, and said the One who wrote it was their ultimate foe.

An hour later, Janice went to bed, while Corban stayed up reading more, then knelt on the floor, folding his hands in reverence. This intrigued Velt immensely. He set aside his TV dinner to scope Corban's actions more intently. Every night, Corban spoke to someone, his lips moving slightly. Whomever Corban spoke to, Velt was certain it was the same Master of the Bible, but Abaddon's enemy was Velt's enemy. Naturally, Velt wanted to know what Corban was saying to their greatest enemy, but he had to rely on reading lips, at which he wasn't very good, and sometimes Corban didn't move his lips at all; he only cried and held his face in his hands.

But this night, when Corban was finished kneeling, he did something different. He came to the living room window and watched Velt's house. Corban's hands were in his pockets, his eyes and face betraying nothing of what he was thinking. Velt shivered. Things that Velt didn't understand about Corban scared him, and Velt hated the man more for it. He wasn't sure if it was the Bible reading, or the kneeling and praying to the Master of the Bible, or—

Corban drew the shades on his window and turned out the lights. Breathing a sigh of relief that he hadn't been discovered behind his own draped window, Velt made a final notation on his pad: *Corban to bed – 10:30.*

†

CHAPTER NINE

Luigi Putelli scoured the internet for any sign of Muhammad ibn Affal. Apparently, the cigarette hadn't killed the crafty man, for the media would have made mention of a recent mysterious death. When he did finally kill the man, Luigi would miss him. Never had he been bested by anyone three times in a row.

In his Naples office, Luigi put all else aside to search every known network for the arms smuggler. There was no sign of a man by his name or bearded description arriving in or leaving Tripoli, Lebanon, or anywhere else, in the last few days.

His next hope was to discover whom Muhammad was to meet at the mosque. Maybe that would shed some light on the man's origins beyond his hideout in Egypt, which Luigi was almost certain was not his home country.

Muhammad's phone calls were usually routed through Crete and Cyprus, then went untraceable through multi-encrypted satellites. And his travel history, traced from years ago, showed that he used the massive airport in Athens to lose any tails and possibly change his identity. Athens was good for that. Luigi had used the hub himself many times.

That Muhammad was not who he seemed to be was the only conclusion Luigi could make. There was something much more sophisticated to him than Luigi had ever suspected. He could feel it in his bones.

By chance, Luigi stumbled upon a Lebanese diplomat who'd been at the mosque in Tripoli, and he had some news of interest. Nearly every known jihadist had purchased weapons through the sheik that day—if not personally, then by proxy. That was of no concern to Luigi. What did concern him was that a man, Omar al-Halil, had been given—not purchased—a brand new Rolls Royce. Luigi had already checked the man's bank records readily available through the Paris DGSE database. Omar al-Halil was his man.

After digging deeper, Luigi found that the automobile had been shipped from Cairo, though the paper and number trail ended there. Maybe Muhammad was from Egypt after all.

Omar, the vehicle recipient, had met with the wily Muhammad, Luigi decided. The two had been there; they knew each other. The car meant friendship, an ongoing one.

Through the night, Omar al-Halil from Beirut became Luigi's target. Luigi pulled up newspapers, media clips, and coverage off the internet, and studied the man who lived lavishly and openly. He studied Omar's resources in the southern, bombed-out regions of the city, and studied Beirut as well. In all his research, he watched for Muhammad's face. There was no trace.

But Omar would know how to find him.

Luigi paced in front of his window through the morning. He had a wad of chewing gum in his cheek. Omar was the key, so Luigi had to find a way to get to him. The man had bodyguards, and bodyguards had guns—especially in the land of Hezbollah guerrillas. Besides, Luigi spoke next to no Arabic. The car was a key, but Luigi didn't know how the car fit into the picture. He had to find out.

Dialing a landline number from his notes, Luigi spoke for a few minutes and hung up. Next, he dialed a cell number, spoke French and German interchangeably, then moved on. Finally, he found the number he wanted and dialed Beirut.

"*Salam alaykum.*"

"*Wa alaykumu salam.*"

"May I please speak to Omar al-Halil?"

There was a long pause.

"Not in English. He speaks no English. I am Adab, his accountant. How may I help you?"

The voice was monotone, unfriendly.

"How about French? German? Italian?"

"No, he speaks only what you would call Levantine Arabic."

Luigi swore under his breath. The time he'd spent following the trail of the car seemed wasted now. His eyes narrowed. Maybe there was another way.

"Is Omar there?"

"He is here."

"I'd like to meet with him."

"He does not meet with Westerners."

"But he drives our automobiles."

"What do you want?"

"Tell him I have information about Muhammad ibn Affal."

There was muffled Arabic spoken.

"What is the nature of your information?"

"The nature that affects their relationship permanently."

More muffled translating.

"Do you know al-Halil's home?"

"Near the market or in the hills?"

"Near the market."

"I do."

"We will expect you tomorrow afternoon, or not at all."

Click.

Gloating, Luigi was enjoying his victory, and then he stared at the pack of gum on his desk. Only two pieces had been taken from it. He knew Muhammad had slipped the gum to him when the two had bumped into one another at the mosque. Just the top stick in the pack had been tainted, one of the two that Luigi had chewed while on the balcony. So clever, this Muhammad.

And now Luigi was forcing himself into Muhammad's circle of friends. He wondered if it was wise to provoke the only enemy Luigi had who didn't wish to kill him. It would be easier to kill Muhammad if Muhammad was likewise trying to kill Luigi. But Muhammad didn't seem to care about the attempts Luigi had already taken in Rome and Tripoli. Surely the man knew how many targets Luigi had already silenced! He'd never failed a sanctioned hit—not before Rome, anyway. Muhammad was different, even special, but Luigi saw no way he could get to know the man without killing him first.

Luigi flew to Beirut that night, taking uppers along the route to stay awake, then downers to sleep once he checked into a hotel in Northern Beirut. The next morning, he slept late, though with the time change, he was still groggy as the taxi drove him to a miniature palace overlooking the Mediterranean.

The palace grounds were beautifully groomed, but near the back driveway was a market of fish and rugs with all their strong smells. Refugees and rubble were everywhere. Israel's bombing of the terrorist-sponsored country had put them back decades, but pockets of commerce still survived—as did the militants.

Since it was already known he was a Westerner, Luigi didn't bother with a disguise; he wore jeans, a collared shirt, and blazer. After a brief frisk, during which his dagger was taken and set aside, he was led down a long hallway. Luigi glimpsed through several doorways, one of which was to a study with a modern computer, another to a prayer room, and one to a porch where two veiled women were lounging. He was shown into a dark, candle-lit room where a man was playing a piano, and another stood leaning on the piano from behind. The man playing the piano had his back to Luigi as he played. The windows to Luigi's right faced the sea, but great, thick drapes hung over them, creating the dark atmosphere.

"I am Adab," the man leaning on the piano greeted as he sucked on a kiwi fruit.

Both men wore *dishdashas*, the long, cotton shirt-dress

of the region. Luigi deduced he was about forty.

"This is Omar al-Halil," the man said, but the pianist continued playing a dreary piece and didn't turn around to acknowledge Luigi.

Though Luigi couldn't see the man's face, he knew it well from photographs and footage. Becoming uncomfortable, Luigi glanced around for a place to sit. There were no chairs, only giant pillows against a wall. He wasn't going to sit on the floor alone, so he decided to remain standing. Luigi folded his hands to keep from digging into his pocket for gum. The three pieces in his cheek were enough.

"I am Luigi Putelli." He saw little reason to hide his identity. It was discovered so easily these days, anyway. Sometimes his name cast fear on the listener's face, and Luigi never tired of that. However, there was no recognition on Adab's face, only boredom. "I have news of Muhammad ibn Affal."

"So you say." Adab shrugged and slurped loudly on his kiwi.

Luigi shifted his weight. He thought he would be accommodated a bit more than this, being as good as ignored by his host. If they kept this attitude, they wouldn't care at all about the perfectly fabricated news he had to share. Perhaps, Luigi considered, if he worded it just right, they would be gracious. Then maybe they would offer him a kiwi as well.

"I found a shipment of BTR-60s that Muhammad intends to sell you in your next purchase." It was a good lie, convincing, Luigi felt, feeling ever so confident the more he spoke. "That's a Soviet, eight-wheeled, armored personnel carrier that can carry up to fourteen people." He paused as Adab translated for Omar. "The version he has in mind includes a small turret armed with a 14.5-millimeter gun."

"We know the BTR series," Adab scoffed, relaying what Omar had muttered over his light piano playing. "What is the news?"

"The news is that the armored plating is faulty. It's as thin as paper and couldn't stop a 9-millimeter round. The sides are hollow and the turret is a coffin. Muhammad seeks to destroy you for a new client."

"Who told you this?"

Luigi smiled. He had them. Soon they would give him Muhammad. Ah, that all men had a mind such as his!

"It is a Kazakh source who wishes to remain anonymous."

"Kazakh. I see. And, Luigi Putelli, what do you propose?"

"For a small fee, I will extinguish his life's fire."

"Kill Muhammad ibn Affal? What is your fee?"

"No more than the value of the automobile he gave you."

The piano playing stopped before Adab could translate. So the man did know English!

"Why would we use you and pay you when we could do it ourselves?" Adab asked. "Muhammad is a Muslim. He should die by our hand, no matter the charge you bring."

"For me, it is personal," Luigi confided. "While I must see to him myself, anyway, I wanted to discuss the matter with you first."

"So, kill the man," Adab stated with a shrug. "You want

to anyway, yes? Why bother us? You do not need permission."

"But to warn you of his deceit is worth nothing?" Luigi shifted the gum in his mouth from cheek to cheek. "I have traveled a great distance at a great price to be here today."

Adab stared coolly at Luigi. Luigi wanted fresh gum. And kiwi. He wanted the dagger they had taken from him. And he was ready to leave.

"You should realize . . ." Omar himself spoke, his English near-perfect. Luigi tried not to appear shocked. His world had its share of surprises. ". . . that I am not a client of Muhammad ibn Affal's, nor have I ever been."

Luigi swallowed his gum with a gulp.

"Truly there must be a mistake. The shipment was labeled to you. Perhaps it was another gift, this one faulty."

"There is no gift, Luigi," Omar stated as he turned to face him. "And we all know there are no BTRs scheduled for shipment here."

As he saw Omar's face, Luigi went pale.

"Muhammad!"

At the sight of Muhammad ibn Affal, Luigi took a step back. He knew he would never make it to the door. There were men waiting in the palace vestibule.

Adab suddenly drew back the drapes, blinding Luigi with sunlight. The real Omar al-Halil emerged from behind the curtains. Luigi had never been as close to fainting in his life than at this moment. Surely Muhammad would kill him this time, and if not Muhammad, then Omar.

"What are you doing, Luigi?" Muhammad stood and allowed the older man, Omar, to sit on the piano bench.

"Did you truly believe I would not be contacted regarding such a meeting as this?" Adab quietly translated for the real Omar. "Omar is a man who knows his loyalties and knows I would not betray him. He is also fully aware that my arms contracts with others prohibit me from selling to him at this time. Do you sincerely believe he would freely give me to you by your evil, lying scheme?"

Luigi's mind flashed back over twenty years of murder and similar schemes, making gain through his own selfishness. Recalling the many who had begged him for their lives, he tried to decide which of them had sounded the most convincing, because that was what he needed to do now—beg for his life. He didn't want to die; he wasn't ready to die. But he saw no way around it this time.

"My greed has made me . . . a fool."

"Indeed," Muhammad agreed as he walked a full circle around Luigi. Omar was listening and watching intently, as if he were engrossed in a movie, careful not to miss any words. "This is very low, Luigi, even for you."

"Yes, Muhammad, I know."

"I have given you opportunities to change. In Rome, and then in Tripoli, I spared your life, showed you mercy. Have you not noticed? Have you not recognized the opportunities to change your ways?"

"I know, Muhammad ibn Affal. I am in your debt."

"Then? Will you never change? Will you persist?"

"Admittedly, I have been deceitful, but I had not decided if I would fulfill the contract on you. In many ways, sir, I only wanted to understand you, why you haven't killed me when you could have. It makes no sense!"

Omar clapped his hands twice, eyes sparkling from such entertainment.

"You flatter me," Muhammad scoffed, "and I sense it is only to your advantage. There is no truth in your words."

"No! Please listen, Muhammad. Three times, sir, I have tried to rise above you, and I have failed." Luigi wrung his hands in defeated frustration. "You already know me well. I have spent so much time in the last month chasing you, my employers are about to retire me. I am no use to them in anything I do. I fear I have only become a failure."

"And you seem to deserve retirement. Have you found out who has hired you to kill me?"

"No. I have made inquiries, but to no avail."

"Omar says he will gladly torture this man for you," Adab relayed for his employer. "Omar is certain this fool knows more than he is admitting."

"That is certainly an option." Muhammad considered it. "Torture. What do you think, Luigi?"

"I've been truthful. I have as many questions as you, I swear it! Perhaps my sponsors knew I would fail, and that was their way of disposing of me. Perhaps I am finished with this life," he said dejectedly. "At a time like this, I cannot be brave. I have told you what I know."

"Muhammad, Omar will dispose of this infidel dog, " Adab hissed. "You will never see him again. It would be an honor for us to do such a minor task for you."

Luigi met Muhammad's gaze. The great smuggler was actually considering turning him over to the Muslim extremist! If Luigi knew how to put his pounding heart into words, Muhammad would know that if he let Luigi live,

Luigi would never cross Muhammad again. Even though the unknown party who'd paid Luigi would surely pursue him for not killing Muhammad. Whether he survived this day or not, Luigi's life was finished.

"There is a place I know of in the desert," Muhammad finally said, "under a fig tree. I will take an iced tea and sit in a chair as he sweats under the sun, digging his own grave. It is a poetic end to a foolish man's life." He turned to Adab. "Could you have him gagged and bound and put into the trunk of my car?"

Adab asked Omar permission. The man approved with some amusement. Adab left the room and returned a moment later with two other men and two lengths of thin cord that would surely cut into the skin.

"Please! Muhammad! Forgiveness! I see my errors!" Luigi begged as the men began to bind his wrists tightly. He didn't fight them. He was defeated. "I'll convert to Islam. I'll serve Allah. I'll work for you, Muhammad. I'll be loyal! I swear it! I have nothing else but to—"

They gagged him and tied his ankles. He wet his pants and sobbed through his gag. This was his end, and he knew he deserved it, but as a devout atheist, he had no entity with which to make his peace in death—not even an empty-faced god of wood or stone. His soul was dark and dead, and an eternity of such terrified him.

Finally, they picked him up and carried him outside. A trunk opened. Luigi twisted around in time to see a spare tire and a tire iron. *Not the trunk!* He wiggled furiously, so much so that instead of setting him in the trunk, they tossed him inside roughly. His skull thumped against the tire, and he lay in a dazed, twisted position long enough for them to slam the trunk door without further incident.

Luigi panted through his gag and nostrils. He seemed to be in complete darkness and intense heat, but his eyes finally found a tiny light on which to focus. His wrists were already bleeding, and his fingers were going numb behind and beneath him.

He hated himself. What a fool he'd been! So many chances to flee from Muhammad, but Luigi had to keep swimming with the sharks. If there was a God, he decided this was His vengeance on his evil life. Luigi could think of no good that he'd done. All was bad and a waste, and he had nothing to show for even the selfishness.

Now he would die in a grave under a fig tree. Understanding and submitting to this sad fate, he lay still in the trunk.

†

CHAPTER TEN

It was midnight before Chloe Azmaveth and Nathan "Eagle Eyes" Isaacson climbed the water tower nearest the Fhatl Lasam Women's Prison. The tower itself rose to an impressive two hundred feet at the edge of the city. Two miles away sat the prison, lit up like an airport.

Nathan first clipped his harness to the water tower's platform midway up the tank, then secured Chloe's. The platform was railed, but with the wind gusting in from the coast that time of year, one could easily be blown over the platform edge. Above them, on top of the water tank, a red beacon blinked a warning for low-flying aircraft. The pulsing beacon was Chloe and Nathan's only light.

He'd been hesitant to allow Chloe to come along on his reconnaissance of the prison, but she'd insisted, reminding him that she'd been inside the prison to see it in detail. Nathan was impressed with the attractive forty-four-year-old and her interest in recon. To him, she was only an attorney for COIL, but here she was in the field, climbing water towers and spying on foreign prisons. She had even climbed the tower ladder faster than he had. And as he secured their safety lines, she carelessly sat down on the edge of the platform, hanging her legs over the side as if she were on a bridge only ten feet above water. Even with the safety line, Nathan approached the edge cautiously. The whole platform was rusty and shaky. He didn't trust it or his line.

"Sit down already," Chloe urged without looking up from her binoculars. "You're shaking everything with your trembling."

"I'm not trembling. I'm just . . . Never mind."

Nathan sat down and hung his feet over the edge. They felt heavy, as if they were trying to pull the rest of his body over the side as well. He could parachute from a plane at 1500 feet, but a feeble nylon cord and a brass clip on a shaky platform . . . *What was he thinking?*

"I could've taken snapshots and brought them down to you," Chloe offered.

"I'm fine!" Nathan snapped. "I'm just getting my bearings." Who did she think she was? Taking his spotting scope from his back, Nathan steadied it on the rail and adjusted the dial until the prison came into focus. His scope was ten times stronger than Chloe's binoculars. He studied the prison for a few minutes without speaking. Everything he saw matched the sketch Chloe had drawn back at the hotel. Glancing at Chloe, Nathan began to realize that she might be more than just their public relations manager or attorney.

She hadn't just done a sketch of the prison; Chloe had drawn a freehand, scaled diagram of the whole prison compound. Nathan now understood her confidence. He wouldn't have known the precise measurements unless he'd seen the prison for himself tonight.

Chloe was a looker and twelve years older than he was, but that didn't matter to him. Looking at the badge on her finger, Nathan had to keep reminding himself she was married, maybe even to someone inside COIL. He didn't know anything else about her, except that she knew German well enough to speak to the hostage, Helena Rauch. Nathan had learned German in the military, and he wanted to know where Chloe had learned it. But he decided he didn't like her. She was too secretive, and Nathan liked to know the people he worked with.

Casting him a quick glance, Chloe caught him studying her.

"Been in the jungle too long?" she asked him knowingly. "Eyes on the prize, huh?" She pointed at the prison. "Eyes front."

"Sorry." Nathan shook his head and put his eye back to his scope. He needed to know the compound inside and out, then describe it to his team. "How'd you know I was in the jungle?"

"You know those reports you write after every op?"

"Sure. You get a copy?"

"I decide who gets a copy."

Nathan swallowed. She definitely wasn't who she seemed to be.

"So . . . you're a little more than a glorified lawyer."

"A little more."

"Is that why I feel you've done recon before? That sketch you drew for the boys back at the hotel was pretty precise."

Chloe again pointed at the prison.

"See the towers? Six hundred feet from base to base. Only the towers are visibly armed, but there's the armory to think about."

"Right. The armory. South side?"

"East. At the base of the northeast tower."

"Oh, yeah. I see it now. You figured that out after only six visits?"

"Sure, but I've only seen Helena three times. See the big building with the stepped-up roof? That's where most of the prisoners are. Across to the southeast tower—"

"How far is it across the yard?"

"Fifty-four feet."

"You're sure? Fifty-four exactly? How do you know?"

"The fence line is poled at three yard intervals. It's all about eyeing the angles and measuring my photographs for the correct hypotenuse. C-squared and all that."

"Okay, I'll take your word for it."

"The long, narrow buildings on the fence east of the southwest tower house three prisoners: one male political, one female political, and Helena's in the third one, farthest east. They're seclusion cells. Special treatment, though it's far from special at all, if you know what I mean."

"I read your brief. But there's something else that bothers me: it's not as big as I was hoping. You say it's six hundred feet, diagonal? That's small."

"Yeah, but think of it like there's less distance to cover once you get in there."

"That's all fine and dandy, but it also makes their guns both closer and deadlier," he said.

If she'd read the Guatemala reports, then she knew

they'd all come out wounded. Toad was still limping. Scooter had a concussion from shrapnel that had nearly scalped him. Nathan's right shoulder was still bandaged from where a bullet had grazed. The others had their share of near-fatals as well.

"I'd rather cover twice the distance to make their bullets less true. Make sense?"

"Fine," Chloe stated. "We just need the right plan."

Nathan grunted. Easier said than done. The perimeter was double-fenced, and the towers had pairs of armed guards. Each tower could easily cover the other with deadly force; it was only two hundred yards from corner to corner. That meant, somehow, they had to take out both forty-foot towers simultaneously. Easy if they could simply blow them up. Not so easy if they didn't want to kill the guards. The towers had sturdy roofs. That could be something, Nathan pondered. The booth in each tower was encased in glass, with sliding windows on all four sides from which to shoot.

"If you read our reports, then you know we're the Flash and Bang Team. You don't need us here. You need someone who can get in and just smuggle her out somehow."

"Not only would that take too long to organize, it wouldn't work. Security's pretty tight. Since they have political prisoners and not just regular criminals housed inside those buildings, they've implemented extra security measures."

"Then it's got to be through the fence, crash through maybe. Or from the sky—parachute in."

"Sounds kind of elementary."

"You have something better?" He found her criticism offensive.

"Not right now. But whatever we come up with is going to need some outside help."

"We've got a chopper and pilot."

"Not that kind of help. I mean intel. We need to know more about this prison. There are still too many unknowns. We just have to figure them out."

"You're saying 'we' a lot."

"Use my sketch to piece together a room-sized model of the prison and go over it with your team."

"Excuse me?" Nathan chuckled and climbed carefully to his feet, shaking his head. "I appreciate what you're doing and the measurements you've calculated. You care about this girl. That's cool. We'll get her out. But I don't take orders from you."

By the time he'd finished speaking, Chloe had climbed to her feet. She was much shorter and had to look up at his six-two, two-hundred-twenty-pound sturdy frame.

"Is that so?"

"Yeah."

"Who do you think you take orders from?"

"Well, this guy named Johnny Wycke, for one, and there's—"

Nathan stopped talking. She wasn't listening, which angered him. He wagged his finger in her face.

"You know what? I don't even have to explain it to you. Go back to the hotel or back to the States. I can tell you'll only get in my way."

Chloe didn't bat an eye.

"I was running ops in Mecca with a cyanide capsule where my molar should've been when you were poppin' pimples and shaving that uni-brow, Nathan Isaacson. You don't take my orders? Wrong. We all take orders. Now, you'll do what I say. Go slow on this one. No wrong moves. No second chances to grab Helena. This isn't like the jungle, or the desert, or a country road. You have to put your ego aside and trust me on this!"

Smiling, he didn't believe the pretty, brown-eyed attorney had been in ops at all. Corban had never talked about her before.

"Maybe we should hear what Corban has to say about this."

Nathan saw Chloe pivot her foot slightly. He didn't believe she'd actually kick him on the dangerous platform. But kick him she did, though only lightly, square on the shin, then she backed away. Looking down at her boot, he couldn't see the tiny needle attached to the toe, but he suddenly knew what she'd done.

He tried to swallow past the lump in his throat before he collapsed.

Forty-five minutes later, Nathan's eyes blinked open to find himself lying flat on his back on the platform. Rolling over to a sitting position, he saw Chloe standing on the other end of the platform near the ladder.

"They don't make 'em like you anymore, Chloe," he said as he shook his head and rubbed his shin. He was humiliated, but he couldn't believe she'd actually tranquilized him! "You were really in ops?"

"Mossad."

"Figures. How long?"

"Twelve years."

"Nice boot trick."

"I don't need the boots, Nathan. They still teach us Israelites a little Krav Maga."

"Look, I'm sorry, Chloe. I should've shut my mouth. I'm used to being on top. I was way out of line."

"Your eyes were doing a little wandering of their own, too."

"Yeah, you're right about that, too. I know you're married. I apologize. We should've brought that taxi driver of yours with us from the hotel."

"Got that right. Come on. Let's go."

Nathan climbed to his feet and offered his hand. Chloe shook it hesitantly. All was well.

But he knew he would never live this night down. He was used to pushing his way around. It was just like Corban to send him an ex-Mossad agent.

Nathan felt like crying.

†

CHAPTER ELEVEN

Corban was still dressed in his Muhammad ibn Affal costume when he pulled his car off the desolate road into the east-central Bekaa Valley desert. He hadn't slept since crossing the Atlantic twenty hours earlier and could've fallen asleep right there, with windshield facing Syria and tailpipe toward the Lebanese Mountains. Another car was also parked there, which had been his doing the night before when he'd been called by Omar for the emergency meeting in Beirut.

He shut the car off. Silence. That was one nice quality about the desert. This desert wasn't always quiet, though. In the recent past, thousands of civilians who supported Hezbollah militants had fled for their lives across this very desert into Syria as Israel stormed into Jordan.

Now Corban had to change vehicles. He would have to change disguises as well—he had a long trip ahead. Flying first to Athens, he had to lose himself there, change disguises again, then fly into JFK Airport.

But first, there was the baggage in his trunk. He knew the usual rules: spy meets spy, one dies. Killing Luigi Putelli would solve a number of problems for Corban, but he knew it wasn't the appropriate answer for a Christian.

Corban thought about what the Bible said about enemies. It wasn't easy, but followers of Christ were to love their enemies, to give them the shirts off their backs if they demanded it. That included Luigi. And all the neighbor principles applied to enemies, for who wasn't a neighbor in some form or fashion? Including Luigi. His neighbor was the guy next door, in the next state, or in the next country. And that included Luigi. There weren't to be any conditions to that love, though Corban knew a lot of Christians who somehow justified killing bad guys. Corban had thought that way before coming to Christ. Perhaps, Corban considered, they weren't reading the same Bible as he was to learn how Christians were to act toward enemies. That was the whole reason he ended up leaving the CIA. Putting a bullet to an enemy's head was hardly loving him.

At the very instant that Corban was asking God what to do about the assassin in the trunk, the answer came to him.

Adopt him.

That was the answer. Show him love, even if it was tough love. Maybe no one had ever done that for Luigi. It meant taking certain risks on Corban's part, certain compromises with his legendary reputation, but he was certain that the answer had come from God through the reflection of what the Bible itself taught. Adopt the man. Show him Christ. And God would work out the details. A brazen decision for a spy who was responsible for so many lives.

Climbing out of the car, Corban opened the trunk. Luigi lay there passively, in his own sweat and filth since he'd been in the trunk for hours since leaving Beirut.

"Whew! You stink!" Corban waved his hand in front of his face at the smell.

Luigi stared up at Corban. His lips were chapped and he'd been crying. All traces of pride had disappeared.

Though Luigi weighed more than he did, Corban grabbed the assassin by the shoulders and pulled him roughly out of the trunk, spilling him onto the ground. With a pocketknife, he cut Luigi's ankle binds and stood him upright. From the backseat, Corban fetched a two-and-a–half-foot trenching shovel and stabbed it into the roadside sand. Then he cut Luigi's wrists loose. Luigi was too defeated to even rub his wounded wrists or remove the gag. As he forced the shovel into Luigi's hands, Corban yanked the gag from his mouth.

"Come on. You've got a hole to dig." Corban smacked the dazed man lightly on the cheek.

He led Luigi by the arm into the desert—where the sand was rocky, though loose—then released him and gestured at the ground. Luigi took a deep breath and, with slumped shoulders, began to dig. Folding his arms, Corban stood watching, admitting to himself that this was a bit cruel. But there was a process to this sort of transformation. Change in people was always initiated by a catalyst.

When the hole was wide and long enough, Luigi climbed into the trench to dig deeper. Corban let him dig, allowing Luigi to decide how deep he wanted his own grave.

"It's important I dig this deep enough, Muhammad, so no wild dogs will run off with my bones."

Though Luigi was dehydrated, he was strong and made

quick work of the hole. When the hole was chest deep, he tossed the shovel onto the pile of sand beside the grave. Turning in a slow circle, he gazed in every direction.

"There's no fig tree, Muhammad."

"I know."

"You said there would be a fig tree. It would've been nice to be buried under a fig tree."

"Get out of the hole," Corban ordered. Luigi obeyed. "Take off your clothes. I don't want anything on you that can be identified as Italian."

"I always thought it would be like this—an unmarked grave." Luigi began to undress. "I never thought I'd be buried naked, but you seem to think of everything, Muhammad. Without my clothes, if my body's found in a few months, no one will be able to identify me."

Luigi stood naked, his clothes heaped next to his bare feet.

"Kick your clothes into the hole."

"Excuse me?"

"You heard me. Everything into the hole. Do it."

Confused, Luigi obeyed. His Italian-bought jeans, shirt, and blazer tumbled into the hole.

"Pick up the shovel now and fill in the hole."

Blinking at Corban, Luigi's face questioned, but he didn't argue. He bent to his work.

While Luigi filled in the grave, burying his past, Corban returned to the cars. It was his turn to strip, peel off his beard, heavy brows, glasses, and costume. After putting everything into a flash-bag, he drew the string and let it burn. From another bag, he drew his red wig, the big nose, cleft chin, and appropriate makeup. He pulled on decade-old clothing and became the well-known author, A.B. Leever.

Taking yet another bagged identity from the trunk of the second car, he also grabbed one of the gallons of water he had stored for emergencies. Luigi had finished filling in the grave and was walking back to the cars when he froze mid-step. He stared at the ugly, redheaded man before him.

"Come on. Put the shovel in the trunk." Luigi obeyed, though not without stealing glances at this new man who had even lost his Mid-Eastern accent. The ugly man handed him the gallon of water. "Wash yourself."

Luigi backed away a few steps. First, he guzzled nearly a quart, then washed the filth off himself. Corban tossed him the bag of new clothes.

"Get dressed. They'll be a little short in the limb for you, but they'll do. Can you dress and listen at the same time?"

"Yes, Muham— What do I call you?"

"For now, I'm Andrew Leever. Call me Andy. I'm a writer. But you—I know you speak French, so you're Canadian. We're flying out of Damascus. The identification is in your bag. Can you do makeup?"

"Yes. I've done this before. What's my name?"

"Reggie Fontaighn. It's one of my legends. You're an oceanographer, but your home is in Montreal. Ever been there?"

"No."

"I'll tell you all about it on the way."

Before they left, Corban poured gasoline over the first

car, then torched it. Black smoke billowed in Corban's rearview mirror as they drove away. Luigi couldn't help but admire Corban's new profile as he drove.

"You're not even an Arab, are you?"

✝

CHAPTER TWELVE

Velt Plavanko was beginning to hate the house in which he lived. He rarely left it unless it was to follow the Dowlers around the city. Even the shopping he did had to be done at night when he was certain the family of three was asleep and he wouldn't miss anything. So it was a relief that day when Janice and her daughter left the house in their hybrid car. This didn't mean Velt could relax, though. On the contrary, he had to follow them at a distance, taking note of everything: their activities, routines, new names, or new faces in their lives. The relief came as a by-product of being able to leave the house in Forest Hills.

They drove only a few miles before they stopped. Velt was an expert at tailing. Veteran agents had even been fooled by his stealth. This mother and daughter were easy. He kept cars or people between him and them at all times and never faced them directly, so he always seemed to be looking elsewhere if by chance his presence was suspected.

Dropping Jenna off at a daycare on the edge of Queens, Janice stayed to talk to a female attendant who Velt knew ran the care center. They came here an average of twice a week. If school were not out, the seven-year-old would be going to a school for the blind in the city. But it was summer, and the care center catered to children with physical disabilities.

Janice spent sixteen minutes speaking to the care attendant, then drove away. Velt followed her through Brooklyn and across the bridge to Manhattan Island, predicting where she was going by looking at his notes from the previous weeks. Sure enough, she paid for parking in Midtown, and walked up Broadway to the COIL headquarters—another location Velt had been warned by Abaddon never to approach. Security was too tight around the two suites for someone like Velt to go snooping about. He didn't fit in around many places since he was strange—and he knew he was strange—so he accepted his place in the shadows and was happy to be used by Abaddon since everyone else rejected him.

According to his notes, Janice Dowler would be at the COIL offices until three o'clock, at which time she would beat the traffic across the bridge, pick Jenna up from the daycare, and go get ice cream. That was their ritual.

Since Corban was out of town and now Janice was out of sight for a few hours, Velt decided to drive back to Queens to Jenna's daycare. He arrived by ten o'clock and parked down the street to watch the children through the front windows of the center with his hand-held uni-scope. If anyone happened across Velt and approached him with suspicion, he had a verifiable private investigator's license, which he'd pulled only four times in twenty years—and it had always done the trick. A badge demanded respect, even when Velt displayed it. The badge was power.

Velt was a little nervous on this day, because he'd

decided to approach the blind girl. He knew his orders, but he was tired of being so far from the action when he was convinced that approaching Jenna all alone was perfectly safe. She wouldn't be able to identify him, of course, and it would be just this once. Besides, he had something for her, a little something he'd put together that Abaddon might have approved if Velt had asked him. It was just a gift, a stuffed lamb. But what made it so special was what the lamb had secured inside its stuffing. Proud of himself for even thinking of it, it made him even more certain that he didn't have to always be at a distance. Not while his handsome friend from the Polish ward got to shake hands and converse with so many important people every day. Velt could do that, too!

The little blind girl was smart, though, already reading children's novels with all the funny dots on the pages. And because she was so smart, Velt would be brief—in and out. He already knew what he would say and how he would say it.

When the children in the center had snack time, Velt had a sandwich. Then, at two o'clock, Velt climbed out of his car with the stuffed animal under his arm. The center maintained a strict schedule of games, stories, and learning. But at two o'clock it was playtime for a while.

He knew what Jenna did every week at this time, and where she went. She always felt her way outside to the fenced-in playground, to the swing set or the slide. Evidently, the center dismissed the idea that a kidnapper would steal a burdensome disabled child, because the fence was nothing more than a chain-link, chest-high on

Velt. The attendant and her helper took playtime as a break for themselves as well. For a few minutes, the two women would drink tea and chat with one another. They probably figured the kids couldn't get into much trouble in that short time. There were twelve kids in all—amputated limbs, a couple deaf, and one in a wheelchair. Jenna was the only blind child. She often reached the playground before the others and played alone for a few minutes.

Velt walked down the street, then crossed it as Jenna opened the glass door and tapped her cane through the playground equipment. He didn't loiter outside the fence since he knew that would look suspicious to normal citizens. After checking the center's windows and seeing nobody was watching, he casually slipped through the narrow gate with no problem.

"Excuse me, Jenna Dowler?"

She'd gone relatively straight to the slide, but she paused at his voice. Turning her sightless face toward him, her cane bumped his shoe.

"Who are you?"

Kneeling in his slacks and short sleeve shirt, Velt came down to her level. Because of the summer heat, he'd abandoned the long sleeves this day.

"My name is George. I'm your father's friend. I came to your house a few months ago to talk to your parents." She boldly reached out to touch his face, feeling his nose and eyes. "I live near here and work for the daycare. Here, I have a stuffed animal for you. You can keep it. It's a gift."

Jenna's hands dropped to his arms and felt his scars where, as a youth, he had cut himself to bleed for the voice. Then she found the stuffed lamb in his hands.

"You talk funny."

"It's because I came from another country. I'm going back inside now. Don't tell the other children about the lamb, or they'll want one, too. This is our secret."

"I don't remember you."

"That's okay, Jenna. I'll never forget you."

Velt was sure he had taken too long. Walking stiffly to the fence, he slid back through the gate. After a ninety-degree pivot, he was casually strolling back to his car. His heart was pounding. No alarms. No sirens. No screams. No problems. He'd done it! Maybe next time he'd be even braver.

Climbing into his car, he surveyed the street. All was quiet. And in the little playground, the attendant was pushing the child in the wheelchair out to be with Jenna. Velt laughed wickedly. He'd been too bold, he told himself, but he was so smart. His handsome friend from Poland had taught him how to make people trust him, how to fit in. It was easy, especially with the blind.

Instead of racing back to catch Janice emerging from COIL headquarters, he waited in his car, knowing she would be at the daycare within the hour to pick up her daughter.

...†...

Janice Dowler had been a nurse by profession, and in many regards, she still was. That was her special place inside COIL—she ran the medical branch of the organization. She was in touch with schools, mission boards, and medical teams around the world to find out what specific medical supplies each needed. The budget Corban gave her wasn't very large, though in unique cases he would allow leeway. But they weren't a medical company, he reminded her from time to time. So Janice kept to her list of priorities and saw to the most demanding, if not the simplest, needs: bandages, gauze, antibiotic ointment, and general medicines. She left most medication concerns for those organizations better trained for such demands.

Even though most would never know who had sent or smuggled the supplies to them, Janice still saw her work as a ministry. The Lord knew; that was all that mattered. And this ministry helped her feel a part of Corban's deep passion. She knew little about the other two COIL directives: to provide early warning and extraction for Christian aid teams in jeopardy, and to screen and train COIL operatives.

Corban and Janice had been married for twenty-three years, but it was only six years ago that Janice learned he wasn't a marketing supervisor for a travel agency. He'd given his life to Christ, and at that time he'd shared his secrets with her and his convictions about leaving the CIA. News of his double life had nearly destroyed their marriage, especially when Corban had disappeared overseas for a full week right after he'd told her everything. Upon returning home, he'd slept on the couch for a month.

Slowly, however, she'd come to grips with his past. The killing was the most atrocious, and she'd become his most avid supporter in leaving the Agency for that very reason.

Now her husband was a spy for Jesus, and she could live

with that. He didn't kill any longer, not even the bad guys. Sometimes he wasn't very nice to the international crooks that endangered God's servants, but when the bad guys woke up from Corban's incapacitating methods, maybe they would thankfully consider changing their ways.

Like her husband, Janice stayed to herself, even in the busy COIL office. She was self-sufficient. Her desk, next to Corban's locked office door, gave her privacy from the caseworkers, since no one approached the boss's door when he wasn't there—and rarely even when he was. The one friend she did have in the office was Chloe Azmaveth. Even though the PR woman was a few years younger, Janice was quite spontaneous and bright-eyed once she opened up, and the two got along splendidly. Chloe and her husband, Zvi, had even gone to dinner a few times with Corban and Janice. Zvi and Corban were like old pals, too. Zvi was in the mining industry, and Corban had spent some time in Johannesburg in South Africa's mines; the two could talk for hours.

Janice had her church friends, too. Every Thursday morning, she and the ladies got together for a Bible study in the church basement. And every Sunday, Corban made it a point to take his family to church—unless an emergency arose and he was called away.

Above all others, Janice preferred her husband's company. His quiet, thoughtful demeanor was the reason she'd married him. Now that he was a Christian, he'd become more sincere than she'd ever imagined he could be. Janice was happy.

The adoption of Jenna had been the most wonderful

gift of all, though it had come about tragically. Jenna's parents had been new missionaries to the Ukraine, when they'd been killed in an explosion from a bomb placed under the chassis of their car. It was a miracle that Jenna had survived, but her corneas and deeper visual tissues had been damaged beyond repair or transplantation.

Corban had been deeply hurt that he hadn't been aware of Jenna's parents' foes in their particular country. He should've monitored the level of danger, he thought, even influenced or directed it elsewhere to save her parents. Feeling responsible, Corban had fully financed Jenna's facial reconstruction after she was released from the burn center. Then it had been just a matter of time before Janice's attention to the girl turned into motherly love. They adopted Jenna the day after Corban quit the CIA.

Noticing the time, Janice realized she'd better get on the road to pick up Jenna before traffic became too congested. She often worked from home on her computer, though coming to the headquarters gave her an official presence that she enjoyed. Besides, most days, Chloe was there and could keep her apprised of Corban's whereabouts—relatively.

Before Janice left the office, she typed Chloe a quick e-mail. She knew there was a situation developing in Malaysia that had drawn Chloe away, but she hadn't heard from Corban in two days. Maybe he was with Chloe, she hoped.

When Janice arrived at the daycare a few minutes late, other children were still about, and Jenna looked like she was having fun. The boy in the wheelchair was giving her directions as she pushed him around the craft room. But Jenna wasn't a very good driver, or the boy didn't know his right from his left, because every other minute, they exploded in laughter as she harmlessly crashed his wheelchair into something. Janice couldn't help but laugh as she watched from a distance. She loved Jenna as if she were her own flesh and blood.

"Mom!" Jenna cried once Janice announced herself. They'd talked about Corban and Janice not being her real parents. Jenna had been quick to assure Janice that she understood her parents were now with Jesus and she needed a new family. "Just a minute. Let me get my lamb."

Janice watched as Jenna left the boy in the wheelchair and extended her cane. The girl crossed to the windowsill and picked up a—

Quickly skirting the table, Janice joined Jenna at the window. As much as she wanted to rip the stuffed animal from her daughter's hands, she didn't want to frighten the girl.

"Where did you get this, Jenna?" she inquired softly.

"The man from the daycare. He said he knew Dad."

"He was here?" Janice peered around the center. She was fully aware that the center's founder was a female, as was everyone who worked there—a mother and a teenage assistant. "When, honey?"

"Was I wrong?" Jenna sensed something fearful. "What's wrong?"

Janice bit her lip. The lamb was hideous. The eyes, normally marble and black, had been whited out. And the lamb's white wool had been dyed a blood-red color, though patches of the wool hadn't taken to the dye. It was a prank . . . or a message.

"Can I keep it?"

"If it was given to you, but you have to let me wash it first, okay?"

"Okay."

Jenna bounded off to say good-bye to her friends, but Janice was hardly settled about her daughter's new toy. Janice was no spy, but she had a mother's instinct. She straightened a number of books and cartons of paint on the sill while discreetly looking out the windows. If a man had approached Jenna, it had happened when she'd been outside. Her daughter liked to play on the slide and swings; Jenna loved to feel the wind on her face as she moved.

It was a good neighborhood with residential homes on the left and right. Cars were parked along the curb, but none that appeared so run-down that she would associate it with a degenerate.

Taking her time to position a spongy dartboard's suction cups onto the glass, Janice looked past the dartboard but kept her hands fumbling with the game. There he was. Nearly a block away was a newer model gray sedan, though she couldn't see the plates; it was too far. But there was definitely someone sitting in the car on the other side of the street. And, she assumed, he was watching the daycare.

Casually turning away, Janice's cheeks flushed. An evil man had targeted her little girl! He'd probably said all the right things. Otherwise, Jenna would've known to scream her head off. She and Janice had even made a game out of the very serious lesson. They'd bought earplugs and taken turns screaming. Jenna knew that was what she was to do if a stranger ever approached her—and the girl had lungs, too!

Janice studied the craft room and carpeted area where she knew the reading time took place. There weren't any other stuffed animals and certainly nothing else painted blood-red.

She caught Jenna's hand as she was petting the lamb.

"Come to the bathroom with me, okay?"

"But I don't have to go."

Exempt from the stern look that Janice was tempted to give her daughter, Janice instead put her mouth to Jenna's ever-alert ear.

"It's an emergency. Please don't argue." As they started walking, Janice set the lamb down.

"What kind of emergency, Mom?"

In the bathroom, Janice locked the door. From her purse, she palmed her cell phone and stared at it. She knew the rule: use for emergencies only. Corban had explained how she was to work through situations. First, she was to pretend she didn't notice anything alarming. That way she wouldn't scare away the tail. Second, she was to call him only in an emergency that didn't require the police immediately.

"Because of who I once was," he'd told her six years ago, "there will be people watching us once in a while— just checking on us. They might follow you for a couple days; you'll recognize their cars. No need to panic, okay?

Fifty percent of the time that you think there's someone there, it's just your imagination. I get fooled all the time, thinking I'm being followed. Forty percent of the time that you feel you're being watched, you are. But there's still no need to panic. They're just those nosy agents seeing what the Dowlers are up to. Then, without warning, they simply go away."

"And what about the last ten percent?" Janice had asked.

"Well, that's when they're not just nosy agents, and you should call my emergency number or the police."

The first year after she knew Corban was an agent, Janice had dialed his emergency number nine times and the police five. She'd been right a couple times, and Corban had called in favors from afar to nab the tails who were frightening his wife. Both times, the tails had been legitimate agents. All the others, they assumed, had been her imagination. And every time, Corban had patiently reminded her not to overreact. But better safe than sorry.

Janice hadn't called the emergency number in two years, but if ever there was a time to call, it was now.

"Mom, what's wrong?"

"Honey, the man who gave you that lamb doesn't work here. He's outside in his car, and I don't think he's a nice man. I'm calling your father."

She dialed the memorized number, and Corban picked up after one ring.

"Jan, what's wrong?"

"We're okay," she assured him. "Can you talk?"

"Yeah, I'm at a . . . Go ahead, Jan."

"I'm at the daycare with Jenna. While I was at COIL this afternoon, a man approached her outside at the slide. He gave her a very strange stuffed lamb. Its eyes are whited out, and the white . . . uh . . . wool, I guess it is, is dyed a deep, blood-red."

"How big is the lamb?"

"Um . . . like . . ."

"Larger than a roll of toilet paper?"

"Yeah, more like three rolls."

"Is it there with you?"

"Yes. I mean, no. I'm in the bathroom with Jenna. It's out in the craft room."

"Okay, let's see here. She trusted him though, huh?"

"Yeah, but he didn't try anything. Said he knew you."

"What else?"

"He said his name was George and that he'd been to our house."

"That's probably just part of his play," Corban said. "Can she describe him?"

"Uh . . . do I need to remind you?"

"She has other senses, Jan."

"Jenna, do you remember anything about him? Anything strange? Think, honey."

"He talked funny."

"Like a lisp? Like your friend Joey talks?"

"No, like Mr. Azmaveth, but different. He said he came from another country."

"What else?"

"He had lines on his arms."

"Lines? What kind of lines?"

"Like . . ." Jenna traced her fingers up her arm. "Like that."

"What's she describing?" Corban asked.

"I don't know. Lines up and down the guy's arms. Anything else, Jenna?"

"I can't remember."

"It's okay. You did good, honey. Corban, I'm ninety percent sure this guy is down the street watching us from his car. I saw him."

"What kind of car?"

She described it.

"Okay. I want you to go home, okay? Tell the daycare gal that you saw a weird guy outside, just to be safe. Most likely, this is somehow about me, however indirectly. Understand?"

"Yes, like a message."

"Exactly. It's really strange, but it might be just some rookie agent trying to pull a stunt and keep tabs on me."

"But the dye, Corban. And the eyes . . ."

"I know. It's creepy. Go home. Call me back after you check it with the wand. Try to stay calm. If he's a creep, I don't want to scare him off; I want to catch him. But not at the expense of my two favorite girls. Okay?"

"All right. I'll go home right now."

"No stopping for ice cream today."

"I know. It's okay."

"And you remember our codes, right? Just in case someone is listening?"

"Yeah, I remember. But when are you going to be home?"

"Jan, my hands are shaking just thinking about what you're dealing with right now. I want to be there. I love you both, and I'm praying for your safety. But I'm on my way to the South Pacific. Remember where Chloe is?"

"I thought you might be going there."

"Call me when you get home. I'll be waiting. Lock the doors. You know the drill. And I'll get someone there by tomorrow, okay? Someone who can keep an eye out for the weirdos and keep you two safe."

Before they left the bathroom, Janice explained to Jenna the game they were going to play and that the lamb might have a listening device in it. Jenna understood. They were going to sing songs all the way home, and that was what they did. The lamb sat in the backseat staring at them with its eerie, white eyes.

"Should we order pizza tonight?" Janice asked as they left their garage and passed into the house. With all the excitement, Jenna hadn't been too disappointed about missing out on the ice cream. "Maybe pepperoni and licorice for toppings?"

"Licorice?"

They laughed as Janice turned up the radio's classical hour. Using Braille messages, Jenna agreed to wait in the living room.

Janice went into the master bedroom closet. Corban hadn't shown her all of his toys but enough of them. She took a taser out of its case and slid it into the back of her waistband. From a flower box, she pulled the wand. Every week or two, Corban checked for bugs and other foreign devices around the house, sometimes even taking apart the smoke detectors. The wand detected metal, nothing more. She turned it on silent mode.

Walking out to the garage, Janice opened the car door and pretended to rummage through her makeup bag. Humming all the while, she swept the wand over the lamb twice. Both times, the indicators beamed green, then red. That was enough. Once back inside, she called Corban's emergency number again.

"All nine lights lit up," she reported.

"Okay. This is outrageous. I'll find someone to send over there, someone from outside our COIL circle, though. I don't want you to be alone."

"Neither do I, but why not someone from the COIL office?"

"I don't know who to trust, so I'm going to handle this separately, quietly."

"Can't we just go over to Chloe's and stay there?"

"Honey, I know you're scared, but we can't jeopardize anyone else. The car may be bugged, even the phone. If you're in danger, we don't want others to get hurt."

"You're right. I'm sorry."

"No, don't be sorry. At times like these, it's okay to voice everything. It keeps our heads clear."

"Okay. I miss you."

"Me, too. I'm praying for you both."

"Come home soon."

"I'll try, Jan. I'll try."

†

CHAPTER THIRTEEN

Nathan Isaacson couldn't stay in his seat inside the Fhotl Lasam Prison visiting booth. He'd been there an hour—pacing three steps back and forth—when the door opened and a petite young woman was pushed roughly into the booth. The door slammed shut.

Helena Rauch had obviously expected to see Chloe. She froze in terror at the sight of a strange man in this enclosed space. Nathan was equally petrified.

He wasn't the comforting type; he was in his element in the field, when he was giving orders and staging the next life-threatening operation. Maybe that was why he was the only one of the Flash and Bang boys who didn't have a girlfriend or wife. But that wasn't why he was there to visit Helena Rauch. The prison had restricted Chloe to one visit a week—security concerns, they claimed. And regardless of his combat physique and darting, eagle-like eyes, someone had to visit Helena. Chloe had insisted upon it, and since the team leader was the only other COIL agent in Malaysia who spoke fluent German, he was nominated.

"Hello, Helena. I'm Nathan, a friend of Chloe's." He tried to focus on her eyes, but his gaze drifted downward. She was so frail. As a combat specialist, he constantly fought against hatred toward those who tortured the innocent. What they'd done to this poor, twenty-four-year-old girl was too terrible to imagine. Memories of the rage from which God had saved Nathan boiled up again. "You can sit. I'm not going to hurt you, Helena."

Nathan sat rigidly in his chair. He wasn't comfortable there. And he wasn't comfortable in the loafers he'd decided to wear at the last minute, either; he preferred his combat boots.

"Where's Chloe?" Helena asked timidly.

Pulling her chair as far away from him as she could, she sat on its edge.

"The prison's giving her a rough time about seeing you too often. She wanted to come, but they won't let her. She'll come as soon as she can. It's all Chloe talks about, like she's your mother." He chuckled. "Helena this and Helena that. She can't wait to get you out of here."

Forcing a smile, Helena seemed to relax some.

"You're the man she told me about from the water tower."

"Yeah . . . she would have to tell you about that, wouldn't she?"

"She tells me about everything: what she does, the friends she has, her husband, Zvi. Do you know him?"

"No, but he must be a pretty tough guy to handle her. And about that water tower issue—it was just a power struggle. She won, but I would never have hurt her."

"I know. She said you're still friends."

"And I learned to never underestimate women!" Nathan laughed.

This made Helena laugh, too.

Nathan was still not completely over the incident—a big man like himself getting outsmarted by middle-aged Chloe. But he believed in full disclosure, so he'd written up an incident report that proclaimed his idiocy and sent it to Corban. Chloe told him she'd done so as well, then the two had exchanged reports and mutually decided they were both in for a world-class chastisement. Corban was due in the city that afternoon, and he wouldn't be happy about his two prized employees butting heads.

"So, where do you live?" Helena asked.

"New York City, in a place called the Bronx, but I go to Manhattan a lot. I haven't been back home for the last five weeks, though. Lots of traveling. You lived in Berlin, right?"

"Yes. Do you know the city?"

"Sure! Where'd you grow up?"

"The borough of Mitte, which is part of Tiergarten now. You know where the zoo is?"

"Of course. I've walked all through there. Southern Tiergarten, with all the museums, right? Oh, and there's that coffee house on—"

"Friedrichstrasse! You have to try their double latte, the house special. It's the owner's secret blend, and he won't reveal it to anyone, so you have to ask for it. It's not on the chalkboard."

"Well, I'll have to try that." He smiled and nodded. Wow, just like old friends. "Maybe we could go there together."

She winced, and Nathan instantly regretted making the offer.

"You don't have to say that, Nathan."

"I know, but I can say it because that's how serious we are about getting you out of here."

"I can't even think about going out in public again."

"Are you serious? Hey, this is hell. It's horrible and nasty for you—"

"I'm a human toilet."

He bowed his head, asking the Lord for the right words, then he looked into her eyes.

"Not long ago, I was in El Salvador. The gangs down there are some of the worst in the world. They make German and American rings seem like playschool. There was this young missionary girl, a daughter of some Australian missionaries, and she had a crush on this one gang member. She invited him over to her family's house for dinner, and they talked over the months. Eventually, the young man accepted Christ, but that's where everything got ugly.

"This fellow wanted to leave the gang and join the girl's church, but his old friends didn't want him to, of course. Gangsters for life, right? So they caught the boy and girl one day, kidnapped them, and tortured them over a three-week period. The boy died, but the girl was found and rescued and—"

"In what condition?"

"Bad."

"You saw her?"

"Yes, I was there."

"What happened to her?"

"She's back in school in Sydney, studying to become a

nurse for missionary work. She's healed. Time passes and the body slowly heals. Of course, there are scars, physical and emotional. The painful memories fade, a little. People who want to move on do so. Somehow God becomes the glue and patches all the broken pieces back together."

"I haven't been thinking about continuing missionary work if I ever get out of here," she admitted. "Mostly, I wonder who would want me now? Will my teeth always feel rotten? Will people think I'm diseased? Is my hair permanently brown instead of blond? All vain things. Then I feel guilty and confused. Have I done something wrong? What good could possibly come from this?"

Helena had worked herself into tears—and Nathan was tearful as well. He knew she had mites burrowing under her skin and laying eggs there. He knew that men had used her. He knew she feared him. But he moved toward her anyway. He had to. He didn't care about that other stuff. Sadly, he'd seen worse in Afghanistan and Iran. Mutilated women. Sodomized boys. Severed limbs. Plucked eyes. Torment and torture.

Covering her face, Helena turned away from him and began to weep, but Nathan wrapped his huge frame delicately around her and picked her up. She weighed no more than a hundred pounds. Sitting down in her chair, he held Helena on his lap as she curled in the fetal position. As she cried against his chest, his tears rolled down his cheeks into her short, filthy hair. He rocked, and prayed, and whispered to her.

But he dared not tell her just how soon they would be rescuing her.

…✝…

There was still a lump in his throat, and his knees were still weak when Nathan strode into the hotel room Chloe had arranged for him and his team. There were other Western vacationers in the area, so they didn't need to worry about their foreign presence alerting the authorities to Operation Helena.

Nathan knocked twice on Chloe's door and was surprised when Corban answered.

"Come on in, son." Corban held the door wide for his operative. "Chloe's just briefing us."

He entered the packed room to find his team gathered about. Corban stood like a general with his hands on his hips behind Chloe, who pointed to her computer screen.

In the corner stood a tall, gaunt-looking man whom no one seemed to be acknowledging. The man, who appeared to be European, studied Nathan with black, penetrating eyes. And he looked like he was chewing a giant wad of gum.

Nodding his greeting to his teammates, Nathan tuned in to what Chloe was saying. Somehow, she was able to maintain her COIL duties via satellite; being in the field hadn't slowed her at all.

". . . So, the Philippines situation is a volatile one, but we're not needed yet. Also, Moldova is having a Russian Orthodox problem. They've firebombed two more churches. I'm monitoring it, but no calls for help yet. And a disaster relief organization asked if we had any nominations for church leaders in Cambodia. They'll supply interpreters, but they're looking for some of our recent missionary evacs who can lead and teach in the churches."

"What about the Vietnamese couple we pulled out three months ago?" Bruno asked. "They still around?"

"Yes, actually . . ." Chloe clicked her mouse. "They're regrouping in Tokyo. I'll send their contact info to the relief agency. Good thinking.

"And lastly, anyone know a Karol Ngolsk? She tracked us down somehow. Let's see . . . She just became a Christian. Says she has resources. It was a strange e-mail—spy-strange, cryptic. And I couldn't find anything on her."

Everyone shrugged and shook their heads. Chloe was about to wrap up her briefing when the lean man in the corner moved stealthily forward and whispered into Corban's ear. All were watching closely, but especially Nathan. The man had a shady quality about him, but seeing him move told Nathan all he needed to know. This guy was a spook, a real spy of the old sort—from Corban's generation.

"Oh, okay." Corban nodded to the stranger, who returned to his spot. "Karol Ngolsk is a black market rep from the Czech Republic."

"Okay." Chloe raised her eyebrows. "Maybe this is something then. In her e-mail, she says she has some information about Abaddon. Corban, can your friend shed any light on that?"

"I cannot," the spook said from his corner.

"Abaddon's in the Bible," Milk said. "The Book of Revelation."

"Yeah, something to do with the Antichrist," Scooter added, his head still bandaged from the Guatemalan incident. "An End Times beast or something."

"He's the king of the bottomless pit," Milk continued. "Could mean Lucifer or someone under him. Abaddon's in charge of the scorpion-locusts during the trumpet judgments."

Nathan knew they were all familiar with End Time events in the Bible, with the exception of the stranger, who appeared to be confused. They understood that the Tribulation years were looming closer, especially with the continued escalation of violence in the Middle East. But this mention of Abaddon made the team's place in the scope of world events seem suddenly monumental. Maybe the End Times was no longer just a distant future prophecy; it might be upon them even sooner than they thought.

"We may be moving into a new age of warfare," Corban stated softly. The team solemnly nodded in agreement. "Abaddon means destroyer in Hebrew, and that's what we've all been seeing around the world lately: persecution and destruction of Christians and their ministries. Either this Karol gal is just out of the psych ward, or she's stumbled across something that would explain this year's escalated attacks on Christians."

"But it's a spiritual warfare," Nathan reminded.

"As well as a physical one," Corban said. "Don't you think the devil's behind these bullets that skin our hides every week? And from everything I've read in God's Word, the Antichrist is a real man—literal flesh and blood, though fully possessed."

"So do we do anything different?" Toad asked. He was

still on crutches, but was due to lose them in another day or two.

"Somehow we find a way to step it up even more." Corban paused, looking at each one in the room as they waited for his next charge for them. "I'm sure you all agree that we're due for even more serious turmoil soon, so beware. And about Abaddon, I have to go to Moscow tomorrow, so I'll stop in the Czech Republic on the way and see who this Karol is. Nathan, how's Helena?"

"She has a firm grasp on what she believes is a hopeless situation." He almost choked up thinking about her condition. "I tried to encourage her. It's tough to know what's right to say to her after everything she's been through."

"And going through right this very minute." Chloe's voice broke with emotion. She focused on Corban. "We know what needs to be done, just not how to do it."

"Okay." Corban nodded. "Let's work it out. When's Memphis going to be in the country?"

"In a couple days," Nathan said. "He and Johnny are in the Sinai helping some Christian archeologists."

"All right. I'll be back from Moscow by the time Memphis joins you here. Do some brainstorming and have something solid that I can approve by then. I don't mean to sound cold, but we're wasting time sitting around here. We have a dozen other cases to jump on—yesterday. Understand? I realize you fellas are healing up from Guatemala, but it's go-time. One week from tonight, you get that girl out. No later."

He gazed directly at Nathan, the team leader.

"Yes, sir."

"Okay. Nathan, Chloe, is there someplace we could . . . The bathroom will do. I want to go over something with you two. Everyone, keep up the good work. Don't neglect your personal time with the Lord. Hold each other accountable. We're all climbing the same mountain. Do what you do. Nathan, Chloe?"

No one else knew why Corban wanted to see them privately, but Nathan knew. And by Chloe's tight-lipped expression, she knew too.

In the bathroom, Chloe sat on the toilet lid, and Nathan sat on the low tub edge. Corban crossed his arms and legs and leaned against the sink counter. At times like these, it was best to shut up and let Corban talk.

But as the seconds passed after the door was closed, Corban didn't speak. His expressionless eyes looked into Nathan's face until Nathan had to look away. Then it was Chloe's turn, until she had to look down at the floor. It wasn't what he said, because he said nothing. What they imagined him saying was worse than any tongue-lashing he could've mustered.

Two adults acting like monkeys on the water tower, struggling for power—was that Christian behavior? Do you two even remember what the fruits of the Spirit are? Have you shut down your brains and sense entirely? Should I fire you? Can I trust the two of you with a project ever again?

The silence was torture.

Surely knowing their discomfort, Corban cleared his throat after five dreadful minutes.

"Is there anything else I need to say?"

"No, sir."

"No, sir."

"Good. Now, Toad could pass as Malaysian. Get him a uniform from one of the prison guards. Build on that."

"Yes, sir," they replied in unison.

And Corban left the bathroom.

†

<u>*CHAPTER FOURTEEN*</u>

Branden Fairchild, CIA liaison to COIL, smiled broadly and shook hands with Deputy Director William "Chip" Buchanen.

"Good to see you, sir."

Though he could never match Branden's smile, Chip smiled back. The teeth, the eyes, the enthusiasm—the thirty-three-year-old ex-pilot from the Air Force was going places. He already had powerful allies in Washington. There was nothing holding him back.

"Likewise, Branden. Please, sit. I got your message. What's this about discrepancies within COIL? I find that hard to believe. Corban Dowler's the most honest man I know."

Unlike most ex-spies on the Langley complex, Chip was glad his field days were over. He didn't mind watching it all happen from the Situation Room. His glory days were over; now he could gloat.

"First off, sir, I know you and Mr. Dowler go back a ways, though no one's certain how far back. You two are friends, that's no mystery. What I have to say, I mean no disrespect. And it won't go beyond us unless you give the word."

Chip considered Branden's speech. The words were almost old school: respect, the implied offer to cover up sensitive information, the suggestion that Branden had dug into Chip's past as well as Corban's.

"By all means, Branden, go ahead. You're something short of an oversight committee, but if you've come upon something, please."

"I believe this Agency's relationship with COIL, particularly with Mr. Dowler, is a matter of national security."

"Corban's been very influential in the success of this Agency for decades. When you say 'relationship', I'm assuming you're speaking of the man's private matters?"

"Aren't we all Christians in the United States, sir? It's a matter of our origins. The danger is that Mr. Dowler and his organization put their emphatic faith first, the security of this country far down the list, and yet he has unlimited access to networks that . . . well, I can't even access everything he can."

"He built those networks," Chip said in Corban's defense, "and I don't mean he designed them. I mean he literally built them—the operating system and the misinformation network. I admit that Corban's level of Christian faith has made me wary at times, but he's always handled himself with moderation. If anything, I trust the man more as a Christian outside of the Agency than I ever did as a so-called heathen when he was with us. Besides, we need him. His old contacts are—"

"They're dead, sir," Branden interrupted. "His and your old contacts are either dead, fully retired and nowhere to be found, or they've become Christians. In two years, COIL has become a force so powerful that foreign ambassadors are wondering if they should rely on COIL to keep them safe when things become too dangerous in their country. Don't you see? The US Armed Forces are made fallible in light of COIL!"

"Yeah, that's Corban." Chip couldn't help but chuckle. "He shames the inadequate establishments into the ground. And what do we do? We hate him for it."

"Sir, this year alone, COIL has recruited forty government and military employees and service members—all of them leaders in their fields of expertise."

"And all of them Christians, Branden. If you really believe they put their God before our country, then you should be glad to get rid of the fanatics!"

"The Christians I know, sir, would gladly do or give anything for this country—even kill if need be. But not those with Corban—I mean, Mr. Dowler. They refuse to kill for country, God, or any other reason. That alienates them right there. They don't and won't stand for anything real when it really matters, and yet they have complete access to all the intel resources the US has to offer!"

"Branden, they rescue people who are in danger! That's what COIL does. Listen to yourself! They distribute medical supplies and spread peace in the name of their God. They're hardly traitors, as you're implying, and they aren't abusing their access to us. That's absurd."

"Breaking the law isn't abuse?"

Chip's eyes narrowed.

"Who's breaking the law? Corban?"

"Yes."

"Just Corban?"

"So far, yes. But I'm sure I'll find others. He is COIL. Without Dowler, COIL would crumble. I'm certain of it."

"Listen for a minute, Branden. You're still relatively new to the intelligence community, so let me explain something to you. Laws are like lines. John Q. Public, he follows a solid line of laws or goes to prison. Actually, ninety-nine percent of this Agency follows the solid line. I expect you to follow the solid line. But for Corban, the line of laws is dotted. Sometimes he runs into a dot or a dash. There's part of a line he won't cross. And then there are the gaps between the dashes through that dotted line. Our charters allow men like Corban to live and operate by dotted lines. It's not against the law; it's a double standard, a necessary one for the very few who have never—I repeat, never—strayed from the honorable path. We watch him closely. We know who strays; we watch everyone."

"He systematically forges your name on orders," Branden blurted, obviously hoping to surprise the deputy director. Instead, Chip grinned as if reliving a memory. "Is forgery a solid or a dotted line?"

"For him, it's no line at all. I'd vouch for every last signature, Branden."

"Even the new identifications? He creates, recreates, and destroys an average of five identities a week. Those are just the ones we know about."

"He has to. Corban's like the unofficial witness protection program—internationally. He has to relocate families so they can live their lives or re-enter a country under a new name to continue their medical aid work."

"You condone everything he does?" Branden leaned forward, as if to catch the old fox in a trap. "Everything?"

"Well, not everything he does privately, personally, or spiritually. What exactly do you want from me?"

"What I want is for the CIA to absorb COIL into its sphere. They have a network we could use. If we absorb them, we'd be able to control them better. And we'd be taking the reins from Mr. Dowler. I think you know he's out of control and too powerful. He's not an agent anymore, Deputy Director. His contacts are washed up, and he's a citizen with a rogue agency of his own now. That makes him a liability, a dangerous one. As a Christian, a devout man, we don't know where his loyalties lie for certain. At best, he's a self-governing civilian. I'm surprised you've left him alone this long. Others have seen it, too.

"Make COIL an asset to this country instead of a liability. Then direct its interests, not on a few missionaries who put themselves into their own hot water, but on our own diplomats, industries, and agencies. COIL is completely set up with everything we need for a takeover. Dowler's days are over; he's a dinosaur."

"A dinosaur? What does that mean?"

"Let's use him for fuel."

PART III

*"Those who sat in darkness
And in the shadow of death,
Bound in affliction and irons—
Because they rebelled against the words of God,
And despised the counsel of the Most High."*
Psalm 107:10-11

†

Corban Dowler and Luigi Putelli climbed onto the water tower platform two hundred feet in the air. They leaned into the wind as the sea breeze whipped at their clothing and hair. Both men put scopes to their eyes and looked toward Fhatl Lasam Prison two miles away. With the sun long down, the prison lights illuminated the perimeter fence, making it shimmer in the distance.

Since leaving Lebanon, Luigi had remained nearly mute. He was alive and felt safe for the first time in his adult life. He asked nothing of Corban—except for a pack of gum—and Corban offered nothing, not even an explanation of their whereabouts. Every hour spent with Corban, Luigi learned a little more about the man. Luigi was in awe of how Corban commanded the undercover operatives in the hotel room. Gradually, as he watched and listened, an image of who Corban truly was, began to take shape. And he liked what he saw—the character—and felt honored to be at the man's side—the same man who could've killed him numerous times, yet had spared him.

"What do you think?" Corban asked over the wind.

"Where's the prisoner?"

"Look at the southwest tower. She's in a cell next to it."

"It's too windy to hang glide over the perimeter," Luigi said. "Too small a prison to parachute in, with the wind. The wind could be an asset, though."

"Are you thinking fog?"

"Fog. Yes. Smoke, too." Luigi turned his head from his scope for an instant to glance at Corban. Corban was truly interested in Luigi's expertise, for which he was honored. He put his eye back to his scope. "The towers are armed?"

"They are."

"You'll need someone inside," Luigi advised.

"That's what I told them, to find a guard's uniform."

"You said the prisoner's name was Helena. What did she do?"

"She was responsible for the Christian conversion of an official's relative."

"And you don't approve of this imprisonment?"

"I don't approve of them torturing her every day."

"Of course." Luigi thought for a moment. "In Rome, you helped other Christians—the family in the villa that was set on fire."

"Yes."

"And Lebanon . . . the automobile was to help other Christians?"

"To purchase their safety, yes. Now you're learning."

"So I am with Christian sympathizers?"

"No, you're with Christians. I am a follower of Christ."

"But as Muhammad, you are not a Christian."

"Muhammad is just a cover to open doors once in a while. I make no compromises as Muhammad. Allah is not my god."

"How can you say Muhammad never made compromises? You are a cruel and vicious murderer. Everyone knows it. I've seen the lists of your victims. And I've heard there are even memorials for your slain."

"It's all a ruse, Luigi. I don't kill anymore. My focus is on saving people."

"A ruse?" Luigi shook his head. "I am confused."

"Misinformation. Like you, for instance."

"Me?"

"You should know that Omar al-Halil has already boasted to his wealthy friends in Lebanon that he was present when Muhammad ibn Affal caught the French assassin and double agent, Luigi Putelli, and buried him in the desert under a fig tree. His body will never be found, yet already the information—the misinfor-mation—is deemed as fact in over twenty agency databases. Luigi Putelli is deceased, buried in the ground of Eastern Lebanon. Muhammad ibn Affal has killed you. And yet I have actually killed no one. You see?"

"Then no one is hunting me for failing?"

"No, I've checked. The DGSE has ransacked your office, closed your accounts, and claimed they never knew you."

"And what of the party who paid me to kill you?"

"They are still out there, but I assume they have followed the false trail as well. Keep your fingerprints and DNA to yourself, or they'll realize you're still alive."

"I am in your debt."

"No, you're in Jesus Christ's debt, my friend. If it wasn't for Him changing my life, I would've killed you long ago."

"But I don't believe in God."

"That's your loss."

"So I am in your debt."

"Have it your way, Luigi, but you'll see in the end."

As the two watched the prison for a while longer, Luigi noticed Corban mouthing words, perhaps praying for the girl chained in its depths.

"Debt or no debt, I need you to go to America," Corban finally said. "A woman and her daughter are in danger. I'm not aware of the details, but my government may be involved. Some have ill feelings toward me since I no longer work for them, so I can't go myself right now."

"But I have no money."

"I know you have money stashed somewhere." Corban cast him a knowing eye. "We all do, for a rainy day, but I'll foot the bill for this. As Reggie Fontaighn, you're wealthy, but use discretion and none of your old resources."

"And I am to help this woman and child? I'm not a savior, Corban." His face was downcast. "I've done things to women and children for my employers. Unmentionable things."

"You're with real Christians now, Luigi. We're trying to stay alive long enough to share Christ and help others. Your past, my past—that's God's business, if you let Him take it off your shoulders. We're the good guys now, you see? As long as you're with us, which I hope is for a long time, you won't kill, either. It's not our way. Help me if you want. If you cross me, I won't kill you, but you will be missing out on more than you know."

"Where are the woman and child?"

"Have you ever been to New York?"

..✝..

The team was sitting by the hotel pool when Corban returned with the lean stranger. Nathan had already questioned Chloe as to who the spook might be, but Chloe didn't know either.

"Keep your eye on that guy," Nathan whispered to Bruno as the team stood to welcome Corban.

Bruno nodded and moved to the side to flank Luigi in case the stranger needed to be handled. However, Luigi stepped to his left and put Corban between him and Bruno. Nathan hung back and glared at the olive-skinned man from a distance.

"What'd you see, Boss?" Milk asked Corban. "See any weaknesses?"

"Maybe. You guys keep working on a plan while I mull over some ideas." Corban's eyes narrowed as he glanced around the room, then settled his gaze on Nathan. "Is there something you want to say, Nathan?"

Nathan squared his shoulders and stepped toward Corban.

"It's not like you to leave us in suspense when we're already in danger in this country. We're all a little offended that you've brought an unknown into the circle. How do we know we can trust this guy?"

"Who?"

"Him!" Bruno declared with a stout finger pointing past Corban. "It ain't right, Boss!"

"There's something about him that gives us the creeps," Toad said.

Corban stood resting his hands on his hips, looking from

face to face, waiting for them to finish with their rant.

"Anything else?"

"No," Nathan answered for them all. "That's pretty much what we all think."

"All right, then." Corban checked his watch. "I have to make a run to the airport. You guys have a good night."

In speechless disbelief, Nathan watched as Corban and the spook turned and walked out of the hotel courtyard. Nathan turned to his men.

"How could he just leave us hanging like that? Don't we have a right to voice our opinions?"

"And that's what he let us do," Milk said from the poolside. "By not responding, he told us it's none of our business."

Nathan growled under his breath and stared after Corban.

"Corban better watch his back around that guy. There's something dangerous about him. I know it."

...✝...

After leaving Luigi at the airport, Corban called his wife and daughter during the drive back to the hotel. They were well and safe and hadn't left the house in the twelve hours since their last contact. But to ensure she was safe and not merely claiming to be so because of an aggressor nearby, he queried by a script, one of several she knew.

"I'll be passing the greenhouse on the way home," he said, testing her. "Have you decided if you want roses or petunias under the rear awning?"

"Oh, let's go with the roses, huh? The red ones?"

If she'd said petunias, Corban would've known she was

under duress, though he wouldn't let on that he knew.

"Okay, I'll be home as soon as I can. A hug to Jenna. No more of that licorice pizza. That doesn't sound too healthy."

Suddenly, he heard Jenna's voice.

"It was just a joke, Dad!" she said, giggling. "We didn't really eat pepperoni and licorice pizza!"

"What? And here I was going to hurry home and try a slice!"

The call home was finished by the time he reached the hotel. His family's safety continued to trouble him, so instead of returning to his hotel room, he roused Nathan from his sleep and told him to gather the others for a small prayer meeting. Corban explained that he couldn't disclose the details, but that they needed to depend on God's spiritual protection now more than ever. Thus, with yawns and sleep in their eyes, the six men knelt around Nathan's bed and didn't budge until each had prayed for the armor of God to fully clothe them.

As the men departed for their own rooms, Nathan signaled Corban to remain.

"Maybe I was out of line earlier tonight," Nathan admitted. "Or maybe I was bothered that you were spending so much time with this guy. We're rarely together in the field, and here you were with someone else while we're risking our lives. I guess I was angry."

"I appreciate your honesty, Nathan. You've got a spy's sense, because that man tonight—he's the most dangerous man I've ever met. But he's gone now, and you can focus on your job, okay?"

"Okay. That's it?" Nathan raised his eyebrows. "It's just us. You can't tell me who he is?"

"For your own protection, I shouldn't have even brought him here." Corban checked his watch. "Better catch some *z's*, Nathan."

Nathan smiled sheepishly and offered his hand.

"You're an iron nut, Boss. I can't crack you."

Shaking the younger man's hand, Corban then slugged him on the shoulder.

"And I thought I was gettin' soft."

Returning to his room, Corban charted his next moves. Like a chess player, he planned several moves in advance, contingency upon contingency. For this reason, he hadn't returned to his family himself. The progression of his strategy forbade him from going home, though it tore his heart in two. He loved his family more than his own life, yet his obligations toward many other lives couldn't be withdrawn.

On his laptop, he arranged flights for his different hops from continent to country, using his various identities. Corban then attempted to log into one of Langley's legend and profiling networks, one he'd developed himself. But upon typing in his username and password, he was denied access. This in itself was no cause for worry, though. Trying a different route, he used the deputy director's name and password, yet was summarily denied again.

This gave Corban cause for concern. In an instant, he understood the implications. The CIA had turned on him, apparently even Chip, his colleague for many years.

Corban could've forced his way into the server, using

backdoors through firewalls and one of a dozen other agents' usernames, but he wasn't one to show all his cards at once. He had other resources available. And he always had a back-up plan.

Sleeping restlessly for two hours, Corban rose, then showered, packed, and checked out of the hotel as the sun rose. Stopping by Chloe's room, he found her wide-awake, well into her workday. Her hotel room had become a battle station and COIL workshop.

As he talked, Corban reviewed her reports.

"I had intended to give Helena US citizenship to get her out of the country, even if just temporarily. My plan was to whisk her to New York, then return her to Germany when the coast was clear. But the Agency has locked me out."

Chloe looked up from her screen in surprise.

"Wow. First time in—"

"Thirty-five years."

"So, we've entered a new phase of cooperation with the US government," Chloe said as it all came into focus. "We'll be running independently, huh?"

"For now, yeah. I'll be looking into it all in the next few days."

"How do we get Helena out of the country after we, you know, get her out of you know where?"

"I'm going to Moscow, anyway. Fost will give me access to the Kremlin's networks. We can give Helena a Russian identity."

"What does this mean for the rest of us?" Chloe clenched her hand. "The Agency's open-door policy with us, though unspoken, has been our lifeblood, our security."

"Our identities are still intact. It's just my access that's being denied."

"But you've never abused that privilege, right?"

"No." Corban tapped his chin in reflective thought.

"Then someone doesn't like what we're doing."

"Right. They're shutting us down slowly, a piece at a time."

"Let me make some calls." Chloe volunteered since she still had old Mossad contacts.

"Yeah, see what you see. I'll do the same."

"So you're still going to Moscow? Even after you know there could be a hunter-tracer team on your tail? They could be targeting you outright, you know. Denied access is a sure sign. I don't like it, Corban."

"We can't stop helping others just because we're going through a rough patch. I'll call from Prague to check in. Be sure to set up a scatter plan for the team here in case we've been officially sanctioned for termination. And be careful with this Helena project. Something doesn't feel right about the timing."

"I'm not leaving her behind."

"Fine, then set up a scatter for everyone else. And notify security at headquarters that we're being—"

"Audited. That's the catch phrase Mario asked for in this circumstance. He'll be on the alert."

Corban thought about Mario Lopez, COIL's chief security officer in Manhattan. He was the ultimate unknown. The trained-though-off-the-radar operative was COIL's fail-safe in the event that the ceiling caved in, if Corban was lost, or if everyone had to be withdrawn back to headquarters.

And since they needed someone for such a position who hadn't been in the intelligence spotlight before, Corban had found him in one of the darkest cells in the Mexican prison system.

Not only was Mario ex-mafia, he'd been so under the guise of a Federale for nearly twenty years. He was a born-again Christian, but his own network of bad boys was not altogether Sunday school material. Mario had so many tattoos and identifying marks, no one would expect him to be the fail-safe operative; thus, he had a one-time-use capacity. After that, his cover would be blown. But until then, he played the uniformed security man at the door of COIL's headquarters and oversaw operations in Chloe's absence.

"And what's his present activation code?" Corban asked.

"Time to swim the Rio Grande."

"Isn't that racial profiling?" Corban chuckled.

"A little, I guess, but he picked it."

...✝...

Corban left Malaysia by flying south, first to change character in Perth, Australia, then to fly the southern hemisphere into Madagascar, where he became Muhammad ibn Affal. He touched down in Cairo and made a fuss over his luggage in front of an airport camera so he could be positively identified. Then he flew into Prague, the Czech Republic capital of over one million people.

Eighteen hours after he'd departed Malaysia, Corban stood in a dark alley in the rain and knocked on a massive wooden door. Observing two cameras, one at each end of the narrow street, he assumed he was being monitored. All they would see, though, was a bearded Arab in costume. After a minute, he heard the dead bolt unlock, then the door swung open wide.

"Yah, sexy, what do you want?"

Being that Czech was a Slavic language, Corban knew more than a smattering of it, so he was able to catch most of what the aged prostitute in front of him said. She was big-boned and ugly, with a low-slung neckline and far too much makeup. He figured her to be around fifty. The woman held a burning cigarette, but her teeth were healthy and white; she wasn't a smoker. Corban had used a cigarette for a prop himself, but he'd always darkened his teeth to support the full illusion.

"Karol Ngolsk?"

"She doesn't live here anymore."

"Perhaps you knew her friend, Luigi Putelli, rest his soul."

"Is that fascist really dead? I heard they don't know where he's truly buried."

"Maybe you'd like to come out here in the rain, and we can talk about it."

The woman studied him a few seconds longer, allowing him to become that much more soaked, then waved him inside.

"I'll put on some tea."

She turned her back on him as he entered and closed the door, taking care to lock the dead bolt. Corban shed his *ghutra, agal*, black beard, and mustache. Hanging them on a coat peg to drip, he followed her down a long hallway.

Open doors greeted him to his left and right. To the right was a massive library. The manuscripts, books, and journals didn't seem to be labeled, and it smelled of mildew. To his left was a small warehouse with heaping stacks of newspapers, computer printouts, and folders. It was into this room that he moved, curiously looking at the careless filing system. Some of the stacks of papers were as high as Corban's shoulders, and on top of each stack was a clipboard that detailed that particular stack's contents.

The aged prostitute stepped into the room and weaved through the mountains of paper. She, too, had abandoned her cover. Her face was clean of makeup, she wore a sweater, and the cigarette had been exchanged for a cup of tea. Corban accepted the cup, and Karol watched as he pretended to take a sip. He didn't know her well enough to drink of her herbs.

"Corban Dowler is Muhammad ibn Affal?" She narrowed her eyes, studying his face. "This is not known by many, is it?"

Though Corban still wore Muhammad's glasses and eyebrows, she'd seen through his disguise—or rather, the facial recognition software on the computer against the back wall had done the seeing.

"My office received your message," he explained. "I'm happy to hear of your newfound faith."

"I searched for years, you know." She waved her hand. "All this junk. I could tell you where Prince Thiamin keeps the Cameo Diamond, but I could not tell you where I would go when I died."

"But now you know?"

Karol flashed a pretty smile, her rough exterior melting away.

"Yes, now I know."

"That's good to hear."

"You are here about Abaddon?"

"That did catch my eye."

"Come into the other room then—and dump the tea. It is poisoned with Seroquel."

She turned away and led him through the maze of paper. Corban carried the teacup and sniffed its contents. Seroquel was an antipsychotic, but its main side effect for a first-time user was irresistible drowsiness and eventual sleep. It had been known to cause death when taken in great quantities—death by coma.

"How much did you use in this?" he asked.

"Four hundred milligrams, but you would be asleep before you had a chance to overdose, and even then you would need more to fall into a coma. I use it on enemies."

They arrived in a back room that looked like the inside of a gypsy wagon. Persian rugs and Afghan pillows cluttered the walls and corners. Corban dumped the tea into a flowerpot. Karol handed him a sealed soda water and sat down on the floor. He sat cross-legged, facing her.

"First, let me understand," Corban began. "You're the famous Romanian archivist?"

"Yes, only I am not in Romania."

"I realize that."

"Being Romanian is my cover. I'm Polish, actually."

"You're far from home."

"True. I have not been back to Warsaw in many years,

and I will never go back. I am wanted there."

"I see."

"No, you do not." She handed him a box of crackers after grabbing a handful for herself. "When I was a child, I heard a voice in my head. My family was terrified. I should not have told them, but I did, and they put me in a psychiatric hospital in Warsaw. It was for the best."

Corban nibbled on a cracker. He was right to assume she was a loony. Why was he wasting his time here?

"For years I was there, but kept to myself. Collected things then, as I do now. I knew I was not crazy, but I also knew only crazy people hear voices in their heads. Some of the other crazies in the home heard many voices, but I heard only one. And you think I am still crazy, I can tell by your eyes. But most people think your face is expressionless, yes? No matter."

She pulled a file from a glass table. Opening the file, she handed Corban one photograph after another as she spoke.

"Here are pictures of two boys who were in the home with me. This one is Velt Plavanko. Velt was older and slower than his friend, who was the handsome, smart one. Everyone in the ward worshiped these two, especially the younger one, Ryan. He made you feel special, listened when you spoke, even put on one- and two-character plays for the patients, but it was all done to impress the orderlies and to gain their favor. Velt followed the other. Ryan was a strong leader and a smooth con. But they heard the voice, too. My voice."

"These two heard the same voice you heard?" Corban

questioned with interest as he studied the pictures. One of the boys in the photos seemed familiar. It was the eyes.

"Yes, but they did not know I knew or heard the voice myself. I would play with my doll near them when they whispered and talked. The voice told me to join them, that we would be an unstoppable force, immortal, but I was too shy, unwilling. My timidity won out over the voice, fortunately. The boys conspired to escape. It was the younger one's lead, but the voice was telling him what to do, directing him."

"What were they in the hospital for?"

"The parents put Ryan away secretly. They were US ambassadors and did not want a crazy in the diplomat's estate. Velt was from the prison, though. His past is much more disturbing. His entire youth is full of crimes: fighting, stealing, and arson. His parents disappeared suspiciously years later. I heard him admit once that everything he did, the voice taught him to do it. All he cared about was making the voice happy."

"The voice was definitely real?"

"Of course it was real! You have heard that the devil's greatest achievement was to convince the world that he does not exist. But the devil is very real. Anyway, one day there was an explosion in the psych ward. Everyone was injured, even the orderlies, but the voice warned the three of us to hide before that. The two boys escaped through the hole in the wall, and I followed them for a while. They fled east into the Ukraine. Resisting the voice telling me to join them, I eventually came here.

"Within one week after the escape, the voice stopped. I

started a new life, a life of secrecy. People pay for information—our kind of people, those of us in the shadows—and that is what I do: collect data that no one else can."

Karol handed Corban a map of the world with lines tracing across it in every direction.

"Here are Velt Plavanko's travels. Though he often returned to places that were familiar to him, I still lost him a couple times. He has never been very smart, but he has had help from time to time. The two set up new lives in America. Ryan joined the military and maintained a cleaner lifestyle. Velt became a shadow and killed dozens of people. As I continue to intercept communication between both fellows and Abaddon, I assure you, there is nothing innocent about any of them."

"How are you intercepting communications if you're not hearing the voice anymore?"

"Someone who claims to be Abaddon sends both men digitally encrypted messages. Sometimes my man in Norway can break them. Sometimes not. The messages talk about the voice the boys heard when they were young, the voice that told them what to do."

Karol gave Corban a number of short messages on computer paper, messages from Abaddon to Velt and the other man.

"Some of these are years old." Corban sorted through the messages, then looked up at Karol. "Anything recent?"

"Decryption takes time." She shook her head. "They send messages back, too, but all I can do is collect them. I have no key. Abaddon's encryption system randomly cycles back through old arrays. Every time we detect an overlap or repeat, we know we have it."

"What's your guy in Norway think of all this?"

"He does not think. I pay him. He breaks the digitals if he can, then I pay him more."

"These messages are . . . well . . . disturbing, to say the least. Abaddon encourages these two to take lives in unexplained missions. There must be a purpose. Have you ever broken a message longer than twenty words?"

"No. Near as I can tell, they do not use the same system to send longer messages. Personally, I believe Abaddon is a demon. When he was just a voice, he used to say I would be a princess in his kingdom, that we would rule together forever, and that the two boys would be my slaves. Similar to the Muslim terrorists who promise mansions in heaven, virgins, and riches to their thirteen-year-old suicide bombers. It is all just brainwashing, unless you take Daniel's vision literally."

"The prophecies of Daniel in the Bible?"

"I am an information specialist, Corban. I collect. I archive. I distribute for a fee. That is all I was doing with these Abaddon messages. Last year, I accepted Christ as my Savior from sin. By reading the Bible regarding End Times events, things started to make sense. So, yes, I am talking about Daniel in the Bible. God used him to give us very real glimpses of the days leading up to Christ's reign on earth."

"Let me get this straight." Corban licked his lips. He rarely came across people who could extract and elaborate on truth from mere suggestion. "When I read these short messages, I see no overall objective. You've had more time to think about this. You're saying there's something more sinister to these communications?"

"Absolutely! The Antichrist is getting ready for his ultimate rule, and I barely escaped the pit. He almost had me, but God pulled me out of harm's way!"

"Now you're talking about the Tribulation era, the Antichrist ruling for seven years. Seeing all of this, it's almost too—"

"I know. It is too real. Imagine me sitting on all of this and showing no one. You are the first."

"It's prophesied, though," Corban stated. "We need to be the salt of the earth; we can try to keep the spoiling from getting worse while we're here, but Satan will still run his course . . . to his eventual doom."

"You are right. We cannot stop it. So, by being the salt, we protect those who we care about. That is why I contacted you. Abaddon has launched a very purposed attack upon those doing God's work in these last days."

"Those would be the international missionaries, aid workers, quick response teams, and such."

"Yes, they are being targeted, along with the man who protects them: Corban Dowler." She gave him two final photos. "This is what Velt and Ryan look like now. According to the origin of the interceptions, they are near you in New York City. Do you recognize either of them?"

Corban felt like he'd been punched in the gut.

"This one. I know this man," he whispered, pointing at the photograph of a handsome man with a flashy smile and trusting eyes. "But he goes by another name now."

"And the other one? Velt Plavanko?"

"I've never seen him."

"Then he is the one you must guard yourself from the most."

t

Running his hand over his smooth skull, Luigi Putelli admired his new look in the full-length mirror. On his way through Paris, he'd picked up an expensive suit and tie, as well as the new head shave. His dome had always been covered with dark hair, with the exception of when he'd joined the Foreign Legion. Now that he was bald, he appeared more sinister and his eyes seemed an even deeper black. He wondered if maybe he shouldn't have shaved his head, since he didn't want to frighten the woman and child Corban sent him to protect.

No, he had to do it. It was his new look, the new Luigi that no one would recognize. Anyone near him would be safer because he looked different.

Passing through Paris on his way to the States had been very daring, but necessary. His caches of gear were primarily in Naples and Rome, but he had drop spots elsewhere that weren't as hot. Just as Corban had back doors into his intelligence mainframes, Luigi had back doors into the DGSE, his old espionage agency. Borrowing Corban's identity had served him well for traveling through second-rate countries, but if he was to go to the US, or someday to England or Israel, his identifications needed to match him flawlessly. Thus, he generated brand new IDs, some with hair, some without. And while he was in Paris, he logged into his old service file and exchanged his fingerprints, DNA, and dental records with those of a dead man.

Luigi also purchased a modest wardrobe and a number of gadgets to fill Corban's requests more fully. Corban had forbid him to kill any longer, so Luigi required a completely new arsenal, but no less effective. Among other items, he traded his poisonous, deadly gum for gum that emitted a sleeping toxin.

Now, as he stood in front of the mirror, Luigi tightened his belt a notch and held his head up a little higher. Yes, he was a new man; he was a good guy now.

He just hoped changing his intentions in life was as easy as changing his wardrobe.

For a few of his new IDs, he'd kept Corban's suggestion that Luigi should be Canadian, since his first language was French and his English still carried a little accent. But instead of Montreal, he chose Ottawa to call home. Luigi slipped through customs into Canada without a second glance. Then, wasting no time, he flew into New York City.

Though he'd been to the city several times, the rushed congestion in the streets still bothered him every time. Yet he was one to blend in, as he had at the mosque in Lebanon, and in no time, he'd assumed the role of a real estate developer interested in several Queens estates. Luigi rented a vehicle and drove into Forest Hills. He'd read the online information on houses for sale in the primarily Jewish neighborhood, so he knew the mindset of the neighbors and the resources they had. Such information was important to his cover as an outsider.

When he arrived on the street on which the target house was located, Luigi slowed his vehicle and spotted the residence at a distance. It was white with red brick trim, with a single car garage, three living room windows facing the street, and an expansive yard in front, as well as one in back. In comparison to the houses nearby, the target house seemed a bit unkempt. But that made sense to Luigi, if only a woman and a child lived there.

As Luigi's vehicle drifted past the house on the left, he looked to the right. If the woman and child were in trouble, danger could be lurking from one of the houses across the street. That was how Luigi would do it—watch his prey for a while, get to know their routine, then pounce.

Across the street was a house for sale. There were no cars parked out front, and the window's white curtains were drawn. Luigi gave it a quick once-over, then moved on. The next house was definitely occupied by a family with children, unless the trampoline and bicycles in the yard were just an elaborate front. No, there was the father in the garage, working on a motorcycle with his son.

Four lots later, Luigi turned into the driveway of a house on the left. He already knew it was empty, and he had a key. It was a furnished time-share house, available for the next three weeks. Pulling into the carport, he carried his luggage in through the side entrance of the four-bedroom, single-story house with a bay window in the dining room. Once inside the house, he didn't take time to unpack. Not yet. He remembered his priorities. Checking the phone for a tone, he then dialed the number he'd memorized.

"Hello?" It was a woman's voice. "Is someone there?"

"Hey, honey, it's me." Luigi did his best to disguise his European accent. "Just calling to let you know that I've got something special for dinner tonight."

There was a pause. He closed his eyes, hoping the woman knew the script as well as Corban had said she did.

"Oh, you're doing the cooking? What is it?"

"It's a surprise, but I'll still be a little while. I probably won't get home till late. Sorry."

"Well, okay. You know about what time?"

"Ten o'clock. No sooner."

"Good. I can't wait."

"You still want the roses, or did you change your mind back to the petunias?"

"The roses are fine."

"All right. See you soon."

"Bye."

Click.

Staring at the phone for a moment, Luigi reviewed every word and analyzed the tone of her voice for fear, deceit, anxiety, or indifference. His own senses worked better than his failed machine back in Naples, anyway. But nothing about the conversation signaled danger. Even though she was only four houses down the street, he wouldn't arrive for another five hours. There were things to do before he showed his face to her—or to anyone else who might be watching.

As Luigi methodically took his time unpacking his three cases full of gear and clothes, he wondered who the woman and child were to Corban. She had responded perfectly to his scripted inquiries. That was agent-like, but an agent wouldn't need outside assistance like this. The fact that Corban was using Luigi told him that Corban's own government and acquaintances couldn't be trusted. He guessed she was a close friend, maybe even a sister. Luigi felt that Corban couldn't radiate the emotion needed to sustain a relationship, evidenced by his expressionless and seeming blasé exterior, so she certainly wasn't his wife. And a daughter? Never. Not Corban—or the Muhammad he thought he knew so well.

Luigi changed into warm-up pants, a T-shirt, and a hooded sweatshirt. It was a cool evening, but he didn't bother to pull the hood over his bald head. That might look suspicious in this neighborhood. Using the mailbox in front of his yard, he took his time stretching. Holding his stretches for a few seconds each time, his eyes focused on a different object at each interval. He'd done this his entire life. Surveillance was one of his specialties because it involved stalking, even stalking an unseen enemy. Except for Corban, Luigi had a perfect success record. As a hunter-tracer, he'd even gotten a few peer spies over the years. They were the toughest to kill. But mostly, his targets had been corporate figures within Italy—under orders of France.

He jogged down the street in front of his target house, head tucked, eyes active. If the danger that threatened those two was in this neighborhood, Luigi would see it. Even if he didn't recognize it as danger right away, he would later. It would be something almost indiscernible.

Later, when he spoke with the woman and learned what the danger actually was, he would be able to recall all the pieces. And it was imperative that he scoped the neighborhood before making contact with her. Peeking into windows would look too suspicious if anyone were watching him, so he had to do so covertly.

Jogging at a pace that showed he wasn't new to fitness, Luigi went out to the county road. Staying fit was mandatory to his role as an assassin—and now as a protector. He noticed everything: the cable and telephone lines were underground, which made them harder to tap; a van with a driver in it, waiting with the engine running. Luigi sensed trouble, but then a car drove alongside it, a transaction occurred, then both vehicles sped away. Selling drugs was a hobby of suburban America that Luigi had read much about.

At the county road, he turned right and circled around to the next residential street that ran one hundred paces behind the one from which he'd started. When he was nearly in front of the house behind the target house, he stopped to retie his shoes. Someone elderly lived here, probably someone in a wheelchair, because a ramp lead up to the front door. He could see the target house through the yard, but there were other houses that had the target house in sight, too. Maybe an enemy was watching it, waiting for an opportunity with a sniper rifle. Luigi had done that as well; he knew all the angles.

Continuing down the street to the opposite county road, Luigi took another right. As he came to his own street, he passed it and turned right at the next intersection. He jogged until he was directly behind the house that faced the target. Luigi stopped to retie his shoes again.

The house was for sale, which interested him, but he hadn't nailed down the reason why until now: it was the curtains. The property looked unkempt and abandoned, waiting for a buyer. So why did it have curtains? Maybe it was nothing. Maybe the previous owner had simply forgotten them when moving.

To get to the vacant house from the rear, Luigi would have to cross another yard, hop two fences, skirt an outdoor pool, and dodge a barking dog. That was no good. Approaching the house at night from the front would be the only way, or not at all. He hoped to remedy his curiosity in a couple hours, after he made a purchase in the Bronx.

Luigi continued his run, took two more rights, jogged up his street, and stopped in front of his time-share. He ran in place while taking his pulse. According to his watch, he'd taken a twenty-minute run, which was the minimum the experts said to take for cardiovascular exercise. But Luigi couldn't care less about a cardio workout right now. This was all for show.

Inside his house, he checked to see if anyone had been there in his brief absence. Twenty minutes was plenty of time for a team to bug the house. But even a single intruder would've disturbed the lint on the tile floor four feet inside the front door. He'd placed two more lint pieces to the left in the living room and to the right toward the back bedrooms. No one had been there.

Luigi changed back into his street clothes, but left the hooded sweatshirt on, even though he knew he stunk from his run. Where he was going, it was okay, maybe even expected.

Replacing his lint pieces, he carefully closed and locked his door. It was six o'clock when he climbed into his car and sped south. He drove onto the Triborough Bridge and took it all the way to the Bronx, to the same neighborhood that Jimmy Carter once described as looking like the bombed-out German city of Dresden after World War II. The area had been considerably rehabilitated in appearance, but not in character.

Luigi parked in front of a tall, low-income housing project. Children in shorts and sandals ran the streets. A gang of youths stood on the street corner nearby, with more young thugs in the other direction. It was time to get into his own character. He pulled the hood over his head and climbed out of the car as he stuffed a square package into his back pocket. Checking his watch, he was right on time. A lone thug on the sidewalk was talking low on a cell phone, his eyes on Luigi. Luigi was obviously expected.

With alert eyes, Luigi walked toward the building. He knew already what was about to happen. The impoverished or drug dependent in America were no different from those in any other country. They were going to try to mug him. Maybe they would stab or beat him before they robbed him. Someone was sure to have a gun, so he might even get shot. But these kids hadn't done this as often as Luigi had, nor had they seen all the different versions of muggings and deals gone bad that Luigi had seen in two dozen countries. And though Luigi wasn't armed with a silenced pistol as he normally was, he wasn't much concerned about these thugs. His only concern was getting back to the target house at the appointed time. He couldn't let the woman and daughter down. And he couldn't let Corban down.

Inside the building, he passed through a group of teenagers grooving to a rapper's beat. Finding the stairs, he started down. At the first landing, he looked up to find the youngster with the cell phone following him openly, whispering Luigi's every move to someone through his phone.

At the bottom of the stairs, Luigi pushed open a door on the basement level to find wobbling, humming washers and dryers. Four young men sat on the machines, but they hopped down as soon as they saw him. One hung up his cell phone as the thug behind Luigi did the same.

Luigi hooked his thumbs in his waistband as the young men approached. Two were African-American, three were white. They all probably lived in the building and had chipped in on this little enterprise to make some cash.

A ruffian with a platinum necklace hooked his foot around a heavy box next to a dryer and, with some effort, slid it out into the middle of the floor. The box was the size of a large boom box.

"Check it out, homes." Platinum Man stepped back, crossed his arms, and stuck out his lower lip.

Luigi stepped forward as the men spread out more, flanking him. Sticking his toe into the box, Luigi flipped open one side. There was no way to tell if the device inside worked by merely glancing at it. Until he got it back to the house and set it up, he wouldn't know.

Moving back, he studied the men for weapons. Their clothes were baggy, making it difficult to see what they could be hiding underneath. He'd seen the same floppy fad in London and parts of Paris. Naturally, such bulky clothing would impede their movements, their reflexes.

"Looks good."

"You got the green? It's all about the Benjamins, ya know?"

"Sure, I've got it."

"It's in his back pocket," the one behind him said.

"That was fast, homes. You get ten *Gs* that fast, makes me think you can pay a bit more."

Luigi chuckled. It was always the same: greed.

"I could've and would've paid more, but this morning I was quoted ten, so I brought ten."

"Give it up."

Pulling the square package of money from his back pocket, Luigi tossed it to Platinum Man, and then put his thumb back into his waistband. The man thumbed through the bills expertly, then passed the brick to one of his partners.

"We'll call that an investment," Platinum Man said.

"The word you're looking for is installment," Luigi said, "and no, we won't. If you want my business again, we'll complete this transaction now. I have clients waiting."

The thug thought about this for a few seconds. The temptation was too much, and the man's face cringed as he fought for control over his greed.

"Anybody want some gum while we're waiting for a close?"

Without waiting for an answer, Luigi pulled out an open pack of gum and selected the top piece, careful so as not to disturb the next one. He popped it into his mouth, tossed the rest of the pack to one of the men at his left, and returned his thumb to his waistband. They shared the gum all around, predictably. Luigi wouldn't have minded using an anthrax pack of cigarettes on these ruffians, but Corban had rules, so Luigi had to use the tranquilizer gum from Paris.

"It's gonna cost you more, homes," Platinum Man said. "Ten more."

As Luigi waited, he eyed each of them carefully. All were chewing the gum. The black market salesmen in Paris had said it worked in less than five minutes. But it could be just plain gum, too; Luigi had been burned before on such purchases. No, that would be bad business for the salesman; he'd been a respectable businessman. With the sort of clients he most often sold to, the salesman would be long dead if he had a habit of selling faulty products.

"If it's ten more for the package, I'll need until midnight," Luigi said. "I've got to go back into the city."

"Midnight it is. Here. Midnight."

"Very well. Ten more."

Those behind him moved aside as Luigi backed away. He ascended the stairs and returned to his car, where he sat listening to the radio for a few minutes.

Stretching, he checked his watch, then returned to the basement. He picked up the box with the device inside and glanced around the basement floor. One of the sleeping thugs had dropped the remainder of the pack of gum with two pieces left. Luigi stuck them back into his pocket. Then he picked up his money and walked out.

$$\dagger$$

<u>*CHAPTER SEVENTEEN*</u>

Back at the house, it took Luigi forty minutes to set up the machine. He ruined one circuit by attaching it to the plasma-screen television in the living room, but he stripped an electrical cord, and it did the trick. Another cord he jacked straight into the house's power, but that was only for the machine's digital display. Its primary power unit was a plutonium core encased in an iridium housing unit that looked like a miniature soccer ball.

Luigi wiped his brow and admired his handiwork. The model was a crude one, probably twenty years old, with pieces from a dozen different sources, but it appeared to be working. The digital display was giving him a readout. All he had to do was turn on the plasma-screen. It was amazing what a man could buy—or steal—in America.

He hit the screen's power button. The machine itself was always on; its plutonium core wouldn't deplete itself for ninety years or more. The screen showed white and black shapes. Luigi turned off the lights in the house; it was dark outside already. Time was running out, and he still had to shower.

Setting a chair in front of the bay window, he positioned the machine on the chair, with wires trailing back into the living room. He moved the machine a little, aiming one end where a red arrow pointed to the right at the houses down the street. The screen came to life. The white and black shapes were joined by red, blue, and green figures, but these colored shapes were moving.

Clicking a button on the control panel, Luigi heard a quiet whirring sound inside the box as the zoom lens focused. He studied the screen. Two figures, red and blue, knelt on either side of a small green object across the street. The green faded to a cooler shade of gray. Then Luigi understood. The father and son were still working on the motorbike in the garage. The green was the engine, then it had cooled down.

Shifting the machine farther to the right, Luigi aimed it at the house for sale across from the target, and zoomed in even more. Getting excited, Luigi shoved three pieces of gum into his mouth as he admired a red blob on his screen. Someone was in that house, hiding behind the curtains, and according to his posture, he was sitting in a chair at the window. Luigi couldn't take his eyes off the figure—presumably a male—as he moved an arm up to his mouth. The figure was eating. His other arm moved to scratch or rub his cheek.

Luigi sat down in front of the screen to study it. The man down the street was watching the target house, oblivious of the fact that four houses from his was a potential assassin with a cheap thermal imaging system, interfaced with a modern-day plasma-screen TV.

Adjusting the machine a dozen times, Luigi made sure the man was alone in the house. Then he positioned it on the next house over and found two people sitting before a blue shape, a television set. They were clearly not a threat.

He glanced at his watch. Time to go. Only twenty minutes before he had to be at the target house, and from what he saw of the man across the street, Luigi would have to use the back door. There was no telling when the woman and child might be in greater danger. Unplugging the imager, he stowed it in the box and climbed into the shower.

…✝…

Janice Dowler's eyes were bloodshot. She hadn't slept a wink, and she wouldn't until someone was there to help her protect Jenna, now asleep on the living room couch. Jenna had tried to stay awake with her mother for the five hours since the call from Corban's contact, but she couldn't do it.

Reaching behind her, Janice touched the taser she'd stuck in the back of her waistband. She'd drawn it fifty times in the last twenty-four hours, just to see if she could get it out in time. In time for what, though? Corban had shown her how to use it, but she'd never fired it.

How hard did she have to pull the plastic trigger? How far away from a foe did she have to be? Ten paces away? Was that what Corban had said? Was five okay? What about eleven? What if she missed? Would the prongs spring back and shock her?

The clock read fifteen minutes before ten.

She heard a car door. Her heart stopped. That was right outside! Two more car doors slammed closed. Now she was too afraid to go to the window to look out.

The doorbell rang. Jenna opened her eyes and sat up.

"Is that him?"

Janice tried to control her breathing. It was too early; the man on the phone had said no sooner than ten o'clock.

There was banging on the door.

"Oh, Lord Jesus, help us! Jenna, go to your room and lock the door!"

Jenna ran to her room. She knew the way in her own house without extending her cane.

More pounding on the door.

Steadying herself, Janice straightened her hair and walked to the front door as she touched the taser gun. Should she draw it now or wait?

"Coming," she called out.

The chain was in place, as was the door's lock and deadbolt.

"Who is it?"

"Federal agents, ma'am. Open the door! We have a warrant!"

"My . . . um . . . husband's not here right now." Cringing, she hoped that would be enough. "He should be back tomorrow."

"Ma'am, if you don't open the door, we'll break it down and arrest you for obstructing justice!"

"There's a child in here!"

"You have to the count of three! One . . ."

Janice fumbled with the lock.

"Two! Three!"

As Janice reached for the chain, the door burst open, slammed into her forehead, and sent her flying onto her backside. She felt blood running from her hairline as she sat up in a daze. Two men marched into the house and past her, then a third closed the door.

"Search the house for the kid!" the third man ordered as he dragged Janice to her feet.

The man was very strong, so she didn't fight him as she was forced into the living room and thrown at the couch. She reached for her taser, but it was gone.

Splintering wood and a child's scream sounded from the hallway.

"Mommy!"

Janice started to her feet, but the man slapped her down. She tasted blood, but she didn't care. As she started up again, Jenna was thrown over the couch, landing halfway on top of Janice. Jenna was trembling. A knot on her cheekbone was swelling and bruising rapidly. Holding her daughter, Janice glared up at the three men in turn.

"Where is your husband, Mrs. Dowler?" The third man seemed to be the leader. With glaring blue eyes and blond hair, he looked too clean-cut and well-dressed to be this cruel. "Where is Corban?"

She wiped the crimson from her eyes.

"I don't know. Who are you?"

"Agent Branden Fairchild, CIA."

"You can't do this! We've done nothing." She glanced over her shoulder. The other two men were moving behind her. They wore inexpensive suits, while the handsome one in front of her was clad in Armani. "If you're agents, then you already know who my husband is. You know better than this! You'll be in so much trouble with your agency!"

Branden leaned forward, hands on his knees, his face inches from hers. Janice decided he was not so handsome after all. He was just a bully. If Corban were here . . .

"Tell me where he is."

"I don't know."

Jenna cried and whimpered, her face in her mother's lap. Janice wondered where she'd dropped the taser. But even if she had it, she couldn't stop all three men.

"If you don't give me answers right now, you'll find yourself childless by morning. You'll be in jail, and your little blind orphan will go to the state. You know how they treat defective kids? The state will give her nothing. Is that what you want? Right now it's you and me, lady. Let me phrase it a little clearer: no talk, no kid! How's that for plain verbiage? I'm the boss, lady. Now talk!"

Janice grit her teeth and held back tears. She needed to buy a little time, only for a few more minutes . . .

"Has Corban done something?"

"Done something? Don't even play innocent, or I'll take you down, too. What hasn't he done? Terrorist acts all the way down to forgery. Is that enough for you?"

"You're lying."

"Oh yeah?" He swung his fist and caught her on the brow. She bounced off the couch cushions and fought for consciousness. "Don't call me a liar! Twelve years ago, your hubby blew up a missile installation in California. Killed a whole bunch of scientists. Claimed he did it for his country. But now the truth is coming out: your husband's a terrorist, lady! An enemy of the people! He's the worst kind because he lives among us, fooling even you. If you tell us where he is, we can protect you. That man will never hurt you again. Never victimize you. Never mistreat you. I know he tells you where he goes. Just tell me which country."

"Stop. Please! Please . . ."

"I'm sorry," he said gently, his eyes seeming kind now. He knelt and placed his hand on her knee. "This is hard for all of us, but it's almost over. I know it's frightening. There's no need for you to go to jail. You can't protect him, okay? I want you and your daughter to be together, but if you don't help me, I have to assume that you're a co-conspirator."

"He's not a conspirator. He wouldn't do those things you said. He's a Christian now."

Branden stood abruptly, snarling again.

"A Christian? How can you be so—"

A loud pop interrupted Branden's tirade. Janice turned to see a stranger—tall, bald, with olive skin and dark eyes—sitting on her kitchen counter. He wore a black suit and chewed a mouthful of gum. Popping another bubble, the man's eyes were on Branden Fairchild. The two agents behind the couch nearly tripped over one another as they backed away and drew their sidearms. They aimed at the stranger and glanced at Branden for instruction, but Branden was momentarily speechless.

Janice felt a chill go up her spine. She trembled with her daughter. The man had to be an angel! He seemed to have been seated on the counter the whole time. The back door was still closed. No one had heard him enter; he had simply . . . appeared. And he was so confident, paying no attention to the two guns aimed at him.

"Sorry. Am I interrupting?"

Branden smirked.

"Who are you?" he asked, shaking his head. "How'd you get in here? Was he in the back room?"

"No, we checked! It was just the girl."

Jenna, though sightless, sat up with curiosity. Janice held her daughter back, sensing that the child wanted to go feel the stranger's face to see what he looked like, as she always did.

The man blew another bubble and popped it loudly. Noticing a framed picture of Corban, Janice, and Jenna next to him, he picked it up, studied it, then set the frame back down and hopped off the counter. He landed lightly on his feet, straightened his suit, and then acknowledged the condition of the woman and child.

"Oh, now look what you've done to them." He shook his head. "Was that really necessary?"

"Mister, we're federal agents performing an interrogation regarding national security," Branden announced as if reading a cue card. "I'm ordering you to leave these premises immediately!"

"Why? So there won't be any witnesses?" He chuckled, sticking his thumbs into the front of his waistband. "Go ahead. Shoot me. I'd like to see you explain that to the police."

"Who are you?"

"I'm the cook. I'm making dinner tonight."

Janice tried not to smile. That was a message for her, to let her know he was Corban's man. She looked him over, but didn't see any weapons. Corban wouldn't want anyone to die. That's why COIL operatives had special, secret weapons with which they could travel undetected. What did this man have? He was too confident to have nothing. Maybe it was his shoes. Corban had told her about a needle with sleeping toxin mounted into certain shoes. But the stranger's shoes looked normal. Maybe he had something up his sleeves.

"I'm ordering you to leave!"

"You have a warrant?"

Branden reached into his breast pocket, produced an envelope, and offered it to the man, perhaps to draw him closer.

"No. Let the lady read it aloud."

Janice read six typed lines aloud.

"Says you can search the premises, seize any property you want, but I didn't hear anything about beating women and children." The man's eyes narrowed on Branden. "You're not too smart, are you? Of all people, you pick Corban's family to harass. Not a wise decision."

"Do you know the whereabouts of Corban Dowler?" Branden asked.

"Have you ever met Corban?" The stranger ignored Branden's question.

"Yes, not long ago."

"But have you ever really spoken to the man?"

"What're you talking about?"

"Think about what you're doing here. Corban Dowler is going to allow you to do all this to his family and let you get away with it? Are you mad?"

"Don't say that!"

"Sensitive about madness? Interesting. Look at me. You bother these two ladies, and I appear suddenly. Do you think that was a coincidence? Whatever the charges are, they're false. Corban would never compromise his faith or his character."

"Sir, leave the house now, or I'll instruct my men to remove you themselves!"

The stranger's eyes became icy cold. The agents with drawn guns seemed nervous. Janice felt the blood drain from her face. Jenna's head was tilted to the side to hear every sound.

"Mrs. Dowler?" the man said, his eyes boring into Branden. "Your husband said you and your daughter scream in unison." A smile spread across the stranger's face. "Show us just how loud you and your daughter can scream."

"No!" Branden gasped, but it was too late.

The high-pitched screaming grew louder as Jenna joined her mother.

Branden dove to tackle Janice. The gunmen wavered, their muzzles swept toward the couch and away from the stranger for an instant. As Janice fought off Branden, Corban's man whipped his belt out of its loops and swung it like a whip at the nearest gunman. Something on the belt's buckle slashed the back of the agent's hand, slicing the skin open.

The stranger swung the belt over his head like a roper as he spun around and kicked the second gunman. The belt's buckle sliced across the soft flesh on the back of the man's neck as he tried to level his pistol. His gun exploded.

Whether by accident or chance, the bullet flew true and slammed into the stranger's chest, throwing him backwards with the force of a horse's kick. Janice screamed even louder at the thought that her only helper was dying.

But suddenly, the man rose to one knee. He moved his belt to his left hand as he stood shakily, panting from the bullet's impact.

Still trying to stifle Janice's screams, Branden was slowly suffocating her. She was getting woozy, but she saw Jenna fighting like a cougar against the grip he had on her with his other hand. He looked up and saw that the bullet hadn't taken out his antagonist. The lean, bald man was back on his feet, with no wound in sight.

"Please . . ." Janice wheezed, her eyes on the stranger.

"Shoot him!" Branden fumed, but then saw his two henchmen were slumped over one another on the floor.

The stranger struggled to take two steps closer to Branden. Branden then released Jenna to reach for his holstered pistol. Corban's man swung the belt as Branden backed off the couch and drew. The belt cut across his wrist, though it made just a scratch.

As the bald man fell against the couch, Branden flashed a victorious smile. He raised his gun and aimed at the man's head.

"Pathetic." Branden scoffed. "Absolutely pathetic, you Christians."

Suddenly, Branden began to stutter and his eyelids fluttered. Janice watched as he swooned while trying to aim his gun at the stranger. Branden hit the floor hard, unconscious.

Janice reached for their rescuer, who was draped over the back of the couch.

"Where are you hurt?" Janice asked. "Tell me. I'm a nurse."

"I'm not hurt," he insisted stubbornly.

"You certainly are!"

"No. My suit is Kevlar lined." His voice was strained. "I just . . . need a moment."

"Mom, where are the bad men?"

Janice grasped her daughter's hand and pointed them out.

"One is there, and the other two are sleeping there."

"What happened to them?"

"Um . . . knock-out toxin? I think. Like sleeping potion, honey."

"Yes." The stranger pushed himself upright. "But they'll wake up in a few minutes. You'll have to help me tie them up. I'm in no condition to—"

"I'll help you. Just tell me what to do, Mr.—"

"Call me Francis. Your husband sent me."

"Yes, I know he did! Thank the Lord!"

"Your husband's a good man," Francis said as he fell against the couch again. "He saved my . . . life."

$$\dagger$$

<u>*CHAPTER EIGHTEEN*</u>

Corban stood next to Fost Ivanovich in a building that had once been a prized Moscow tavern. Only weeks before, in the basement, Fred "Memphis" Nelson had been tried and tested by Fost and COIL's Agent, Johnny Wycke. A big man in his late fifties, Fost was overweight, bearing a physique that said he'd drunk too much vodka during his youth.

Fost ran COIL's Moscow office, though long ago, during a much different time of strain upon the world, Corban and Fost had been enemies. But they'd been much different men long ago, as well.

Seven men of average height and build stood at attention in front of the two veteran spies. Most were middle-aged, and their slightly overweight midsections bore a resemblance to Corban's own gut.

"All volunteers?" Corban asked Fost in perfect Russian.

"Yes, from various Moscow churches."

"They know the risks?"

"I've not lied to them."

"And if they're caught?"

"Two men or women have been assigned to each of these," Fost explained. "The two will follow each man at a distance. If any are captured, I'll be notified and take the necessary legal measures to free them. It won't be difficult. They won't waste time with these."

"What about makeup?"

"Each has applied three masks so far, some only partials." Fost shrugged. "They're not experts, but they'll be ready."

Leaving Fost's side, Corban stepped directly in front of the first of the seven volunteers and looked him squarely in the eyes.

"What's your name?"

"Corban James Dowler!" the man replied with a rich, Russian accent.

Turning to Fost, Corban nodded and smiled.

"That's good."

"You must understand that none of these know English, but they can print the name perfectly and say it like this one."

Corban moved to the next man.

"What's your name?"

"Corban James Dowler!"

"Where were you born, Mr. Dowler?"

"New . . . uh . . . Jersey! USA!"

"Vineland, New Jersey. Good." He went to the next.

"What's your age?"

"Fifty-six!" The man grinned.

The next man.

"What's your wife's name?"

"Yani Dowler!"

"Janice Dowler."

"Yanice Dowler."

The next man.

"Where do you live?"

"New York, New York!"

Corban returned to Fost's side.

"They are adequate for you?" Fost asked eagerly.

"They're perfect, Fost. Begin tomorrow?"

"Yes. Or the next day. Not before they're ready. I have their identifications to complete. My printer is a genius."

Repeating his thanks to the men, Corban excused himself to ascend the old tavern's back stairs to a furnished apartment. The apartment had five beds separated by partitions, a small bathroom, and spacious living areas at each end. For now, Corban was the only tenant, but it was often used by COIL employees traveling through Moscow: an evacuation team, operatives, or new recruits who were enduring their training under the management of Fost Ivanovich. And Corban funded it all.

On a sofa at one end of the apartment, Corban keyed into his inbox through the apartment's complimentary laptop. There was an e-mail from Chloe:

"Corban— Getting the uniform this afternoon. Also, Abaja, Nigeria - pulling out two from refugee mission. Two others insist on remaining. Soldiers certain to kill all within 24 hours. Also, see news from North Korea? Fifteen escapees. Tunnel. All captured. One dead. Torturing. Source says will torture till dead. Can you assist? They're all confirmed Christians. Also, when will you be back in M? They've rejected me from seeing Helena now entirely. Nathan visiting though. Write soon. –Chloe"

Closing the email window, Corban found articles that the North Korean communist press had posted on the escapees. North Korea's press releases said notorious criminals had dug a tunnel out of a Pyongyang prison, but all were captured and routinely executed. However, Corban knew better. The extremely censored country lied through its media outlets as much as the Arab countries of the Middle East lied through theirs. Chloe's more accurate information came from a COIL operative. Rather, he was an undercover Christian, a contact of COIL, whom Corban didn't even know. The contact maintained a position of some type of authority close to the dictator's staff.

North Korea had always been a hot spot for Christian persecution. Certain watchdog groups had estimated that 200,000 Christians were imprisoned in labor camps where they were enslaved, tortured, or executed on a daily basis. There'd been some escapees from the camps, men and women who'd fled to South Korea or China, some even without assistance from agencies like COIL. A few of those escapees had testified in Washington, DC and elsewhere about the brutalities, but so little could be done.

Corban wrote to Lin Quanhai, the woman at the Nanjing-based COIL office in China. Lin was only twenty-one years old, but she ran the office as her late father had before her. In China, atrocities toward Christians were constant, though some American evangelists claimed they were receiving open sponsorship from the government to share Jesus.

"More like government censorship," Corban mumbled to himself.

It bothered Corban how some American evangelists flew to China and saw ten percent of the "churches" that the government allowed them to see, then returned to America to report that China was experiencing a revival led by the government itself.

The truth was, however, that the other ninety percent of the churches—the true Church—were meeting in homes. These were illegal and unregistered churches where true Christians met. They had to worship Jesus Christ underground. China's Religious Affairs Bureau raided house churches, confiscated Bibles, and arrested believers all the time. Christians had been beaten to death in recent months, and the persecution wasn't getting better. Reeducation through labor camps was quite the norm. Lin and other sources within China gathered intelligence to share with COIL and other interested parties.

A few minutes later, Lin responded to Corban's message:

"Mr. Dowler— I can confirm the fourteen are still alive and being held separately for discipline. They killed the fifteenth, a man they claimed was the leader. Inside source says he died on knees, praying. Another matter: lacking hymnals. Can you help? —Lin"

Right away, Corban wrote a message to Johnny Wycke, COIL's operation staging manager:

"J.W.— Hymnals to China ASAP. Include tracts and Bibles if space. Keep up the good work. —C"

Johnny was responsible for most of the initial recon and field prep for the Flash and Bang Team, but he also smuggled materials into more countries than any other organization did. His cover was as a geologist, and his equipment was often hollowed out to fill with Christian material, especially Bibles. Since no country in the world wanted to deny the world-renowned geologist the opportunity of discovering a valuable mineral inside their borders, he was readily given permission to move in and out of nations that even Corban couldn't access without altering his identity.

Corban wrote Chloe back:

"Chloe— Addressing N.K. issue. Delayed from return to M. Suspicions of Abaddon true. Trouble at home. Enemy infiltrating COIL. Beware. Check prison's sewer system. Will bring fog machine. —C"

For three hours, Corban set up his North Korean detour, a mission he didn't relish, but it had to be done. His flight left that afternoon for Pyongyang. When finished, he stood and stretched, but there was no time for a much-needed nap. He had to slip into his Muhammad ibn Affal guise.

Just then, his emergency phone rang. Only a few people had the number, so he knew them all, but this wasn't a caller he recognized. Hesitating, he thought of how Abaddon's agents were creeping ever closer—faster than he could ward them off. But he had to make certain . . .

"Hello?"

"My Rome friend."

Corban tensed. It was Luigi.

"Where are you?"

"I am where you sent me, and I have your two roses. But three petunias are in the bathroom—tied up. It is a slight mess."

"Which petunias?"

"A fair child and two others from the same school."

Corban reflected upon Karol Ngolsk's cluttered rooms and the photos she'd shown him of the two who served Abaddon. A fair child? Agent Branden Fairchild of the CIA.

"The roses are well?"

"Slightly bruised, but fortunate. Another petunia watches the garden, unaware that I know."

"I don't understand. He's not with the others?"

"No. He's across the street, hiding."

"The house for sale?"

"The same."

"It was the curtains." Corban shook his head. "I knew those curtains didn't belong on the windows."

"What shall I do with these three petunias? The fair one had a warrant."

"Oh, wow." Corban sat down. The CIA wasn't playing around. "We can't fight all the gardeners. The warrant makes the fair one legit. You have their car?"

"Yes."

"Dump the weeds unharmed somewhere."

"I would rather break their necks," Luigi said. "I was shot."

"Are you all right?"

"Yes, I'm fine."

"Okay, then do as I say. Do you have a safe place to take the roses?"

"Yes, but I do nothing more about these three?"

"Things are being done. Eventually, all dark-hearted ones bring destruction upon themselves."

"And this fourth petunia across the street?"

"Keep him at bay. He may be worse than the fair child, if he is who I believe him to be."

"You know, I'd rather trade places with you," Luigi admitted. "You come here, and let me go out there to hunt the ones responsible."

"I'm not hunting anyone—yet. What name are you using?"

"Francis."

"Francis, I'm allowing the enemy the space to destroy themselves. I'm opening the door. God is watching. Regardless of what the devil is doing, our work must go on."

"So you say. Your rose wishes a word." Corban heard Luigi give the phone to Janice with a whispered reminder not to say her husband's name.

"Honey?" Janice cried. She sounded stressed. "When can I see you?"

"Not very soon. Maybe a week. You're okay?"

"A week!"

"Yes. I'm sorry, sweetie. Will you be all right?"

"Yeah. Francis seems to be able to handle things."

"And the little rose?"

"She's pretty shaken up, but she's okay."

"Do everything Francis says. He's one of the best."

"I will. I love you. The little rose says ditto."

"I love you both, too. Bye."

Corban hung up and said a prayer. The lion's jaws were ever so near.

...✝...

"This feels wrong."

"You haven't done anything yet, Toad!"

Nathan rode with Toad and Scooter in Fuzzi's taxi. The Malaysian taxi driver hadn't been too keen on letting the vehicle out of his sight, but somehow pretty Chloe had convinced him to loan it to the American soldiers.

And that was the problem, Nathan thought. They looked like combat soldiers: his own size and handlebar mustache; muscleman Scooter and his Mexican smart mouth; and Toad, the Chinese militant, who wore the same combat boots as the others. Since they didn't blend in, at least the taxi gave them some cover—as long as they stayed inside the car. It would've been so much worse if Nathan had allowed Bruno and Milk to come along.

Toad slowed the taxi as the Fhatl Lasam Prison guard they were tailing hopped off his bicycle and walked up to a squat home that appeared to be constructed out of cardboard. The nearby houses were the same, but this was still the lower-middle-class neighborhood: small front yards, maybe some plumbing, not as many animals darting about as the lower class.

"You think he lives alone?" Toad asked.

"Doesn't matter." Scooter sat forward to get a better view. "He's the one. You need his uniform."

They watched the house for ten minutes, then bowed their heads for a moment of prayer.

"Time to go, Toad," Nathan said. "Surprise is on your side, but use the taser if needed."

"Can't we wait until dark?"

"Who knows what kind of nightlife this guy has? We

have him here and now." Nathan would never ask his men to get worked up into a frenzy of anger or hatred to carry out a job. He could've reminded Toad that this guard could be one of the men raping Helena, but they already knew the details. "You have the money?"

"Right here." Toad patted his breast pocket. "But I still don't like doing this. The guard could get punished for losing his uniform. And I don't even know if I'll be able to fit into that skinny guard's clothes anyway!"

"We're leaving the guy seven times the value of the uniform," Scooter stated. "That should be enough to keep him from reporting it missing."

"That still doesn't justify this attack—not for me, anyway. I wouldn't feel so bad about this if it wasn't for the taser. It just feels like an assault or a mugging rather than a covert op. Sure wish Johnny had gotten our NL-3s and other non-lethal weapons into the country in time. But I know this is all we have for now. I'll roll with it."

Without stalling any longer, Toad climbed out of the driver's seat. He did look Malaysian in the face, but he was a thick-chested Chinese man who knew no Malaysian at all.

Nathan and Scooter watched Toad walk through the yard, then step over the bicycle on the porch. He didn't pause or look around suspiciously; he just entered the house without hesitation. Checking their watches, they decided to give him two minutes, then they'd go in to rescue him if need be. There was no telling what was inside that house. A woman with a butcher knife could already have Toad backed against a wall, yelling foreign words at him.

But it didn't come to that. After about a minute, Toad exited the house with a brown paper bag. He hopped lightly over the bike and was in the taxi a few seconds later. Nathan opened the top of the bag to spy the brown uniform within, as Toad started the car.

"See? No problem!" Scooter ruffled the man's hair. "You leave 'im the cash?"

"Of course. But it still feels wrong."

Luigi pulled the agents' car into the Dowler garage. His chest hurt as he moved the three agents from the bathroom of the Dowler house to the car. It even hurt to breathe, and he found himself holding his breath and taking more rests than he normally would have during the required lifting. He was constantly wary of the man in the house across the street, who was sure to be watching intently. Curtains restricted the stranger's view of activities inside the Dowler house, and he couldn't see anything happening in the garage. The hidden man was no doubt curious as to why one car had been pulled out and the other one driven in.

Janice had helped Luigi tie the men up with extension cords, but after that, he asked her to stand aside. It was an unseemly job to move the bound men about, a job no woman should have to do. She cringed as she watched Luigi lift the men, bouncing their limbs this way and that off the walls on the way to the garage. Except for the chest pain, Luigi was not bothered by the chore. He was sorry Corban wouldn't let him kill them, but he understood. Killing the agents would be an act of war, and the CIA would certainly win. But Luigi wondered what would happen when Branden Fairchild woke up from his nap. The fact that the man had obtained a warrant in the first place said he had some juice.

When the men were finally in the car—one in the trunk and two piled in the backseat—Luigi walked back into the house.

"You have everything?" he asked Janice.

"For now, yes."

In front of Janice and Jenna sat three suitcases filled with clothes and important belongings that the family couldn't do without. They were leaving the house, probably for good. There was no telling what would become of the residence once the CIA came back to it— and they surely would.

"I'll pull the agents' car out of the garage," Luigi explained, "then I'll pull your car in. We can load everything without the petunia across the street seeing what we're doing. You two ride in your car. Follow me closely, understand? Don't let any cars between us. The petunia is sure to follow us, so we're going to lead him on a little ride through the city."

"But we'll be safe, right?"

"Yes. He seems to just be watching us for now. Besides, I have a plan."

"What about that stuffed lamb in the backseat I told you about?"

"Give me a moment."

Luigi took a knife from the kitchen and went to the garage. After swapping the cars, he took the lamb by the throat and gutted it on the cement floor. He would've thrown the animal aside since they were leaving, but Luigi was a man who knew his surveillance equipment, and he wanted to see what kind of people had left it.

Inside the lamb, he found a crude, handmade sound transmitter. It was sound or voice activated, so the AAA batteries would last for days. The microphone had been mounted near the lamb's nose, but the rest of the gadget was too basic to be government-made. Stripped bread ties and cheap tape held the fist-sized electronic device together. The wire to the end of the microphone doubled as the antenna. The power source—mere drugstore batteries—told Luigi that the receiver was within a few hundred yards. Chances were, the lamb was a product from the man across the street, Luigi deduced.

Having learned all he wanted, he crushed the electronics under his heel and kicked it aside.

Janice and Jenna climbed into their car. It was too dark now for the watchman to see Luigi's face, but in case the man had a night vision scope, Luigi kept his hand over his brow to hide his features as he left the garage and got into the agents' car.

The two goons in the backseat were waking up, moaning and grunting against their binds. Luigi had gagged them and didn't care what they had to say, so he ignored them. He couldn't let them go just yet. As he drove away from the house, he heard dull thumping from the trunk where Branden was bound. Remembering his own trunk experience in Lebanon, Luigi knew the trunk wasn't pleasant. Branden was lucky it wasn't a hundred degrees out!

Janice followed Luigi, staying on his bumper as instructed. After a few blocks into Brooklyn, Luigi had no difficulty picking out the square headlights following both cars a full block behind. Tailing at night through strange neighborhoods, and doing so secretly, was not easy. It was tough enough in the daylight.

Luigi worked his way south among buildings along the East River and zigzagged his way through the warehouses until he found what he wanted. Stopping the car, with Janice behind him, he climbed out and acknowledged the tailing vehicle two hundred yards back. Its headlights suddenly went dark, but Luigi didn't care. That man's tailing days were over.

"Are we going to leave the cars here?" Janice called from her open window.

"No, we're just covering our tracks."

He spent ten minutes rolling barrels out from under one building's awning and standing them on end across the road. Then he hauled railroad ties out and laid them behind the barrels. Luigi paused often for breath because of his bruised chest. In all that he did, he kept a careful eye down the road to make sure their tail didn't sneak up on foot. But all was quiet and the surrounding warehouses were dark. On top of the railroad ties, he piled wooden crates and cans of paint and an assortment of trash. All accumulated, it came to a height of three feet behind the barrels, a barrier no city car could breach.

"I'm going to drive fast now." Luigi warned Janice then climbed into his lead vehicle.

It would've been great amusement to watch the man

try to break through the barrier, but he would have to pass it up this time. Following Corban's wishes to get the girls to a safe place was of utmost importance to him. He drove to the river, then circled west and north and deep into Brooklyn. Only after he'd reached Crown Heights on a winding route, and still saw no tail, did he park on the side of the road. Taking the gag off one of the men in the backseat, he force-fed him one of the two remaining pieces of gum. Four minutes passed before the man drifted off to sleep. Luigi untied the man's binds and left the keys in the ignition. It felt quite foreign to Luigi to leave these men alive, but he had to trust Corban—that the dark-hearted would destroy themselves.

Climbing into the driver's seat of Janice's car, Luigi drove east, entered Queens, and then went to Forest Hills.

"We're not going back to the house, are we?" Janice asked anxiously.

"No."

A few minutes later, Luigi helped them take their luggage into his time-share four lots from their old home.

"Stay away from the windows," he warned. "Don't touch any of the equipment without asking. And the TV doesn't work. I have to go dump your car. I'll be back in a couple hours."

"Where do we sleep?"

"Pick any room you like. Do what you want, just don't leave."

Janice led Jenna to the back rooms as Luigi checked the house across the street for movement. Clear. He hated to leave the girls, but he had to. Besides, he'd be back soon.

†

CHAPTER NINETEEN

Muhammad ibn Affal strode proudly between the massive marble columns that guarded President Lon Jong's estate. Military personnel saluted at his passing as if he were a general in their own armed forces. But Muhammad didn't smile at their anxious welcome. His arrival was a surprise, but Lon Jong had made rapid arrangements. It had been too long since Muhammad had graced North Korea with his presence. All in the estate seemed curious as to what brought the notorious man from the Middle East to the Pacific Rim.

"Ah! Muhammad!" Lon Jong greeted him warmly. They would speak English, since it was their only common language, though both claimed to detest the language of the West. "So long you come!"

In greeting, Muhammad nodded a shallow bow, and Lon Jong touched the Arab's hand in friendship. Like Lon Jong's father, his teeth were horribly bucked and his comb-over was almost a miracle, his hair was so thin.

"The pleasure is mine, President," Muhammad bowed again. "I trust your health is well. You look much younger in the flesh than on television."

"Yes, and I punish them for that! Come. Eat!"

It had been two years since Corban had been in North Korea as Muhammad ibn Affal. The leader of this suppressed country depressed him so deeply that he avoided nearly every request by Chloe for his personal intervention in situations of persecution. He'd often sent operatives to the country in his stead, or he stayed out of the business altogether and left COIL's assistance in the region to the Nanjing office.

Corban was confident that God had given him the abilities to deal with anyone he happened across. That included the North Korean dictator, who had successfully achieved the status as the worst violator of religious rights in the world. But another reason Corban personally avoided North Korea was for the same reason he avoided places like Sudan, Uganda, or Eritrea: the suffering was all too great, and Corban could do so little to fight it.

There were fifty-two countries considered most dangerous for Christians, where they were regularly persecuted and martyred, and Corban had been to all of them. He'd held the children, kissed the scarred women, and hugged the men with amputations. But he felt he was of more help to the volunteers and field agents who worked those regions by remaining at a distance.

True, Corban felt he could outwit the evil men of the world with disguises, but when he came face-to-face with those who suffered so tremendously for the same God he served, he felt weakened by their strength. The madness that injured those dear servants was beyond him, so he designated their needs to people who were more prepared emotionally for that battle. However, in any situation where Corban felt his skills—and his skills only—could be utilized to help even one believer, he went to their aid, regardless of the country or its conditions. Corban didn't hesitate to don his makeup, apply his hair coloring, and change the pitch of his voice if he could make a difference.

It was with this distaste that he sat down with President Lon Jong for tea and something that tasted like pita bread. Lon Jong boasted of his achievements as Corban sat patiently listening and studying the man.

The last time Corban was in North Korea, he'd delivered to Lon Jong three Palestinian suicide bombers who'd supposedly escaped from one of Israel's prisons. The entire situation had been staged, however, worked out between Chloe and her old Mossad contacts. It'd been quite a ruse, since all three "escaped prisoners" had been Hamas' most prized bomb makers. Lon Jong had been ecstatic for the gift and showed his appreciation by delivering to Corban—as Muhammad ibn Affal—a captured missionary from Japan, which was a trade that Corban had requested. The irony came when Lon Jong realized that his own scientists knew ten times more than the Hamas "experts" did. He punished the three by gouging out their eyes and cutting off their fingers so they could never make another bomb as long as they lived.

Back in Gaza, Hamas leaders still boasted of the three men who'd escaped an Israeli prison. However, Israeli intelligence coordinators knew the three had received far worse punishment than they ever would've received in Israel custody.

Nevertheless, Lon Jong was forced to show Muhammad

favor, for the exchange of three for one had been done in good faith, as far as Lon Jong knew. He needed every ally he could muster in his fight against democracy and the West. And there was no one more anti-American than Muhammad, the weapons smuggler.

"No more small talk, Muhammad. You have come to my great country for a reason. How may I serve you?"

Corban reached into his *bisht* and withdrew four photographs of beautiful snow leopards, their thick winter coats giving them added size. He set the photos on the table for Lon Jong to view.

"Ah, yes. Such creatures! Yes. These are for me? A gift?"

"No, they are mine at home in Egypt. I stole them from Mongolia's Gobi Altays when the animals were cubs. My request of you is more of a glorified bloodlust which I hope you might accommodate."

Lon Jong's eyes sparkled at the mention of blood, his love for violence apparent.

"Go on."

"My pets grow weary of the prey I feed them inside their habitat. I am forever searching for food for them. When they grow bored, they do not eat, and when they do not eat, they become like bones and their coats become mangy." Corban pushed the photos closer to the president. "You may keep these. I understand you have fourteen individuals that would serve my pets' appetites rather nicely. And as escapees, they surely know how to run. My babies love a good chase."

"Ah. You know of my escapees. This we can do, but how may I watch?"

"I cannot bring my babies here."

"But I cannot go to Egypt, Muhammad," Lon Jong said with some disdain. He was a prisoner within his country. If he left its borders, he was a man certain to die by the hand of any number of governments for atrocities he'd committed against visiting diplomats. "May I purchase one from you? I would love to feed one myself, Muhammad."

"Separating my babies is out of the question. They would cry worse than my loudest wife. No, our only option is for me to take the food by chartered flight to Alexandria, my summer home, and I will digitally record the feeding for you. What do you think? Will two visual angles be enough, or shall I bring in a third camera crew?"

"More is always better, but must you take all of my escapees?"

"Certainly," Muhammad stated with a frown, as if anything else would be unacceptable. "The cages are being built as we speak, and I have promised my babies seven kills apiece. I cannot disappoint them. Think of them, Lon Jong, stalking the Christians, killing them as they pray to their God for salvation!"

As Lon Jong eyed the photographs of the two leopards, he seemed to picture the bloodbath.

"This is much better than I could have planned, Muhammad," Lon Jong said. "It is of Roman genius—killing Christians with cats!"

"Only yesterday did this come to me. That is why I gave no notice of my arrival. Besides, we have to celebrate a new age in our friendship, and what better way than with blood?"

They toasted one another.

"I do hope all fourteen are still alive!" Lon Jong stood abruptly. "Come with me."

"They are here? On the estate?"

"Oh, yes. I cannot supervise discipline and execution elsewhere. Of course, now it is in your able hands, though I do wish we could do it here. If they were not such good laborers, I would kill all the Christians in my country."

Lon Jong led Corban on a short trek through more marble columns to the back of the mansion. They skirted a number of hedges where gardeners were working, eyes downcast. Finally, they arrived at a swimming pool that was empty of all but six inches of water, in which stood fourteen naked men and women. Along the edge of the pool, three men paced with rifles and whips. By the look of the captives' shoulders and backs, the whips hadn't been spared.

"Good! All are still alive—and after two whole days!" Lon Jong exclaimed. "It is something my father designed. The water draws mosquitoes. That is torture. They cannot sit or lie down, or they will be whipped. Their feet swell to the size of watermelons as they stand. Soon, the blood pooled in their feet will burst through the skin. And if they thirst, they have plenty of water to drink!"

Corban nearly vomited from the sight and smell, but he forced a grin for the president and said a silent prayer for the suffering servants.

"It is quite . . . masterful," Corban said. "How long will they last?"

"Two weeks. No more. They die from their own filth and

disease. See? It is not I to blame!" He laughed at his sick humor. "If you listen, Muhammad, you can hear them pray; they take turns. But no angels save them. No God hears them. It is best if they die quickly, but they hang on for no reason."

"But how are they to run from my babies if they are in ill health?" Corban asked. "Look at their feet already swelling! You would give me diseased food for my kittens?"

"No, no!" Lon Jong clapped his hands and gave the guards orders in Korean.

"And get clothes on them," Corban added. "I want to see no more of them than I must."

Some of the prisoners helped the more crippled ones to the pool's edge, where they were roughly lifted out by the guards. It took every bit of strength for Corban to not jump into the filth himself and lift them to the lawn.

"Surely you will stay the night, Muhammad? They will not travel well until they rest."

"I am your most humble guest. Might I request a computer so I may arrange a jet for tomorrow?"

"Of course. And tonight we will talk of future transactions!"

…✝…

"I want news, people!" Branden Fairchild yelled at the nine men and women who worked at the computer terminals around him. It was the first time the young supervisor had been given charge over the CIA's Situation Room. And he loved it. "Watch Athens. The man likes using that airport. And Cairo. He has an alias that frequents that city."

Branden ran a hand through his blond hair. After he and his men had freed themselves from the car in Brooklyn, he'd driven straight to the office. Too furious to do anything but work, he wasted no time in searching for the bald, lean man who had attacked him and saved the two Dowler females. And, using everything available within the Agency, Branden was going straight for the big prize as well: Corban James Dowler.

Shutting down COIL's headquarters in Manhattan wasn't Branden's goal. But he'd posted a number of junior agents inside the two suites to monitor any communications between Corban and his staff. Corban must have anticipated that.

The young CIA supervisor cursed. Corban had vanished! He was last seen in Bursa, Turkey, but that last trace was two days old, and Branden knew he was no longer there. Branden had even gotten his hands on airport security footage, but he couldn't identify anyone for certain. He still had nothing.

Branden hadn't taken time to shave yet, but he'd changed his clothes and bandaged his wrist where the belt buckle had slashed him. And he refused to eat until he heard some news on Corban.

The door behind him slid open. He turned to see Deputy Director William Buchanen enter the Situation Room. Branden rolled his eyes; that was all he needed. He hated this sixty-two-year-old has-been—his athletic frame that nearly matched Branden's and his thick, white hair. But it was the steely, gray eyes that really got to Branden. They reminded him of Corban's eyes—the confidence, maybe some amusement, and definitely secrecy.

Chip stopped next to Branden and observed the terminal screens. The consoles and giant wall screen before them revealed the world's continents and several blinking dots.

"Pulling an awful lot of our scouts from other projects, Branden. What's going on?"

"You wouldn't let me shut down COIL, sir. I had to go over your head. I got the okay. I got the sanction. I got everything I wanted. Corban is finished." Branden watched Chip for his reaction, but the old man was stone-faced.

Abaddon's spirit was in Brandon's heart; he could feel it. The feeling was like a drug, and he didn't want Chip to bring him down. Abaddon, Branden, Velt—they'd worked too hard and for too long to be stopped now!

An alert on the screen drew Branden's attention. His people needed him. He left Chip to observe the new order of things.

...†...

Chip Buchanen watched Branden Fairchild run the operation in the Situation Room. The young agent had gone over Chip's head to the director to chase down Corban Dowler and COIL. And of course the director had given his approval to Branden. Branden had supposedly saved the life of the man's son back in Iraq. At least Branden had convinced everyone that it was he who'd done the saving.

Someone had run an airstrike west of Baghdad and saved a platoon of coalition forces. Yet Chip knew it hadn't been Branden at all. It'd been Branden's wingman.

Meanwhile, Branden had fired on Iraqi civilians in the north. Not a rifle had been found amongst them. Maybe, Chip considered, it was time to memo the director about the "hero's" real success in the war. His kills were innocent civilians: twenty-three women, nineteen children, and twelve men. Chip had the reports to prove they were the only successful kills Branden had made during his deployment. Other strikes that Branden claimed responsibility for had been abandoned holds: a bridge, a couple bunkers, and a water hole. Nothing too flattering; nothing at all heroic.

Though not a godly man, Chip was wise enough to recognize that men and women paid for their indiscretions. Sometimes it took time—a lot of time—but Chip was patient; he liked to watch. He figured he'd let Branden run his course. He'd come up too fast; he'd go down fast. But he was certainly making a mess of things while he was on top.

"Any sign of him yet?" Chip asked Branden.

"No. He must have ten different legends in his suitcase. Even if we could track him from point A to point B, he'd be someone different by the time he got to point C."

"Unless he skips point B and point C and goes straight to point F," Chip said, just to confuse the issue.

"Is that comment to help or to hinder me, sir?"

Chip chuckled.

"Look, you've never been in the spook business, Branden. What makes you think you can catch Corban Dowler?"

"I've got him outnumbered about a hundred to one

right now, and I don't know how many freelance hunter-tracer teams are on him out there."

"And you think Corban carries legends in a suitcase?" Chip shook his head. "You have a lot to learn, son. A lot to learn."

"How else would he transport his disguises? He's moving around too much and too fast to do it any other way."

"It's called stage-prepping, Branden, and me telling you isn't going to help you much. I suggest you shut down all of this before someone gets hurt."

"Tell me anyway. You taught him, didn't you? How's he staying out of sight?"

"That was thirty-five years ago. The world was different then. Who knows what he's learned since then. He's years ahead of me now, and I used to be the best. You know, he's probably listening to us right now. It wouldn't surprise me."

"I had the place swept an hour ago."

"Then he's got one of these techs here whispering in his ear."

"These nine were hand-picked by me."

"And you don't expect him to stump you? What do you know about him? Everything you know is what he's allowed you to know. Corban James Dowler." Chip cursed under his breath. "His real name is Bill Weber or Devin Manson or Jud Patacky, or something like that. He may not even remember his own real name at this point."

"You're telling me Corban Dowler isn't his real name?"

"Right now it's his real name. We used to call them our

base names. You know, like base numbers. Alias names are built off base names. Base names are complete legends, and the best operatives back in the day, forty years ago, had two or three, even five, base legends, then four or five aliases on top of each of those—depending on how much traveling was done.

"Depends on physical appearance, too. When my hair was long, I had one name that had four other legends. If my hair was short, I was a man who had two other legends. Both men were different identities. Once I was even a woman. That was when the wall was still up in Berlin, but that was before your time. We had to do everything right back then—or we died. Many died anyway. Friends. Today, everyone's sloppy. Too much dependence on technology, like this, instead of old-school skill."

"So what's stage-prepping?"

"Let's say I'm going to Cairo. Most guys would go in two stages, which means he'd handle two different identities. I start in New York as John One. Fly to Paris. Still stage one. Fly to Athens where I change identifications. Now I'm in stage two as John Two. Then I go off to Cairo to handle my business.

"Two-stagers are pretty easy to trace if you know how to look for them, since the beginning and the end—the origin and destination—aren't too distant. A two-stager can even carry his disguises with him, maybe a wig sewn into his overcoat so even customs doesn't see anything.

"It's the three-, four-, and five-stagers that are too tough to track. Corban? He's probably pulling four stages, at least, between points A and B. Because he knows you're watching. But just because he knows you're watching doesn't mean he'll hole up and hide out. He's too busy. Innocent people are depending on him for safety as you hunt him. And you're right: he's moving around too often to do all of his own handling. That's what stage-preppers are for.

"Over the years, you get used to working with some stage-preppers that are real reliable; they never question your movements and never try to make unnecessary contact. Go back to our Cairo trip. Before I even leave for Cairo, I contact my stage-prepper in Paris. I tell him I'll be there at this time on this date. If I know I can trust this guy and my phone's secure, I might even tell him all four of my stages so he can call ahead and coordinate every stage-prepper for me. He'll want to do that for me, because he knows I'm going to drop him more cash for handling more details.

"So, I fly to Paris. I go into the left stall of the first bathroom in terminal B at the airport. He's in the next stall. We exchange money for a flashbag. If the money's good, and it always is, he leaves. No words. No risks.

"In my flashbag, I find my new legend for the next leg of the trip. Maybe I shipped that particular identity to this stage-prepper a month prior. Maybe I shipped him ten duplicates of the same disguise. I change clothes, wigs, identifications, whatever. The old clothes go into the flashbag. As I pull the string, I cough. A little smoke, and I walk away a new man.

"Next, I fly to Hamburg where there's another handoff from a different stage-prepper. It takes five minutes. I become another man. Then to Rome. Change there, too. That's three stages already. Maybe one more in Casablanca, then off to Cairo."

"That's too much work." Frowning, Branden studied Chip's face. "I can't see him doing all that at every layover. It would cost a fortune. And handling the plane tickets with all the different names? The details would be a nightmare."

"Stage-preppers make it easy. Aren't you listening? Of course, you've got traveling stage-preppers, too, though that's rare. Maybe you've got two—which is smart—who relay along with you or work in tandem on your flights. They take care of your legends, your tickets, and even watch your back. No one even knows anyone's really traveling with you. They're called roamers. But they don't come cheap. The others are called stationaries."

"Which one does Corban use? Roamers or stationaries?"

"He probably uses a combination of both."

"You're a lot of help." Branden clapped his hands for his technicians' attention. "All right, listen up! From now on, we're keeping an eye out for Dowler's stage-preppers, both stationary and roaming. Watch for patterns. Pay attention, they might be traveling in tandem or relay!"

Those at the consoles glanced at one another and snickered. They'd all heard Chip telling Branden about an operative's travel strategy. When they shrugged, shook their heads, and continued working, Branden turned red-faced. He grabbed Chip's arm and turned him so he could see the older man's face directly. Chip was barely suppressing a grin. Branden's hand on his arm didn't anger him; he was too pleased with himself.

"What'd you do? Make all that up? They don't know anything about stagers and roamers!"

"Of course they don't. Branden, Corban's worked for this country for over thirty years—not just for the government, but for the people. He's never injured this country by selfish ambition, not like you have."

"What's that supposed to mean?"

"This is the intelligence agency, Branden. We can access anything. And something more: Corban's too careful to trust even me with his travel secrets. Of course there's no such thing as stagers and roamers. You're so green, you just sucked in a ten minute lie."

"How dare—"

"Oh, be quiet. I'm not even worried about your little exercise here. Corban's too good to be caught by the likes of you. Oh, but . . . uh . . . keep up the good work. Maybe you'll catch his stage-prepper!"

And Chip walked out, the roomful of techs doing their best to hide more snickering.

PART IV

"And this is the condemnation,
That the light has come into the world,
And man loved darkness rather than light,
Because their deeds were evil."
John 3:19

✝

Corban sat cross-legged in the Gulf Stream twin-engine cabin and watched the fourteen prisoners President Lon Jong had given him. The prisoners were bound wrist to ankle—one person's wrist chained to the next one's ankle. Lon Jong had jeered at them when they'd awkwardly boarded the jet, taunted them about their fate. And here they sat on the floor in the back of the corporate jet, muttering prayers, fully aware of the death due them by two beautiful snow leopards.

All fourteen of the captives were North Korean; four were women. They were all apparent converts through some of the many underground churches in the communist country. And they spoke only Korean. Corban had checked. But he couldn't speak to them even if he knew Korean, since Lon Jong had sent two of his most trusted bodyguards from the mansion to both guard the captives and witness the feeding. Denying the guards passage wasn't an option, either, after Lon Jong had so freely given away his recovered escapees.

Corban considered how he might free the captives and separate them and himself from the two guards. The guards were armed, one with a Chinese SKS and the other

231

with a pistol. The two pilots were Egyptian. One spoke a little English. Neither had batted an eye at the weapons or the captives, as if trafficking humans was something they'd done before.

To make matters worse, Corban knew Agent Branden Fairchild was on the prowl, so contacting COIL headquarters in Manhattan was out of the question. Now Corban would need to do much of his maneuvering through the Moscow and Berlin offices. Branden, as the CIA liaison to COIL, knew of the international offices, but as near as Fost Ivanovich could tell, neither Moscow nor Berlin had been infiltrated. Both offices were relatively small, so the agents knew one another well. This group of godly men and women had given up their previous lines of work, as Corban had, in order to serve Christ. If there were a blatant pagan amongst them, he would stand out.

Though Corban was sipping pineapple-orange juice from the complimentary bar, he hadn't offered the guards anything to drink. He wondered when the guards would become thirsty on the long flight. Corban would insist on fixing the drinks himself, at which time he would spike their drinks and put them to sleep for a while so he could communicate with the prisoners in private. He immediately reasoned against that idea, though, because at some point, the guards would wake up, and they would know he'd drugged them. If Corban weren't concerned about ruining relations with North Korea, he would've already put the guards and the two Egyptian pilots to sleep. He could fly the computerized jet himself.

But he did care about maintaining relations with Lon

Jong. With the man's instability toward Christians, there was no telling when Muhammad ibn Affal would need to intervene again. That bridge couldn't be burnt quite yet.

Corban curiously eyed the captives. For the most part, their heads were bowed, and they made no eye contact with him. He was the Arab who was to kill them, so why would they wish to look at him?

Little did they know that before he freed them and set them up with new lives, he was going to take three-dimensional photographs of their faces. His technicians in Berlin would fabricate a most believable video of two leopards attacking and eating the fourteen. It would be an animation, but Lon Jong would never know the difference. The graphics engineers would take pre-existing footage of snow leopards killing a large monkey in a caged habitat. They would then reproduce it from different angles with patched-in human faces and features.

Interestingly, Corban had used the scam years ago on a Honduran drug lord who had captured two Australian missionaries in the jungle. Technology was better now, and the footage would be even more realistic—which meant bloodier, as Lon Jong preferred.

Corban was working on his second glass of juice when he saw it: a gesture. It was so slight that he wasn't even sure of what he'd seen, or if he'd seen anything at all. A gesture between a guard and a captive. Just a nod. Then a nod in response.

Five minutes passed before Corban saw it again. This time the gesture came from the guard with the SKS and was directed at a different prisoner.

He didn't want to jump to any hasty conclusions, but it was certainly some form of communication. It could simply be encouraging, sympathetic nods coming from the two guards who'd been given the duty to witness the prisoners' demise. But no, these two had made a point of requesting this long-distance job. Corban wasn't one to read minds or hearts, but he knew body language, and he realized what was happening before he could entirely believe it.

Pretending to read an in-flight magazine, Corban continued to watch for an hour, though slyly, glancing up every several seconds. Sometimes he caught more than a nod—mouthed words back and forth—and then nothing for a few minutes.

That was when Corban spied the safety on the guard's SKS rifle. It was on! The guards had been ordered to remain vigilant at all times, so the safety should've been off. Perhaps the safety was on just to avoid an accident. But that didn't make sense either. These guards were supposed to be the type of men who would shoot the captives first and worry about their own safety later.

The gestures could mean only one thing, Corban decided. The guards and the captives were co-conspirators. Maybe they were even planning to jump Corban and escape once they reached Egypt. But they couldn't be certain that the robed Arab didn't have a weapon under his loose clothing. And surely there was some concern about the pilots, as well, who seemed loyal to Corban—the infamous Muhammad, the client with money.

The fact that the captives and guards were communicating secretly told Corban that he'd better stop watching and speak up before he was stuffed into the cargo hold with or without the pilots. He could never fend them all off, nor did he have a weapon besides the falaco dart inside his glasses. And there was no need to fight them off, for if the guards and captives were truly friends, then Corban could speak to them openly. Or at least he could signal to them openly since he couldn't speak Korean.

Corban began to sketch pictures on napkins from the snack bar: a cross on one and a tomb with the rock rolled away on another. On a third napkin, he drew one stick figure baptizing another in a river. And on yet another, he drew as many stick people as he could between two walls of water—the parting of the Red Sea. It was the international language of the Bible.

After that, he sketched a number of Jesus' miracles: the blind seeing, Lazarus coming to life, and a man being lowered through the roof by his friends. The guards and captives were becoming increasingly aware of the mad Arab's scribbling, so much so that they ceased communicating amongst themselves and watched him intently.

Finally, Corban had sixteen drawings that depicted well-known biblical events. He approached the guards first and gave them each a napkin. Then he reached out to the captives and did the same. Returning to his seat, he watched their realization unfold. Each prisoner admired his own napkin. One napkin alone wasn't particularly meaningful or profound, but once the captives began comparing sketches, their eyes widened. The guards knelt beside the captives and shared their sketches as well, until everyone had seen them all—and they were speechless.

Then a rare occurrence took place: Corban grinned. Only his God could arrange something this fantastic. Smiles and excited chatter soon broke out, and the guards stepped up to Corban to ask him questions he couldn't understand. Crawling through the chain of captives, Corban unlocked their ankles and wrists one by one. Just yesterday, they'd been scheduled to die. Their bodies still bore signs of insect bites, and the crimson stripes on their shoulders showed through their clothing.

They wept with Corban and held one another in turn. The guards, who had refused to eat or drink since their captive friends couldn't partake, now dispensed the snacks, juice, and water from the bar. Since there were not enough seats for them all in the rich man's jet, Corban sat on the floor with the others who were now free of their chains. Forgetting about their guns, the guards sat amongst their brothers and sisters in Christ as well. They rambled on and on about their experiences, but Corban could only nod and smile. He wished he'd learned Korean.

...✝...

". . . and then when he looked inside the lions' den the next morning, he saw that Daniel was okay, and he took Daniel out and put the bad people in. The end."

The voices had woken Janice, and she now stood at the corner of the living room, unnoticed, observing the unique scene before her. Jenna, the early riser, still in her pajamas, was reading her Braille children's Bible to this man who had his shirt off while working on his belt weapon. The man she knew only as Francis had a torso much like her husband's, with multiple little, round scars on his front and back. And there was the ugly, black bruise from his most recent confrontation with a bullet the night before. He was repositioning tiny shards of glass on the belt buckle after painting them with a thick, toxic paste.

Luigi looked from the blind girl to the Braille book she held on her pajama-clad lap.

"And how do you know this story? From all those dots on the paper?" Luigi's mock fascination made the little girl giggle. "These are only dots! Dots don't tell stories, Jenna!"

"Well, I don't think all those squiggly writing marks you call letters can tell stories, either!" She argued in a very mature way. "I've heard your *s* is just a zigzag, and your *x* is just two things crossed. And don't even get me started on your *o!*"

As they both laughed, Janice joined them in the living room of their temporary home.

"What're you two doing up so early?" she asked as she collected their cereal bowls and deposited them into the kitchen sink.

"She's convinced me that I must learn Braille," Luigi said as he used pliers to remove another piece of glass. "It's not often a man in my profession spends the morning being read to by a seven-year-old."

"I'm almost eight. And then in ten more years I'll be on my own."

"I believe you should stay with your family as long as possible," Luigi said. He paused to focus on his belt and the intricate placement of toxin-covered needles and shards. "I left my family too early and, therefore, didn't become what I wanted to become."

"And what was that?" Janice sat on an overstuffed chair next to the sofa.

"An oceanographer. But perhaps it wouldn't have worked out anyway. I'm terribly afraid of sharks."

"Oh, I hate sharks, too!" Jenna said. "Huge teeth—as sharp as knives, Dad said."

"Yes, and they can smell you a mile away—through water!" Luigi shook his head. "Yes, it's best I didn't go into that profession."

"Well, when did God get ahold of your life?" Janice asked with curiosity.

"You mean, when did I become a Christian? I'm not a Christian. I'm an atheist."

"What's an atheist?"

Janice was too dumbfounded to answer. *Corban had sent someone who wasn't even a believer to protect his family?*

"It's someone who doesn't believe in any god," Luigi answered.

"What? You don't believe in God? Are you crazy?" Jenna exclaimed incredulously. "How can you not believe in God? Did something happen that made you mad at Him, like your child or your family died?"

Luigi had probably never been confronted like this before. He glanced at Janice for help, but she didn't offer him any. She just gazed at him with a puzzled look on her face.

"No, no one died in my life, not anyone I cared about,

anyway. I grew up in Italy where everyone believed in God. It's tradition in my country, and I find traditions something like entrapment."

"What's entrapment?"

"In this case, entrapment is believing in something only because everyone else does, but in your heart you don't really believe."

"So they don't really believe God is real?" Jenna asked.

"I don't think they do."

"Of course He's real! I'm blind and I can see that!"

"Then you have better vision than I, little girl."

"How did you and my husband meet, Francis?"

"Ah, perhaps it's not something for the ears of ladies."

"Come on!" Jenna pled. "Dad will tell us if you don't."

"I highly doubt that."

"It's okay," Janice said. "We'd both like to know. After all, we've let you into our lives. With all we've been through, I think we should know."

"Very well, but it's not a very nice story. You see, for many, many years, I wanted to kill Corban Dowler."

"What?" Janice suddenly believed this truly wasn't a story for ladies.

"But I didn't know his real name at that time," Luigi claimed. "I only knew him as . . . I will call him 'M'. I watched him travel all over the world and hoped he would come to my country, Italy, where I could kill him. M is a very well-known man all over the world because he is the very best at what he does. I imagined if I could kill the best, that would make me the best.

"Then, a man—though I know not who—paid me a

great deal of money to kill M, so my dedication became even greater. M finally did come to Italy to help some people in peril, even though I now believe he knew it might be a trap."

"What's peril?"

"Danger, sweetie."

"You were waiting for him?" Jenna asked softly, her bottom lip trembling.

"Yes. I was waiting with very dangerous weapons. But M shot me with a tranquilizer dart, which made me fall asleep right on the street."

"And that's it?"

"Oh, no. There's much more. After that first time when M chose not to kill me, I became curious. What kind of spy doesn't kill his enemy when given the opportunity? I even tried to kill him again, once with a poisonous cigarette and another time with a knife. But he was smarter than I was, and he again let me live, even though he knew I was trying to kill him.

"Then I came up with a new plan. I decided to make one of M's powerful friends mad at him, so I went to this man and told him lies about M, and I thought he believed me. Until I realized that the man I was speaking to was M himself! His friend came from behind a curtain and wanted to kill me for my deceit, as a favor to M. But M said he would kill me himself.

"He took me into the desert where he made me dig my own grave. I was certain I was about to die, but then M told me to put all my clothes into the grave and bury them. He gave me new clothes, new identification, and a new life—

safe from the enemies that were pressuring me to kill him—and that's how I came to serve your father. He saved my life many times. He's a great man."

Jenna and Janice were speechless for a minute as Luigi finished his work on the belt and began to clean up the materials and tools.

"Um . . . Francis?" Janice asked. "Through all this, you didn't see how God was keeping you alive, maybe for something very important? Maybe to save us? That's how God works, you know."

Luigi considered this, then stood and tightened his belt around his waist, careful not to cut himself on the tiny shards on the buckle.

"I don't know," he finally stated. "There may be something to it all. I have more work to do. Please stay away from the windows."

And with that, he turned and left the room.

✝

CHAPTER TWENTY-ONE

"**A**gent Fairchild!"

Branden flinched, suddenly awake, and spilled half of his cold coffee onto his lap. Cursing, he stood and shook the fluid from his hand.

"What is it?" he growled.

One of the nine technicians pointed to the wall map inside the CIA's Situation Room.

"We've got Corban Dowler!"

"Where? Show me!"

He led Branden to his console, where a number of other specialists had gathered to confirm his findings.

"Here. In Moscow."

"How long ago?"

"Only a few hours. He boarded a plane to Athens. They should be touching down there within an hour."

"Alert the team in—"

"Already done, sir. They'll take him down in the airport terminal before he has a chance to disappear."

"Excellent. Athens is perfect. We have a good team in Greece, don't we?"

"Yes, sir. Team Foxtrot."

Just then, Chip strode through the back doors of the

Situation Room. The ex-spy looked too refreshed, Branden thought.

"You have him on radar?" Chip asked, seeming to already know the answer.

Branden scowled. The room was definitely bugged, or one of the techs had alerted the deputy director. The shaming Chip had given Branden earlier still stung his pride. Once this COIL business was handled, Branden had already decided to make the old man disappear. He didn't think Abaddon would mind.

"Yes, we have him, sir," Branden replied triumphantly. And, for now, he needed to show respect to the man, but soon . . .

"Yeah? Where'd you catch 'im?"

"We'll have him in Athens within the hour. You should stick around and watch us take him down."

"Without force, I hope."

"Unless he resists." Branden shrugged. "I expect he'll resist. He knows we have evidence against him; he's a doomed man. Actually, he's better off resisting. If we can take him out permanently in Greece, he'll save himself and the American people a lot of embarrassment."

Chip studied the screens.

"This says he's traveling under his own name."

"He is. Corban Dowler."

"Pull up the airport footage," Chip ordered.

"It's coming in now, Deputy Director," a specialist said.

They viewed a full-sized image of a busy airport terminal in Moscow, freeze-framed on the wall screen. Then it began to move. Everyone watched for several minutes before Chip touched the console and paused the picture. Branden watched as Chip zoomed into the frame's upper right quadrant, his fingers flying over the controls. Moving to the larger-than-life screen, Chip studied the man in focus.

"Well, it appears you really have the old boy. That man on the screen is Corban, all right. Maybe a little more tan than I remember, but it's him. So, why's he using his own name?" Chip asked the room of agents.

"We flushed him out," Branden claimed. "Full-court press. He ran for a while, had us fooled, but eventually he had to use up all of his disguises. All he had left was his own name."

"But he could've run . . . or stayed put. Corban knows how the sleeper agents do it. They lie dormant for weeks, even years, until it's time to come out of hiding."

"Nah, that's no life. He's finished, and he knows it. We've got him; his glory days are over."

Turning, Chip clapped the confident, young agent on the shoulder.

"I've got to hand it to you, Branden. I didn't think you could do it. Clearly, Corban Dowler's not the top dog we thought he was. You're coming up. Might even have to start calling you Agent Branden Fairchild myself, pretty soon."

Chip offered a smile and his hand.

Branden sighed away old feelings. Maybe this old man would stand behind him as he stormed to the top. Abaddon did say to collect allies as he climbed the ladder—the more powerful, the better.

"Sir! You'd better see this!"

Branden bolted back to the console, but Chip remained where he stood.

"It's Corban Dowler, sir. He's been spotted in Naples, Italy!"

"How long ago?"

"The call just came in. Uh . . . five minutes ago."

"That's impossible! He's on the flight from Moscow! Show me the footage."

"Just a minute."

"Now!"

"The team is still piping it through, sir."

"And I want facial recognition software on that guy from Moscow. Someone check him! If he's got a double running interference for him, I want to know who's real and who's not."

"Maybe there's simply more people named Corban Dowler in this world than you thought?" Chip asked snidely.

"Here's the Naples' stream."

The stream appeared on the wall. There was Corban Dowler—same height, weight, hair, and eyes.

"Recognition software? Is this him or his double?"

"It's running. A few seconds, sir."

"Ah-hah!" Branden snapped his fingers. "Hey, Deputy Director, a mask can fool our eyes, but facial measurements are too unique, right?"

"That's right," Chip said, "but it's the eyes that not even a plastic surgeon can rearrange. The space between a man's eyes is something that can't be easily disguised."

"This is impossible!" a wide-eyed technician said. "It says they're *both* Corban Dowler—one hundred percent positively identified as both being our Corban Dowler! I've never seen a hundred percent before, not even on the real thing. The computer always has some margin for error."

Cursing, Branden punched the console, cracking the frame.

"He got into the mainframe, didn't he? Didn't he?"

"It seems so, sir. Somehow, he's convinced our database that there are multiple choices to one man's facial features. We'll never be able to identify him now, not with this software."

"Sir?" A different specialist called. "I've got another Corban Dowler who just landed in Oslo. He looks exactly like the other two!"

Too furious, Branden didn't bother to approach the console. Chip had known this was going to be the result all along! Where was that white-haired old geezer, anyway? Growling, he looked around, but Chip had left the room.

Branden slumped into a chair as more Corban Dowlers continued to surface in other parts of the world. He needed a new strategy to take over the masses, Branden decided. Maybe he wasn't cut out for this espionage career after all. But he couldn't walk away from his assignment. Corban Dowler was standing in his way. Abaddon would know what to do; Abaddon always knew what to do.

...✝...

Two hours later, Branden Fairchild, dressed in a silk robe, prostrated himself on the floor in a secluded, dark room. He was ready once again to put into practice what he'd learned as a youth in a Polish church—though he'd seen many in America do it, as well. Repeating a mantra over and over in a whisper, he entered a self-induced trance.

Branden suddenly sat upright, his eyes glazed, and stared at a broken piece of mirror. By the glimmering light from the six candles around him, he could barely see his reflection.

On the floor to his right, his cell phone rang. He answered it before the second ring.

"Abaddon."

"Hello, my child," a deep voice answered.

"Why don't you speak to me in my mind as you did when I was young?" Branden's eyes didn't blink; he bordered on unconsciousness.

"You know I inhabit a physical body now. But I still hear when you call for me."

"The man whose soul you've entrusted me to destroy has evaded me."

"This I have seen. And you grow weary?"

"Yes, I grow weary."

"Look into the mirror."

"I am looking."

"I have sculpted you into a beautiful man. Say it."

"I am beautiful."

"Beside you, there is no equal. You hold the power within you to conquer all of your struggles. You are wonderful."

"I am wonderful."

"Corban Dowler believes you are an evil man, but

believe what I tell you—you are a great man."

"I am a great man."

"Because Corban serves a weak master, Corban is a weak man. You serve a prince, a powerful being of might and intelligence. And I impart this might and intelligence to you, because you deserve it. Many will worship you in the kingdom we are building, because we are gods. You are a god."

"I am a god."

"You will find Velt at Corban's old house. He is there."

"I have been there. My men have searched it. The house is deserted."

"Velt is there. Do not doubt me. Have faith in me, as I have faith in our supreme master. And as you grow wiser day by day, have faith in the god within yourself. You are worthy."

"I am worthy."

"Look in the mirror more often. Worship yourself. Praise the spirit that has been placed inside you. You will prosper."

"I will prosper."

"Go to Velt. He will obey you. Sacrifice him if you must. Velt will understand. It is the order of things. But you are royalty. You are a ruler. You are a god."

"I am a god."

"Do not dwell on the recent setbacks. Corban is crafty and deceitful. He helps the weak people because he is weak. You are strong, and you will crush the weak. You will spit on the weak and intimidate them until everyone around you worships you."

"Yes. They will worship me."

"Because you are beautiful, they look at you and they are jealous. They wish they could be you. I have seen it, so do not despair. Many will follow you when it is time. Use your crafty tongue to lead them from our enemy. You have the gift, but you cannot find your place while Corban's soul is on this earth. Wipe him away by using his family."

"What about the deputy director?"

"He knows some of your secrets. He must die soon, but he is not a great threat. He enjoys watching."

"Is he a foe?"

"Yes, he is a foe because he is loyal to Corban. They must both be destroyed, but Corban must be first."

"Yes, I will do it. They will love me because I am wonderful."

"That is true. I am so proud of you. My pride is everlasting, and in it I hold you; in my embrace, you are invincible."

"I am invincible."

"Yes, my child, you are."

$$\dagger$$

<u>*CHAPTER TWENTY-TWO*</u>

When Corban reached Cairo with the fourteen escapees from North Korea, he didn't linger with his new brothers and sisters in Christ. Though he never shared an intelligible word with them, they were all brought close by their Lord and His preservation. Corban left the escapees in the able hands of two of Fost's operatives from Moscow, one of whom spoke Korean. As soon as the leopard animation was completed, the two guards would return to North Korea to boast of the horrific feedings they'd witnessed. And there, those two brave men would continue their secret work for Christ, until they were caught and killed. They knew the risks, and they took them joyfully.

The fourteen would be given new lives under Fost's direction. Most likely, they would go to Seoul, South Korea, where much of the aid effort for North Korea's Christians was coordinated and the language was the same.

To maintain appearances, Corban flew on to Alexandria as Muhammad, then became Christopher Cagon, the International Red Cross ambassador for the UK. He changed identities two more times before he reached Malaysia as red-haired A.B. Leever. As soon as he was clear of the airport, he ditched his disguise and took a taxi to the hotel. None of the team members were in their rooms, so he picked the lock to Chloe's room to gain access to her laptop.

For two hours, Corban read reports from other teams who'd recently rescued Christians or extracted missionaries from danger. Twelve new incidents had sprung up in the last forty-eight hours. The laborers were few, and the devil was trying to make them fewer—though the harvest was ever more plentiful. Corban praised God for the end he sensed was near, when the last person would be saved in this age.

Lying on his back at the foot of Chloe's bed, Corban woke suddenly to find Chloe sneaking into her room with a clothespin-sized dart gun. He asked her to call the rest of the team over to her room so they could all participate in a briefing session.

The team had been busy under the mutual leadership of Chloe and Nathan. Chopper pilot Fred "Memphis" Nelson was on loan from Johnny Wycke. Johnny had arrived to deliver their combat gear, then left a few hours later. If they needed a pilot for the mission, Memphis was their man, and it would give the new member a chance to work with COIL's primary ops team.

"Okay, tell me what you've got figured out for this extraction," Corban said.

"This is what we have so far," Nathan said as he pulled the prison model from under the bed. "We've sketched in the city's sewer manholes that access the inside of the prison. There are no body-sized tunnels or pipes through that muck into the perimeter, but we received your fog machine, Boss. We can crank that baby up from two blocks away, about here, underground, and force fog down this way so it seeps out the holes of the sewer covers inside the prison here, and here. There's a playground about two miles away, so we've been testing our theory on that. The wind is a little difficult, but we can at least see how the fog is going to spill out of the ground. After monkeyin' around with the density, we've got it so the fog isn't so heavy that it drifts too low to the ground, but not so light that it rises and blows away either."

"And it works," Bruno added. "At night, we'll be able to fill that compound with soup so thick, we could drive a tractor through the fence."

"But we're not doing that." Nathan chuckled. "We were able to get the uniform."

"That was my job," Toad announced.

"Toad's going into the prison at 2000 hours, shift change," Nathan continued, "and directly to the southwest tower to climb the internal staircase up to the tower's observation level, which we'll call the nest. He'll tranquilize the two guards, tie them up, and signal Scooter and me. We'll anchor a cable over the two perimeter fences and to the ground outside before we climb up the far side of the tower. From the ground to the nest is a good climb—forty feet.

"Now here's an anomaly: every other prison we've researched has its perimeter towers outside the perimeter fences. Why this old men's prison is built with its two towers *inside* the fence line is a mystery to me. But I do know that our job and this plan are a lot easier because of it.

"Okay, moving on. Scooter, Toad, and I will be in the southwest tower, dubbed Tower One. Cue in the fog. That's Chloe's job. As the fog develops, Toad leaves Tower One, crosses the yard, and ascends to Tower Two's nest, where he takes out the other two guards. He drops a cable over the fence to Milk and Bruno. They climb up and secure Tower Two.

"At this point we're within range to cover every angle of the prison. Toad will go back through the fog to Tower One, where he'll wait with Scooter and me until the fog is thick enough for me to go get Helena."

"Why doesn't Toad just get Helena himself?" Corban asked.

"Because he looks Malaysian, he's wearing a guard's uniform, and he speaks no German. Helena might cause a scene and draw attention if he tries to drag her out of her cell."

"All right. From the second we cue for fog, how long until you can cross the yard?"

"About eight minutes."

"That's a long time to wait," Corban said. "I can fly in another fog machine."

"Boss, the fog from one fog machine looks unnatural enough, and by the time a second one arrives, it would take two or three more days of testing before we could be ready."

"Okay. Continue."

"As soon as the fog is soup—which happens pretty fast,

once it starts emerging—I descend Tower One and fetch Helena. Toad and Scooter cover me. I take Helena up to Tower One's nest, and we exit down the outside cable to a vehicle driven by Chloe. Milk and Bruno make their departure into the city to the water tower, where Memphis will be in communication, watching over everything from above. That's it."

All looked expectantly toward Corban for his approval or criticism. It was nearly a minute before he opened his mouth.

"Perimeter vehicles?"

"They have none. There's no need for more security," Nathan explained. "The only prisoners who cross that courtyard are under escort and the eyes of two towers. No one else is allowed outside."

"And what about the gatehouse? You haven't said anything about that. What are there, two or three guards at the gatehouse?"

"Right. Two seems to be the norm at night, three during the day. We don't know exactly what to do about them, though they seem to be under Tower Two's view."

"What're you packing in with you, Toad?"

"The NL-1, sir."

"The air pistol. All right. After Tower One is secured, you'll be going back toward Tower Two. Can you approach this gatehouse?"

"I could."

"Well, they have to be taken out before Milk and Bruno scale Tower Two. According to this model, they have a line-of-sight at the backside of the tower. That won't do."

"So I visit them with Tower Two looking down on me before Tower Two is secured?"

"Chloe, after you get the fog rolling, can you get northeast, about here, and set off about a dozen fireworks when Toad's ready for Tower Two's diversion? Something colorful. Will that do the trick, Toad?"

"That'll do, sir."

"All right, there's still one distasteful thing I must mention, since no one else has." Corban moved to where he could stand with his back against the wall and see them all. "This is a pretty good plan. For a girl and a bunch of guys who don't speak the language, it's a real good plan. But what if Helena isn't in her cell by the fence?"

"What do you mean?" Nathan frowned. "That's where they house her."

"They never take her anywhere else?" Corban asked, implying the worst, though their confused looks told him he had to be more direct. "You're telling me that the guards who use her for their own pleasure go into her infested cell?"

Nathan paled. The others fidgeted uncomfortably.

"You're right," Chloe said. "They do take her somewhere else."

"Do we know where?"

"I haven't been able to ask her." Nathan sighed. "She avoids the whole topic."

"And do we know which shifts they take her?"

"Surveillance is tough because we don't want to be seen on the water tower too often," Nathan said.

"I think it's at night when they get her," Chloe said.

"One time she said, 'They took me again last night.'"

"So this is a problem," Corban concluded. "At any one time, what's the minimum-maximum number of guards on the premises?"

"Twenty to forty."

"Is this the only armory, here by Tower Two?" When no one answered, he continued. "I don't think it is. It's probably the armory for the towers only. The truth is, we don't have a clue what lies inside these buildings here and here. Other prisoners, yes. More guards, yes. Is there an officers' lounge? There usually is. How about a warden's living quarters? They take her somewhere private, I'm assuming, but where?"

"And it's not every night," Chloe added.

"We have one shot at this," Corban said, his hands on his hips. "This is a little more extreme and exposed than you're all used to, but that doesn't mean it's impossible. Memphis?"

"Yes, sir."

"As soon as you can get on that water tower platform without drawing attention, you need to get up there. We can back out of this operation up until Toad goes inside at 2000 hours. But after that shift change, we're all in. At that point, we'll assume she's in her cell. All we can do is hope to get her before they do. And Toad, you realize there'll be other guards around you in that courtyard, even if they're just walking past you? The fog will make a few of them curious."

"Yes, sir. I'm learning a few basic Malay phrases."

"Good. At least you know what you're facing. Well,

you're the best at what you do. Take no personal effects. You know the drill. Use the brains God gave you. You've got my go-ahead."

"You won't be joining us, Mr. Dowler?" Milk asked.

"No. Chloe and Johnny Wycke have been informed, but the rest of you should know, too: there's a faction within the CIA that's trying hard to shut COIL down. They've taken over our Manhattan headquarters, though not with violence. I've been in hiding for a week. They're after me, but they'll take you all down to get to me. Even my family was attacked."

"That's crazy!" Nathan exclaimed. "Who is it?"

"It's our old friend, Abaddon." Corban placed two photographs on the table: one of Branden Fairchild, and one of Velt Plavanko. "These two are his most loyal subjects. Their days are numbered. But to answer your question, I won't be here because I have to squash this thing back in the States before it starts to affect operations. Pray for my family—and all of us. I'd say the devil's quite aware that his time is about up."

"Bring on the Judgment, I say!" Milk cheered.

"In due time, everyone, in due time. Get Helena out. Chloe has your scatter plans to get you back to Berlin for debriefing, and then it wouldn't hurt for you all to go home and see your families before the next job. Make it quick, though. Just a short recess."

"If I wanted a desk job, I woulda asked for one, Boss." Milk nodded at Corban. "My wife knows what we do. She misses me, but she's supportive."

"All right. Lord willing, I'll see you all safely back in the

States—or sooner, if we're called up yonder. Let's have a word of prayer together before I leave."

Corban was in New York City fifteen hours later.

"You see? If we're ever separated, I can still find you," Luigi explained.

He tightened two screws on a bracelet around Jenna's right ankle. When he finished, she felt it with her fingers.

"It feels like a dog collar." Jenna giggled. "What color is it?"

"Red and black."

Sitting nearby in the living room, Janice was watching the shapes and shadows of the thermal imaging system on the plasma television screen. During the night, the mystery man had returned to the house for sale down the street. Janice and Luigi had been watching him all day. The man had paced a lot, punched the walls, and sat at the window for hours as he observed the empty Dowler house.

Glancing over her shoulder, she looked at her daughter's new tracking bracelet. Both of their faces were healing from the assault a few nights prior, and Francis said his chest wasn't paining him any longer.

"How's it work?" Janice asked.

Luigi held up a cheap cell phone.

"Call the bracelet and it speaks to you. GPS."

"It works through the phone?" Janice sat next to her daughter and took the phone from Luigi. "What's the number?"

"Ask Jenna."

"How would I know the number?" Jenna frowned then

she jumped up, excited. "Oh! Can I make one up?"

"No, no. I've stenciled the number onto the top of the bracelet."

Jenna brushed her fingers over the otherwise smooth surface.

"It's in Braille! Francis, you wrote it in Braille!"

Janice dialed as Jenna read the numbers aloud. A smile spread across Janice's face as she listened to a digital voice give the latitude and longitude of her daughter's position. She held the phone to Jenna's ear so she could hear.

"That's not our address!" Jenna noticed quickly.

"No, it's a satellite address." Luigi collected his tools. "And it's accurate within inches."

"I need one of those on Corban." Janice joked as she pulled her daughter's pant leg down to hide the device.

"There are many people who would like to put one on him, I believe," Luigi agreed. "I'm sorry, Mrs. Dowler. I'd give you a tracker, but I only have this one."

"It's okay. I'm not leaving her side anyway. She's my own little tracking device." Janice tickled Jenna until she laughed breathlessly.

"Quiet!" Luigi snapped.

The girls jumped and shrank into the couch.

Luigi knelt in front of the plasma screen. Janice was considering a reply to his sharp order, when she, too, noticed the screen. She leaned forward.

"What is it, Mom?" Jenna whispered. "What's happening?"

"Someone else is with the spy down the street," Janice said.

Gripping the sides of the screen, Luigi studied the red and blue hot spots.

"I wish I knew who these guys were, and what they want with you and Corban," Luigi said with concern. He adjusted the focus and sat on the edge of the chair to watch.

Janice moved closer to watch with him, occasionally telling Jenna what was happening on the screen.

Jenna trembled with fearful excitement.

†

CHAPTER TWENTY-THREE

Branden Fairchild drove alone to the old Dowler house. He knew it was empty, but he obeyed Abaddon's command anyway. Parking in front of the mailbox, he climbed out, scowling at the house in which he'd failed so miserably a few nights before. It wasn't his fault. The Dowler trash had made him fail.

He turned around slowly, a demonic gleam in his eye, studying each of the neighboring houses in turn. A man with a boy on a motorcycle waved and smiled at him, but Branden ignored the pair. He wasn't on a public relations tour. Yes, he knew he was irresistible, a model of perfect maleness to be worshipped, but he had other things to do. These lesser subjects would have to wait in line for his attention.

The next house he analyzed was one for sale. His eyes were wandering elsewhere, when the curtains suddenly flew open. Velt stood at the window wearing a devilish grin, his arms open to receive his boyhood friend. He waved Branden to the front door, which he opened as Branden jogged up and embraced him. They moved arm in arm into the house and closed the door.

"This place is a mess, Velt!" Branden touched his nose.

"It smells like a sewer in here!"

Hanging his head, Velt nudged an overflowing trash bag.

"I haven't been able to leave the house for a few days, and the plumbing hasn't worked right for a week."

"You've been here in this house that long?" Branden crossed the cluttered living room to the window where snack wrappers crowded a spotting scope. He gazed at the Dowler house across the street. "You mean you saw me the other night? And did nothing? Why didn't you help me, Velt? We could've had them! We could've had Corban by now!"

"I . . . I . . . That was you? Their drapes were closed. It was dark. I tried to follow in my car, but they . . ."

Velt punched his leg in frustration. Branden crossed to his friend and hugged him.

"It's okay. I know they're full of deceit and trickery. Now it's our turn to make them stumble. Let's eat, my friend. Feed me, and we'll share the adventures of our missed years."

Heating some canned stew, Velt found some nearly expired milk for the two of them to drink. They spoke their old Polish language and laughed as they recalled the days when they'd first begun to rise above all others. Velt recounted how he'd spent his years doing Abaddon's bidding, how he'd murdered and thieved from the weak.

Branden took his time giving Velt the details of the Iraqi war during which he'd bombed so many innocents and how the event was now known by the authorities, particularly the CIA's deputy director. His time with the Agency was limited, Branden knew. Velt relished the story of blood, gore, and broken bodies. Laughing at the memory of his bombing error, Branden cursed the authorities for their stupidity; they could've figured it out and pinned the massacre upon their star-studded pilot long ago.

Together, Velt and Branden scoffed at the enemy's God, at how weak and ignorant He was of His subjects' suffering. And soon, very soon, when the protector Corban Dowler was eliminated, Abaddon would make them princes and give them loyal followers to serve their every whim. In turn, they would give their subjects freedom to torture and kill all Christians and burn their houses and churches to the ground. It would be a glorious day of cleansing. And they knew they would succeed, because no one could stand in their way.

The ones who bowed the knee and read from the strange book that so confused Velt would be diminished soon. Most of them had already begun to live like the rest of the world, which meant they were never real followers of their Christ in the first place. Yes, Branden and Velt agreed, taking over the world for Abaddon's beloved was so near! Mankind was primed; hearts were as dark as night. They were already subjects of Abaddon, and most of them didn't know it—or if they did know it, they didn't care. People were comfortable in this world.

"And then we'll not hide any longer, my Velt," Branden declared. "We'll live openly and people will cheer for us. The world will rejoice for the peace and unity Abaddon has brought the world! There will always be small uprisings, but we'll have great armies by then. Corban will be gone, and those without Abaddon's mark will be led to the slaughter. Princes and generals we'll be! We'll be great! We'll be gods! We are so close!"

"What do we do next?"

Standing, Branden thrust his hands deep into his pockets and walked to the window. It was nearly dusk outside.

"Abaddon sent me here for a reason. He said you and I, together, could catch Corban."

"But he's gone into hiding. He hasn't been here for over a week, and his family is gone now, too."

"I know, I know, but they must've left some clue behind. A sign. Have you seen anything suspicious? Perhaps they told a neighbor where they were going? Anything, Velt. Think!"

Velt thought about it for a moment.

"There is one new neighbor. Four houses down."

The two men stood at the window together.

"The one with the carport and bay window. He moved in the afternoon before you came to the Dowler house. Could it be? I saw him jog past the house. Let's see . . . Dark, like an Arab. Maybe darker, like an Indian. But not black. Narrow face, bald head, and—"

Branden shoved Velt away from the window.

"Stupid! That's the one who attacked me! It has to be. It's no coincidence, not in this neighborhood!"

"I didn't know! He hid his face that night!"

"He's with the Corban's trash even now, I bet, laughing at us as we look for them elsewhere. And here they are so near!"

"Corban could be there, too!" Velt said.

Their eyes widened as visions of glory and wealth flashed before them.

"Abaddon has blessed us," Branden said. "He's making this easy for us."

"He loves us."

"Listen. Give me two minutes to circle around to the back of that house, then you go through the front." Branden drew his pistol. "Don't even ring the doorbell."

"What if it's not them?"

Branden slapped Velt hard on the cheek.

"Do not doubt! I know it's them! I feel it. Either way, we kill them or use them to find Corban. I'll decide that when the time comes."

"If we kill them, can I do it? Please?"

"Kill the bald one," Branden said. "If Corban isn't there, we may have to use the females for bait."

"And where should we take them?"

"Where we started when we came to this country, Velt. Where we were first welcomed with open hearts and empty minds."

Velt's laughter was maniacal.

"They loved us there."

"And they'll be our most loyal subjects." He gazed afar as if remembering a past vision, then snapped to attention. "Two minutes, Velt, then go straight through the front door."

Branden exited the back door, and Velt checked his watch. Despite his excitement, he was still calm. He wanted to kill the enemy, but he knew there were other ways they might be used to serve Abaddon.

Jogging in place, Velt took deep breaths and tried to stay loose and ready. Finally, he was a soldier again—and with his greatest companion, Branden!

It was time. He drew his weapon from his shoulder holster. Pausing by the front door, he gripped the handle and took one last deep breath. Velt knew there would be nothing subtle about the next few minutes, but he wasn't afraid; he loved this part. Abaddon gave him courage.

Whipping the door open, he leaped off the porch and sprinted down the footpath through the grassy yard. The house wasn't much farther; he was already halfway there. He was strong from doing pushups, but he was already getting winded.

Velt crossed the street at an angle. He bounced off the car in the carport and used his momentum to head straight at the front door. Ramming the expensive door with his right shoulder, it gave way under his weight. He stumbled over the splintered wood and skidded to a stop on the tile floor.

A bald man stood in the entryway, tugging at his belt and blocking access to the woman and girl as they scrambled into the back hallway. As Velt leveled his gun, the bald man swung the belt. The buckle sliced a dozen scratches on his knuckles. Stepping closer, Velt tried to use his size to crowd and intimidate the man, but the man held his ground, no fear on his determined face as he continued to swing the belt. Every time Velt raised the gun, the belt buckle attacked his knuckles. With his hand bleeding, Velt felt the room begin to spin. He fell against the wall and fired two rounds into the floor.

As he sank to his knees, he saw Branden step quietly into the living room. Then Velt slumped to the floor.

"How long is your belt?" Branden mocked the bald man.

Spinning around, Luigi raised his leather whip, but Branden was too far away. Branden fired four shots from his hip. All four bullets slammed into Luigi's chest. A crimson spot darkened his polo shirt. Luigi dropped the belt and fell backwards, his head landing on Velt's still body.

"Get off him!" Branden hissed and dragged Luigi by one leg away from Velt. Checking Velt's pulse, Branden slapped him twice on the cheek. "Velt! Velt! Wake up! Come on! That stuff shouldn't even bother you, not after what you eat!"

Leaving Velt on the floor, Branden strode down the hallway. When he came to the locked door, he kicked it twice to break the flimsy lock. He stepped into the master bedroom and muttered his thanks to Abaddon.

Janice held a lamp over her head, ready to batter him if he dared to step closer. The child sat on the floor next to the bed, behind her mother, drawing dots on the wall with a marker.

"I can shoot you, or you can come with me," Branden said calmly. He aimed at the blind girl. "Of course I only need one of you."

"No!" She lowered the lamp, then dropped it to the carpet. "Don't. I'll go with you. Leave her here. She's no good to you anyway. She'll just be a burden."

"A blind burden, yes, but a pure one." He took two paces toward Janice and clubbed her on the brow with the pistol. She spun, bounced off the bed, and lay still. He grabbed Jenna by the hair. "Come along, little one."

Jenna stood faster than he expected and stabbed blindly upward with her marker. Branden took a full two inches of the marker up his left nostril until it sank into his sinuses. Pain and tears exploded across his face. He released Jenna, who felt her way out of the room. Blind now himself, he tripped over Janice and fell onto the bed, jamming the marker even deeper. Branden screamed like a wounded animal. With a trembling hand, he blew his nose and pulled out the marker, his anguish-filled, high-pitched scream waking Janice.

Wiping away his tears and blood, Branden rolled over on the bed in time to see Janice crawling from the room. He emptied his clip in her direction, then reloaded his weapon as he sobbed in pain and anger. Never in his life had he been wounded; now he bled profusely from the nose—and at the hands of a child! Even in the Air Force he'd avoided the slightest scuffles to protect his beautiful face.

Branden staggered to the hallway. There was blood on the carpet. A bullet had gone through the wall and hit Janice, but she'd kept crawling.

"I got them, Branden," Velt called.

While wiping his eyes, Branden ran down the hall. He found Velt still lying on the floor, but holding the blind girl by the wrist and the mother by the ankle. Janice was kicking feebly at Velt with her free leg, blood matting the side of her shirt. Jenna was trying to peel Velt's claws off her wrist.

Branden pistol-whipped the woman on the head to still her, then backhanded Jenna so hard that she flew against the wall and crumpled onto her mother.

"Get up, Velt!" Branden ordered. "The police'll be on their way. Load them into their car. You drive it and follow me. I'll drive my own car."

Velt rolled to his knees, then his feet. His right hand was scratched and bloody from the belt and kicks, but he just licked his knuckles. Picking up both girls, he carried them out to the carport. Jenna squirmed and fought his grip, but Velt just laughed.

"Amazing," Branden said as he bent over Luigi. "You're still alive. It's a pity we don't have more time to spend with you, but we have a little homecoming to prepare for Corban, you see."

Luigi tried to protest, as blood pooled on the tile floor beneath him.

"No . . ."

"No? Oh, but it must be so."

"No," Luigi panted. "Their God . . . is too . . . strong."

Branden cackled. He aimed his gun at Luigi's heart and fired one finishing shot. Then he turned and walked outside.

...✝...

Corban pulled into his driveway as an ambulance zoomed down the street, its siren wailing. Even though the flashing lights were at the far end of the street, Corban knew it had something to do with his family. A rushing ambulance was a good sign, Corban thought. It meant there was still hope for the passenger. The quiet, slower-moving ambulances were the ones that worried him.

He wasn't even sure he was staying in his house that night, so Corban didn't bother with his single piece of luggage. Crossing the street, he approached a group of neighbors who had gathered on the curb.

"What's going on, Jerry?"

Jerry was wealthy by inheritance and spent every moment he could with his family.

The two men shook hands.

"Big ol' shoot-out, Corban," Jerry said. "About twenty shots. Even some guy carrying a body out. Too dark to see too much."

"Twenty shots, huh? All from the same gun?"

"Now how would I know a thing like that?" Jerry raised his eyebrows at Corban. "And who would? That many bullets, we'll probably be finding holes in our own walls and roofs for the next year."

"Who lived there?"

"Don't know. Some bald guy just moved in. Seemed friendly enough. Quiet. Jogged some. It's that same time-share that saw a lot of parties a couple years ago.

Corban stood watching, judging, and making hasty conclusions with his neighbors for a few minutes, then excused himself. As he walked into his house, he noticed the door had been unlocked. In a glance, he saw that the place had been ransacked.

Jerry had said some bald guy lived in the time-share. Corban didn't know many bald men, but he still had to check it out. A shoot-out on his street had to be more than a coincidence.

He went into the kitchen, opened the cupboard under the sink, and reached far into the corner for something he hadn't touched for several years. Tearing loose a sealed plastic bag, he ripped it open. Cash, credit cards, and clean identifications spilled into his hand, including a billfold with a badge.

Corban washed up, combed his hair straight back, and picked up a wrinkled suit off the floor. Ten minutes later, he looked the part, complete with glasses and a new mustache. His neighbors paid him no mind as he walked down the street to the time-share. As he ducked under the police tape, a uniformed officer raised his hand.

"Sir, this is—"

"I'm Agent Brown, FBI. Who's in charge here?"

The officer stood up straighter.

"Whoa. FBI." He pointed at the carport. "Detective Marsh. He'll want to see you."

Corban continued and stopped in front of a curly-haired, broad-shouldered man. By his features, Corban guessed he was Greek. The man looked from his notes to Corban's face, then to Corban's blue-lettered identification hanging freely from his suit breast pocket.

"Name's Marsh," he said as they shook hands. "Don't tell me this guy was one of yours."

"Let me take a look and I'll tell you."

"Ambulance just took him out. He was alive—so far. Probably won't last the night, though. Thought he was DOA when we got here. Looked like four or five to the chest. Close range, too. Go figure. Made a swimming pool of the living room. Wasn't new to the game either. I figured it was possible one of you boys might show up."

"Why do you say that?"

"He had old scars. Bullet wounds. No wonder he was hangin' on; he'd been through this bit before—just not this bad."

"What'd he look like?"

"Dark-skinned, like a Mexican, but maybe European. Tough guy. Bald. Maybe forty."

"Mind if I take a quick look? It's all yours. I'll just be in and out. See what I see."

"Yeah, okay. Watch where you step, though. The place is a real mess."

Corban moved slowly through the open door, his eyes taking in everything. A quart of blood had to be hurdled before he could access the house and the walls were spattered. As he jumped the mess, he noted a bullet hole in the floor and the shape of a body chalked around it. Behind him, the forensic team was prying more bullets from the drywall.

In the living room, Corban spotted an antique thermal imaging system hooked up to the plasma screen, but no one else noticed it yet. The machine was still on, aimed at the house for sale down the street.

On the coffee table, there were gum wrappers and a child's Braille Bible. Next to the Bible was a bottle of thick, clear jelly with a French name on it. *Boneve*. Corban looked around before pocketing the bottle. He might need the sleeping toxin later. No telling when he'd get to his stash of falaco.

Studying the kitchen, he found evidence of three

people. And more gum wrappers. In the hallway to the bedrooms, a junior detective was picking up a white cane, collecting it for evidence. Corban didn't share his insight.

Farther down the hall, Corban found more blood—a few drops—and signs that several bullets had passed through the wall. To study the downward angle, he entered the master bedroom. Nine bullets had been fired from the bed. Blood and mucous had been drooled across the bedspread. The lamp and an empty gun clip were on the floor. Corban studied a marker coated with blood and mucous, like someone had choked on it. The marker was Jenna's; the type with which the blind wrote. The tip left raised ink marks on paper. He tried not to draw any conclusions as to whose blood was on it.

Then, at the bottom of the wall, behind the discarded lamp, he saw a number of dots. To the ignorant eye, the dots were mere clumps of paint. But Corban knew better. Janice had taught Jenna Braille two years before, after the girl had come to live with them. Naturally, all three had learned the letters, but Jenna had been a whiz. After the alphabet came the more difficult sounds, like *ch* and *sh*. Corban had helped her with those characters and her numbers, too.

Squatting next to the wall, Corban studied the Braille cells. He remembered that Braille letters were structured in a single cell pattern of no more than six dots each, two by three. But Braille numbers were preceded by four dots in the previous cell to announce that the next cell contained a number rather than a letter, since the *A* and the number *1* are essentially the same. What Corban saw on the wall, though it slanted downward, was a series of numbers. He counted five before Jenna had been interrupted while writing the precursor to the sixth number. Not sure what they meant, he memorized the five numbers and jogged through his memory for a familiar phone number. Or maybe it was a license plate. Whatever Jenna had been writing, it was incomplete. If it was a phone number with seven digits, the two missing digits presented exactly one hundred possible combinations. But he didn't believe it was a phone number, because it didn't have any prefix he recognized. Jenna was an intelligent little girl, though. She had picked up on something and left a clue for him. Who else would she leave it for, but her father? Who else would search for her without ceasing?

Outside, Corban was approached by Detective Marsh.

"What'd ya think? One of yours?"

Corban made sure they were alone. Marsh recognized the hesitation and stepped closer.

"Handle this carefully."

"Well, of course. What do you know?"

"This was a safe house for a former CIA agent's family."

"Go figure." Marsh scratched his unshaved jaw. "So who's after him? Old pals or old enemies?"

"It's inter-agency. Fella named Fairchild seems to be running his own hide-n-seek squad. See the house down the street? The one for sale?"

"Sure. What about it?"

"A house for sale . . . an abandoned house . . . a house with curtains when no one is living there?"

"Oh, I see. A stakeout?"

"That's what I read. Since there was gunplay, they probably left in a hurry. Maybe they left something behind. If you look at the front door, you can see it's still open."

"Yeah, I see it. Maybe some DNA or fingerprints got left behind."

"I don't have it all put together yet, but that's where I'd start."

"What about the guy sporting the five new buttons?" he asked. "Ours or theirs?"

"Last time I saw him, he had hair, but he's one of ours. He was guarding the family."

"Okay. That's a start. How many in the family?"

"Two. Mother and daughter. Ages fifty-seven and seven. Daughter's blind."

"Blind? Go figure. Can you give me names?"

"Can you keep it quiet?"

"Sure, but if this is a kidnapping, we can muster a multi-state bulletin right now."

"It's more like a hostage situation."

"I'll do what I can. The names?"

"Janice and Jenna Dowler."

"And they're being held hostage for . . . ?"

"This rogue Fairchild fella wants the father. Fairchild's obsessed, or possessed, or both."

"And the father, you say he's ex-CIA?"

"That's right."

"Well, who is he?"

"Me." Corban looked the detective square in the eyes. "Corban James Dowler."

The decision to cooperate with Detective Marsh had

been made at the last minute. The man was simply doing his job, and if Corban proceeded on his own, he might cause more trouble than he was willing to handle. Besides, he liked the way the detective referred to the "bad guys" as one of theirs, and the "good guys" as one of ours. This was an ordinary, no-nonsense cop, and as far as Corban was concerned, that was the best kind—slow to judge, few biases, old fashioned. Sometimes those three qualities didn't come together, but when they did, an open-minded detective emerged.

Corban told him about the thermal imager and his own residence down the street. He even told him about the five-digit number written in Braille, but he instructed him not to mess with it for now. Then he shared with Marsh that he was on his way to the Agency's deputy director's house to work out the investigation from that end. Marsh agreed to handle it as a burglary on a time-share, mixed with a hate crime against a Canadian named Malvao.

As Corban and Marsh talked, the detective admitted that he liked the idea of coordinating an investigation with the CIA, where he would play the fumbling detective, when all the while, he was in charge and privy to all the details. And because Corban had been around the block a time or two, Corban would know how the Agency would want to keep the situation civil.

"Fairchild will be isolated, now that he's crossed the line. And you'll even receive a commendation for cracking the case of a corrupt agent," Corban said, slapping Marsh on the back.

The two exchanged contact information before Corban

sped away to begin his own hunt. His heart ached for his two girls, the two he loved so much. Then he briefly gave in to doubt.

He wondered if God was even watching, or maybe He was busy elsewhere. Was God allowing this for some reason? Corban saw enough suffering in the world to know that bad things happened to good people, even to the faithful. But it was always harder to see God's purpose in difficult situations when it was personal.

As Corban sped to Virginia, he wept and prayed. What unimaginable things would he have to do to get his wife and daughter back?

†

CHAPTER TWENTY-FOUR

Corban abandoned his vehicle near a beach in Eastern Virginia and crept up to an iron fence. He was dressed in black under the bright moon, but he wasn't as invisible as he wished. Cloud cover wasn't something he could wait for that night.

Studying the estate on the hill, Corban was reminded that one hundred seventy years ago, a man had sailed a small boat from the beach north to Maryland as he ran for his life. That man had been a slave during the days of the Underground Railroad. Times hadn't changed much; men and women were still hunted and persecuted, even in the Land of Liberty.

The estate was surrounded and sheltered by elm trees. Corban had been there a few times, and each time he'd wondered at the level of security the deputy director maintained. A twenty-four-hour guard stood watch at the main gate. There were also men with Dobermans and German Shepherds. The guards and dogs were terrifying. If the guns didn't tear a man to pieces, the dogs would. The men wore overcoats as if they were reliving Berlin's past, which was actually part of Chip's history. A mix of Gestapo and KGB was alive and well on Chip's estate.

In Corban's fist was an NL-2, COIL's machine pistol. It fired the same water-soluble pellets as the NL-3 rifle, but since the pistol was smaller, it held two hundred fifty rounds with a rapid-fire cycle rate of six hundred rounds per minute. The selector switch offered single shot or fully automatic firing. Corban had it on automatic.

Pulling a black mask over his face, he vaulted over the fence, then crouched and waited. It had been a long time since he'd infiltrated an establishment by stealth, but it still felt as natural as it had when he was twenty-three years old. This time, though, his calf muscles trembled, his stomach did flip-flops, and his mouth was dry. But his breathing was even and his eyes were steady.

Corban ran across the hill rather than up it. Only a fool would rush straight at a fortress. He knew there were cameras in the elm trees, but they were stationary and aimed toward the colonial-style house, rather than outward.

Halfway across the expanse, Corban dropped to his belly. Sliding a bit on the wet, short grass, he lay still. A Doberman and its master were emerging from the elms, walking toward him. Maybe they were taking a walk down to the beach to check the eastern perimeter. The man carried a strapped Tech-9 machine gun. Corban had tangled with a Tech-9 before, somewhere in Camden. He'd also tangled with a Doberman before, somewhere in Dublin.

Trying to merge with the grass as one of the many night shadows created by the moon, Corban hoped neither the man nor dog would know the difference between him and a rift in the ground, a lumpy tract of grass the mower had missed. But the difference between this shadow and others was that it had two arms extended above its head, grasping a non-reflective black object.

Unfortunately, the NL-2 pistol only had an effective range of fifty yards. After that, the pellets slowed in velocity so hastily, they would bounce off a target rather than break open and vaporize on impact.

Nevertheless, Corban wouldn't hesitate to fire at seventy-five yards—where the guard was—because most men who were shot with the pellets believed the sting was a real bullet. The initial gasp and clutching was a few-second delay that often decided the victor.

Sixty-five yards.

The Doberman's pointed ears perked as it spied the shadow in the grass. The dog sniffed the sea breeze. The wind was blowing across the expanse, but Corban hadn't showered for two days, and the canine had a keen nose. It gave an excited yelp and pulled against the leash. The guard paused, studying the shadows.

Corban pulled the trigger. In less than a second, a dozen pellets slapped into the man's chin and throat, though only half the pellets broke on impact at that distance. But it was enough. The guard clawed for his trigger, but his leather gloves were a hindrance. He fell backwards, asleep before he hit the grass.

The Doberman, though, was not distracted. As soon as its master's grip loosened, the four-legged killer flashed forward with bared teeth.

Rising on one elbow to get a better sight on the smaller,

lower target, Corban pulled the trigger. The dog flinched and snapped at the pellets biting its face and muzzle. At twenty-five yards, at a dead run, the dog's legs folded, and its pointed body torpedoed into the lawn. It skidded to a stop, steam rising from its overheated body.

As Corban watched and waited, it seemed that no one else had noticed—for now. He rose to his feet, approached the Doberman, and tugged on its collar to pull the dog's nose out of the dirt. There was no point for him to kill the beast; it didn't know any better.

Since no one came to the aid of the fallen guard, Corban guessed that his side of the house was clear. He jogged up the gradual hill to the nearest elm tree. It was about thirty yards across the lawn from the elms to the porch. That was far enough for him to star on Chip's funniest spy videos if Corban wasn't careful.

Every other tree had a small box camera mounted ten feet up. Each was focused on its own section of the house. Chip's security had covered all bases: the camera views overlapped so if one camera was taken out or damaged by a storm, the angle was still covered by the next camera. That meant a minimum of three cameras had to be disabled for Corban to approach the house without straying into the sight line of other active cameras, though it was an invisible line.

Recalling the layout of the house, Corban knew he'd have to act fast. Someone would be in the control room, just to the right of the coatroom, watching the monitors. Even a lazy, inattentive security guard would notice a snowy screen.

He located the four closest cameras that had the back porch in view. Standing under the first one, he fired at it for a half-second. The result at that range was a half-dozen, pea-sized hailstones pelting the lens. At the very least, the lens would crack and the image would be distorted.

Running to the next tree, Corban fired a burst, and then did the same at the next two before sprinting toward the porch. Through a window, he saw someone moving toward the door. Aiming at the side entrance, he decided he couldn't shoot through the screen effectively. The man needed to emerge.

A guard rounded the corner of the porch. His dog barked, but Corban kept running. He fired as he took three porch steps at a time. The pellets peppered the side of the house and raked across the man's chest. The effects of the vapor were immediate. Though he fell to the porch, asleep, the man's left hand still held fast to the leash. The German shepherd cowered below Corban, as if accepting its fate at the stranger's mercy. Corban fired five pellets at the floorboards in front of the dog.

Not waiting for the dog to drift off, Corban leaned flat against the house as the pitter-patter of feet echoed from within. Everyone on guard would've heard the barking.

But the man didn't rush through the screen door as Corban had hoped. This man was cautious. He stopped in front of the screen and peered outside for danger. Corban had no time to wait; he heard another foaming Doberman approaching from behind him.

Using the muzzle of the NL-2, Corban threw the screen door open and reached through the doorway. With his left fist, he punched the man square on the jaw, hard enough for the guard's senses to blur and his knees to weaken. The man held a drawn pistol, but Corban slapped it to the floor. Gripping the man by his Hawaiian shirtfront, he pulled him through the door. Then, taking a quick two-step, Corban hurled him down the stairs to the grass. As the man rolled away, Corban fired a dozen rounds at his chest and head.

Corban slipped through the screen door, then eased the great wooden door to a close and locked it. Though there were other entrances to the house, he didn't bother with them; there was no time. He heard yelling and radio chatter nearby. Outside, radios crackled orders and dogs barked as they looked for him. Corban ran across a Persian rug which was far too nice to be walked on, but Chip was careless with his spy fortune, most of which had been smuggled into the country.

Passing an impressive display of New Guinean artifacts, Corban swung over the banister and crept up the carpeted staircase, his back to the wall. He knew a butler and maid slept in the house, and both were trained in defensive and offensive arts. But where were they?

As he reached the top of the stairs, he heard muffled pounding as men rammed their shoulders against the locked door outside, but the lock was holding.

A door opened on the second floor. It was the maid. At the sight of Corban, she quickly snaked a revolver from an inner-thigh strap. But Corban knew he still had rounds left in his NL-2, so he used them before she used hers. As she slumped into a corner for a twenty-minute nap, Corban continued to back down the hall.

When he reached Chip's bedroom, Corban eased the door open and slipped inside, relieved to find Chip snoring and undisturbed. He closed the door, tiptoed to the overcrowded walk-in closet at the far side of the room, and found a place to hide amongst the hanging shirts.

A heavy fist pounded on Chip's bedroom door.

"Mr. Buchanen! Sir!"

Chip flopped over and sat up. He switched on a lamp as the pounding continued.

"Come in! What is it?"

A guard entered and swept the room with his weapon. His canine companion pranced and barked, unfamiliar with the interior of the house.

"We've lost three men and two dogs, sir!" the man said. "Natalie was taken out at the end of the corridor!"

"Find them!" Chip tugged on his trousers. "Go! They must be in the house! And lock my door! "

"Yes sir!"

The guard turned the lock, then slammed the door behind him. Footsteps pounded down the hall as the men checked all the other rooms.

Chip fumbled for his service pistol. Corban raised his NL-2 through the hanging wardrobe and fired a burst into the wall above Chip's head. Hearing the pellets slap the drywall, Chip spun around, his eyes darting across the room. He aimed his pistol at the closet, squinting to see who was inside.

"Easy does it, sharpshooter," Corban said in German.

"Corban? Oh, it's you." Though a fit sixty-two-year-old, Chip clutched his chest and sat on the edge of the bed.

"What're you doing, giving my security some exercise? Look, I know you don't kill people, but you better not have hurt the dogs, either. They cost more than the grunts!"

"Lose the pistol, Chip."

He tossed the gun to the floor. Only then did Corban emerge from the closet and kick Chip's gun under the bed.

"After everything I've done for you, you still don't trust me?"

"I don't even trust myself, Chip." Corban sat on a low bureau that faced Chip and the door. "Someone took Jenna and Janice tonight. Guess who that someone was."

Swearing, Chip ran his fingers through his white hair. Corban kept his pellet pistol aimed at him. He knew some of the tricks the old spy could have up his sleeve.

"Corban, I'm sorry. Jenna, too? I didn't know. Fairchild?"

"My gut told me I shouldn't have allowed you to involve him on COIL matters. The man was unbalanced from the start—more than you told me!"

"It was just a harmless liaison job, Corban. Besides, he was supposed to be answering to me, but he got ambitious. He's had it out for you. You know I had to find out who he was working for."

"Yeah, I remember that part of the arrangement, Chip. What happened? He's off the grid! I can't even find him!"

"He went over my head. Kissed up to the director. I thought I could handle him. And I thought you could handle him!"

"Well, it's time to shut him down, Chip. Cut off his resources."

"Is that why you snuck in here like this? To force my hand?"

"I'm not above twisting your arm. COIL's network is in chaos right now. I wasn't sure where your loyalties lay. You let him bring COIL to a standstill, Chip. People are dying overseas. My own family is in jeopardy. You said if I agreed to let him nose around, maybe you could figure out who his principal was. Well?"

"No, I haven't learned a thing." Chip shook his head. "His methods are well hidden." He rubbed his eyes and yawned. "Okay, let's think. Janice and Jenna. How does taking them fit into his agenda? You're not even an active agent anymore, so what's his deal?"

"When are you going to realize that this isn't about an opposing foreign government agency?"

"His obsessions are unnatural, Corban. He's working for someone, I'm telling you! He has an agenda. And his Polish is too flawless."

"I know. I know his agenda."

"You do?"

"Yeah, I found his origins, even his parents."

"Where are they?"

"Poland."

"See, I knew it!"

"But it's not what you think. They were American ambassadors there. Get dressed. We both need some coffee. Then I'll tell you all about Abaddon."

"Abaddon. What's that? An op?"

"More like a code name. It's who Branden Fairchild works for. No, scratch that. It's who he serves."

†

CHAPTER TWENTY-FIVE

"Nathan!" Helena Rauch exclaimed as she was thrust into the prison visiting booth. She wrapped her bony arms around Nathan. The top of her head reached only midway up his chest. "I missed you!"

He squeezed her back, but reminded himself why he was there.

"I missed you, too. Your hair . . . Did they let you wash it? It must feel so much better!"

Helena blushed.

"Yes, they let me shower. My hair is growing out, too. Do you like it? I mean, since it's clean, finally?"

She stepped away and twirled around for him. They'd even given her a clean uniform gown.

"You look brand new," he said, but he wondered what the prison administrators were up to. For what were they getting her ready? It was a good thing his team was getting her out of the prison that night. No, it was past time.

Helena pulled her chair close to his, facing him. Taking his hand in hers, she smiled and looked up at him. Something stirred inside him against his will. Her eyes looked clearer than they had before. And her teeth had been brushed; they were whiter than his. That was puzzling.

At most of their visits, he'd held her as she cried, and he'd felt so helpless. But now he didn't know what to think of this new side of Helena, this unusually joyful Helena. He attributed it to her newfound cleanliness and the fact that he was visiting.

"Do you think . . . if I ever get out of here . . . that you could ever see yourself with someone like me?"

"Oh, um . . ." Nathan broke his gaze. In the past, he had implied that they would do things together when she was out, but he'd only said that to encourage her to look toward the future. "You mean in a relationship?"

"Yeah." She smiled. "Would you . . . ever?"

He knew it wasn't possible, though his heart was drawn to her.

"Helena, I've just been trying to focus on getting you out."

"Do you think I'm pretty? I mean . . . now?"

"Yes, I think you're pretty, Helena."

"And you like pretty girls, right?" She giggled at his discomfort, tracing his hand with her finger.

What was happening? Nathan was at a loss as to how to respond to Helena. Why was she acting this way?

"Uh . . . sure."

He hadn't meant to lead her on; he'd only wanted to comfort her. But he had to admit he liked being needed. It hurt him to be unable to protect her. Should he be honest and tell her it couldn't work out between them? Maybe that would be too hard for her to hear right now. Nathan wished he could talk to Chloe to get her input, but that was out of the question. And now he wished he hadn't come today. They could've just come in and rescued her. But Chloe had wanted him to find out any last minute details that might be helpful for their mission that night.

Helena looked into Nathan's eyes and reached up to touch his face. Suddenly, her nails dug into the flesh of his left arm, and she clawed him from bicep to wrist. He jumped up and backed away, knocking his chair over in the process. She leaped clear of him and cringed against the wall. Nathan panted and stared at her in disbelief. His arm was on fire. A trickle of blood was beginning to surface from the superficial wound.

"Are you . . . going to hit me?" Helena whimpered.

"I'd never hit you, Helena. I just don't understand what's happening here. I . . . can't do this. This isn't right."

"I thought you liked me, Nathan." She began to cry. "I feel so stupid. I'm such a fool . . ."

"No, Helena, I do like you. I like you the way Christ has told us to care for His own." He considered going over to her, but hesitated. She needed help. She needed to talk to someone—a mature Christian woman, not him. Helena was looking for the wrong kind of love and needed something more than what the guards were giving her, but it couldn't come from him. "Please don't cry."

"Could you hold me, Nathan?" She started toward him. "I'm sorry. Just hold me."

Nathan wrapped his arms around her, and she wept against his chest. His heart ached for her, but it made him even more certain that they needed to rescue her that night.

When the guards came to take Helena away, she cried

and clung to Nathan. It broke his heart.

"I promise you, I'll be back as soon as I can, Helena." Nathan felt so helpless as he watched the guards take her away.

...✝...

"Please tell me you found something out from her," Chloe said as Nathan entered her hotel room. They had agreed to meet for an informal debriefing after his final visit with Helena.

"I couldn't get much of anything out of her today." He sat on the edge of the bed, in the only spot not covered with papers. "I've got to tell you, her emotions were a little . . . uh . . . raw and overbearing."

Chloe looked up from her laptop.

"Raw and overbearing? How do you mean? She's a woman in a terrible situation."

"Look, Chloe, I don't know women. I'm just admitting that I was uncomfortable today. She got a little close."

"Not to sound insensitive, but playing a boyfriend role isn't so horrible, is it? Helena just needs the attention. But it's all over now, anyway. We're on for tonight even if you didn't find out anything else. The weather looks good—clear skies, not much wind. Nothing tropical expected in the vicinity."

"Chloe, listen." Chloe met his gaze. "I need you to be serious with me for a minute, all right?"

"Fine, Nathan. What's going on?"

"I'm just a guy. I've spent too many years in jungles and deserts. I admit I don't have much experience with women. But I'm telling you, Helena wasn't herself today. This was a side of her that . . . Look, I'm a Christian, so the Spirit of God is in me. I've been going over the visit in my head and praying about it, but I'm sensing that there's something extremely wrong here. There's something wrong with her, something deeper than what we know."

"Well, Nathan, you know how she's been treated. That would create some emotional baggage after a while, don't you think?"

"Of course, but there's something off here, something dark. I've been around rape victims before, rescued them from the worst conditions imaginable. No, she seems more intact than I thought. This is something else, something that she . . ."

"What? I'm not really agreeing with you, but go ahead, Nathan. Say what's on your mind."

"Today, I felt like she was a fake. She's not for real."

"Nathan, that girl is anything but a fake! How could you say such a thing? I've spent hours with her and never saw anything."

He shrugged and shook his head. Then he pulled up his jacket sleeve.

"And there's this."

Chloe picked up a lamp and held it close to his arm. Four fresh nail scratches traced from his upper bicep to the wrist. One gouge was deeper than the others, having removed all of the flesh.

"That one looks pretty nasty. I'd worry about infection."

"Yeah, I know. I've cleaned it with alcohol. Sure smarted."

"So why did this happen? Were you getting too close?"

"No, Chloe. She wanted reassurance that we could have a relationship one day. I had to tell her that I cared for her as a Christian brother. Look, you think I'd be saying anything at all to you about this unless I was really concerned?"

"So she took a chunk out of you. I don't understand what you're worried about. Add it to your list of scars and move on."

"Chloe, I don't care about scars! Helena was seducing me!"

"What?" She guffawed, then caught herself. "Sorry. Didn't mean to laugh. Why would she seduce you?"

"I don't know. But she'd been extensively cleaned, combed, and brushed—the works."

Chloe sat down again.

"Okay. Why?"

"She wouldn't say, but I think she knew. My first thought was that she was to be the center of entertainment."

"That's what you first thought. Then what?"

"Then I was thinking it was all for me, and that there was something deeper here, and I felt used."

Chloe bit her lip to keep from smiling.

"Listen to yourself. First you come unglued on the water tower. Now this? I don't understand. You're hesitating about tonight because you've got a few scratches on your arm? What about her? We leave her here?"

"All right. It's all in my mind." Nathan took a deep breath and nodded. "This is almost over. Maybe I'm overreacting. She was strange today, but I'll get over it."

"Yeah. Okay. Work it out. And you might want to put some antibiotic on that one scratch."

He started for the door, then turned back.

"And Chloe, no one else—"

"Needs to know. Don't worry. It won't make the report. Go get the boys. Head count here at 1800 hours."

...†...

Janice Dowler blinked at the darkness several times before she realized a hood had been pulled over her head. The throbbing pain from the bullet wound in her side tugged her senses back from her drugged state. She moved her arms. No longer bound, she ripped off the hood.

Jenna lay next to her without a hood. Janice put her ear to her daughter's mouth and found her to be breathing normally. They'd both been drugged when taken from Francis' safe house. It was all coming back to her now, and it was almost too much to bear. She remembered their protector, Francis, lying on his back on the floor, bleeding to death.

Only after she was sure Jenna was okay did Janice acknowledge her surroundings. They'd been left in a tiny, windowless bedroom with metal walls. The only light in the bare room came from a flame that flickered from beneath a curtained doorway.

Touching her side, Janice could tell she was no longer bleeding. The bullet had only grazed her, but it still burned like fire just below her ribs. Tucking her T-shirt snugly into her waistband, she hoped to keep enough pressure on the wound so it wouldn't reopen as she moved about.

The sound of chanting was coming from somewhere

outside the metal walls. She didn't know the language, but Janice had visited enough indigenous tribes overseas to recognize the sound as a pagan mantra. The chanting gave her chills, and she mouthed a silent prayer for physical as well as spiritual protection.

Janice crept toward the curtained doorway, pushed past the curtain, and stepped into the next room.

"Going somewhere, woman?"

She tensed and saw Branden Fairchild sitting like a stone in the midst of a pentagon of candles. Naked to the waist, his eyes were closed. But he wasn't the source of the chanting. Eyeing a flimsy, wooden door that led outside, Janice realized they were just in a cheap shack.

"Where are we?"

"Does that matter? You're mine now. You will serve me."

Shuddering, she looked at the outside door again. Branden wouldn't be able to catch her before she reached the door, but she couldn't leave Jenna behind.

"Who's out there? What's that chanting?"

"They pray to the master."

"What master is that?"

Branden's eyes flashed open. They were blood-shot and demonic. He took a deep breath, then closed his lids again.

"You'll learn who your master is, woman. Return to your room. Unless I permit it, you're not to leave."

"Corban will deal with you. You know my husband; you can't win," Janice proclaimed.

"I've already beaten Corban Dowler, because I have you!"

Janice wanted to argue, but decided against it. She needed time to contemplate an escape or to access a phone. And knowing Corban, he would be canvassing the East Coast for her. Hopefully they were at least still in North America!

Backing through the door and into the darkness of her room, she could still hear the chanting nearby. Both men's and women's voices mingled in a monotonous, whining hum that forced her to cover her ears with her hands for a moment.

"Mom?"

"Sweetie!"

Thankful that her thoughts were interrupted, Janice knelt next to Jenna, touching her forehead.

"Where are we? What's that noise?"

"Whisper, sweetie, okay? I don't know where we are. The bad men have taken us somewhere. The noise you hear is chanting. They're praying to Satan. We need to pray to God for them, okay?"

"Is Dad coming?"

"He's looking for us. I'm sure he'll find us. We need to be brave. No matter what happens, trust in Jesus, okay? I love you so much."

"It's okay, Mom," Jenna assured. "Dad really will find us."

Jenna grasped her mother's hand and guided her fingers to the hidden bracelet around her ankle. Janice felt the locator device under Jenna's pant leg. Her heart skipped a beat.

There was hope after all.

PART V

*"And have no fellowship with the
unfruitful works of darkness, but rather
expose them."* Ephesians 5:11

✝

Corban studied the transponder screen from the backseat of the SUV. Another SUV with tinted windows followed on their bumper. Both were full of task force agents from Philadelphia, who had gathered in the City of Brotherly Love under Deputy Director Buchanen's command. The task force was CIA, except Corban, who was a civilian "observer." Though Corban had been out of the Agency for only two years, he knew none of these agents. He'd never crossed them in the field because he'd often been overseas in deep cover. The few who'd heard of him had passed the word as they were staging that the civilian observer was an ex-spook and no one to mess with.

From Philly, the SUVs crossed the river and drove east into southern New Jersey. Unlike the northern part of the state, this area was covered with farmland and forest.

"Take a left up here," Corban instructed the driver, his eyes focused on his screen.

With the help of Detective Marsh and his good equipment, they'd been able to figure out the full number for Jenna's tracking device through a process of elimination. Corban was thankful and confident that the device was leading him to his family. To rescue them safely was his primary goal, but almost as much, he wanted to catch the men who had abducted them.

It was night, and the men and women around him loaded and chambered live ammunition in the darkness of the SUV. They wore Kevlar vests, blue jeans, and hats that read FEDS, but they wore them backwards so they could also wear their night vision goggles. Corban sensed that each one hungered for action. He hoped his speech back at the staging garage was not ignored: they were to take Branden Fairchild and Velt Plavenko alive.

Though Corban had an NL-2 machine pistol, he doubted they'd give him a chance to use it. The feds knew who their targets were, and they had orders from Chip that superseded any authority Corban could muster here. This was their job. When they found the kidnappers, they would give him his wife and daughter, but the feds would have their way with the two creeps, as Chip put it. Corban was fortunate to be riding along at all.

His cell phone rang.

"Yeah."

"It's me. Chloe."

"What's up, Chloe? You've got two minutes."

"You get 'em back yet?"

"Almost there."

"We're going into Fhatl Lasam Prison tonight."

"Be safe. I'm praying for all of you."

"Off the record, Nathan's been having some reservations."

"What kind of reservations? I didn't see that in your latest report."

"He's nervous. Just letting you know. He's sensing some kind of manipulation by Helena."

"Nathan isn't one to speculate like that. Are his nerves compromising the op? Or is this legit?"

"No, sir. It's nothing. I'll let you go. COIL's headquarters are back to normal, right? You're witnessing Fairchild's permanent fall?"

"That's affirmative. The CIA has labeled him for what he is. By the way, I don't expect you back in New York until after a brief vacation. I gave Zvi the same order."

She laughed.

"Roger that. Out."

A man with biceps as thick as Corban's leg knocked the slide back on his M-14 assault rifle. He looked down at Corban.

"So what do you do, now that you left us?"

"I help out with an international assistance program. What do you do?"

"You're lookin' at it, dude. Maybe you haven't been where I've been, 'cause I could never leave. Once I started killin' the bad guys, I couldn't quit."

"Yeah, I never thought I'd quit either, but God got ahold of me. Nothin' else worked. He can get ahold of anyone, even you."

"Whatever, dude." Bicep Boy rolled his eyes. "It's your life."

"Look alive!" the front passenger yelled, then spoke into his headset. "Rover Two, this is Team Leader. Do you copy? The compound is on the right. Yes, ram the fence. The satellite shows twenty to thirty persons on the premises, judging from the thermal imaging. We'll set up a perimeter; you go straight in. Over."

The team leader eyed the SUV occupants. He had a scar through one eyebrow that told Corban the man had seen action.

"We scatter left and right. Rover Two will make first contact. Try to weed out the crazies from the perps we're after. The data sheet might say this cult is unarmed, but don't trust 'em."

"I'm with Rover Two," Corban said. "I'll be making contact with them. That's where the buildings are."

"It's your call, Dowler. The deputy director said to let you do what you want."

The SUVs crashed through a tall, barbwire fence, then rolled to a stop at the end of a dirt road. In the distant darkness, against a stand of trees, dozens of figures danced around a single bonfire. The agents piled out of Rover One, Corban being the last. The Rover One team split up and disappeared across the field to surround the compound.

Rover Two team wasted no time approaching the cultists around the fire. The teams knew their roles; this wasn't their first cult infiltration under cover of darkness. Rover One, with the heavier artillery, surrounded a number of squat buildings as stealthy agents moved to the edge of the throng.

Now that he was close enough to hear and see the dancing figures, Corban noticed the cult members were entranced, perhaps even drugged. They danced dangerously close to the flames, and their black, short-sleeved robes made them indistinguishable from one another. Worse yet, their faces were painted an eerie white.

Corban touched the NL-2 tucked into the back of his belt, then knelt to study the cultic ritual. Beside him, agents paused at the edge of the firelight to communicate on their headsets with the team leader. The worshippers didn't realize they were surrounded by government enforcers, and even if they did, they seemed too drugged to respond.

The team leader tapped Corban's shoulder and crouched next to him. He leveled a shotgun at the cultists.

"We've sealed off any escape. Now that we're up close, how would you proceed without a massacre? We can't tell who's who here. You've seen at least one of the guys in person, right?"

"If you fire a gun right now, these folks will probably go mad, stampede, maybe even attack us in a craze, with teeth and nails."

"That's why I'm talkin' to you."

"We're only after Fairchild and Plavanko. Hold the perimeter. Search the shacks first. Let these people exhaust themselves till we're ready to deal with them. There's no identifying anyone with that face paint."

The team leader relayed Corban's orders to his team. The agents swept across the compound to search the buildings.

"So we just wait 'em out?"

"It's called patient containment, young man," Corban said as he rose to his feet. "So, contain."

Corban turned his back to the firelight as he approached

more than a dozen metal shacks erected without foundations. Agents widened their containment perimeter as others paired off to search for the kidnapped victims.

Alone, Corban drew his NL-2 and stepped up to a shack the agents had yet to search. Since he had no night vision goggles like the others, he had to utilize the flicker of bonfire light to see the shadowy shapes around him.

Turning the door handle quietly, he pushed the door inward. He moved aside, half-expecting gunfire to erupt from within. His girls had been abducted violently, and Luigi had been shot, so he was sure Branden and Velt wouldn't surrender peacefully.

The shack consisted of two rooms. Corban ducked into the first to find a storage room full of black short-sleeved robes like the worshippers wore. He cleared the second room—a tiny bedroom—then returned to the first. Throwing a robe over his shoulders, he hoped the agents didn't shoot him in his disguise.

Leaving the shack, Corban studied the dancing cultists again. His wife could be there, drugged, or forced to join them. Jenna wasn't among them; the dancers were all adults. But Jenna was definitely near. The GPS signal from the number Jenna left him had led them here.

When Corban reached the team leader, the agent aimed his shotgun at Corban for an instant before he realized who he was.

"I almost shot you!"

Corban didn't slow his pace.

"Keep your men searching for my family. I want a closer look at these characters."

Hiding his pistol under a fold of his black robe, Corban entered the fray of twisting, twirling worshippers. Almost ghostlike, they floated past him as they chanted. Wandering amongst them, he bumped shoulders and studied their painted faces. He knew Branden's features well enough to see through any face paint, but he worried about picking out Velt, whom he'd seen only in photos.

A clumsy, bulky man bumped into Corban from the side. Corban reached out and steadied the man by his arm. The man's forearm was covered with scars, and his eyes were glazed over. Just as suddenly, the man moved on, twirling, bowing intermittently toward the crackling flames inside the circle. But Corban didn't lose sight of the man; he tracked him around the circle. The man was almost a head taller than the others.

Corban had seen the aftereffects of men and women who had attempted suicide by cutting. But this man's arms . . . This was something different.

Thinking back to his daughter's description of the man who'd approached her at the daycare, Corban remembered what Jenna had said: "He had lines on his arms."

"Velt Plavenko," Corban mumbled and raised his pistol.

Simultaneously, as if he'd heard Corban say his name through all the commotion, Velt seemed to come to his senses and stared across the fire at Corban. Corban expected to see surprise register on the man's face, but it remained expressionless, though he definitely recognized Corban because he didn't look away.

After several seconds, Velt looked over the heads of his

worshippers, then back at Corban. He'd obviously seen the agents at the edge of the firelight and realized there was no escape. Velt smiled as he walked toward the fire, as if to say he'd rather die by the fire than be taken captive.

Corban fired a burst of pellets through the flames. The pellets slapped Velt's chest and caused the cultist to pause. He touched his chest, uncertain of what had hit him. Five seconds passed before he stumbled sideways. Reaching for the fire, he seemed to strain for it desperately, but he collapsed instead. The twirling worshippers trampled him as they continued to dance in oblivion.

Hiding his pistol, Corban browsed the faces around him for Branden, but he wasn't there.

Two agents pushed through the worshippers and dragged a sleeping Velt away from the circle. Stepping clear of the cultists, Corban couldn't mask the anger on his face as he strode up to the team leader.

"Fairchild's not here." Corban grumbled.

"Maybe not, but look!"

Corban followed the agent's gaze toward the shacks. Relief flooded his heart. Two armed agents escorted his wife and daughter toward him. One carried Jenna in his arms, and Janice was holding her side.

"When he comes around," Corban said as he pointed at Velt, "find out where Fairchild went."

"You got it, Mr. Dowler," the team leader said. As Corban stepped toward his family, he heard the leader turn to another agent. "How'd he identify Plavenko in all that?"

"Dad!"

"Corban!"

He embraced his wife and daughter, one in each arm. Janice wept against his shoulder as Jenna strangled his neck.

"Dad, I was so scared!" Jenna cried.

"C'mon. Piggyback ride," Corban said as he boosted the girl onto his back.

She pulled up her pant leg to expose her ankle bracelet.

"Did you get my message, Dad?"

"I did. You taught me my numbers, remember?"

"What about Francis?" Janice asked, her eyes tearful with relief and dread. "Did he—?"

Corban squeezed Janice's hand as they walked to the SUV.

"They don't think he's going to make it. Are you okay?"

"I'm okay." She pulled her hand aside to show him her bloody side. "It's just a scratch. I was more worried about the demonic side of things, you know?"

"Sadly, I do know."

"Dad, I want to change houses."

"Me, too, kiddo. Me, too."

Corban helped his family into the backseat of the SUV.

"Is this over?" Janice asked quietly as Jenna snuggled on his lap.

"I'm afraid not. Branden Fairchild got away."

"He was here earlier today. I spoke with him."

"We have to find him before he finds us again."

"Do you know how?"

"I think so. Somebody named Victor will help." He kissed each of his girls. "I can't go with you now, but I'll be with you as soon as I can. These men will keep you safe."

Corban slipped through the crowd of chattering agents. The team leader caught at Corban's elbow.

"Where are you going? We can drive you back to Philly."

"You go. I have to find Fairchild." Corban shook the man's hand. "Thanks for your help."

Then Corban jogged down the road alone, darkness closing in around him.

...✝...

"Hello. I'm here to see a patient, Francis Malvao."

"Are you friend or family?"

"I'm a friend. My name is Corban Dowler. Francis was protecting my family when he was shot. Please tell me—did he make it through the night?"

"It's . . . well . . . very odd, Mr. Dowler. Your friend . . . he disappeared on us."

"Pardon me? He had five gunshot wounds to the chest!"

"Believe me, sir, I know how bad his wounds were. I'm his nurse. And if you find him, I'd like to know how he left as well!"

†

CHAPTER TWENTY-SEVEN

"Lookin' good, Toad. You're almost there. Everything's cool. You're just one of the fellas pullin' night shift. Nice and easy."

Smoothing down his guard uniform, Toad listened to the voice in his earpiece.

Memphis—their eye in the sky—was also the voice in his ear, because with his high-powered scope he could see everyone and everything from the water tower two miles away.

Toad swung his lunch pail casually as he neared other guards approaching the Fhatl Lasam Prison gatehouse. He tried to fit in, but like the others on his team, he preferred the straightforward methods of combat and ambushes instead of the covert technique of secret infiltration. But he knew both strategies were needed at times. And how was he supposed to keep a straight face when he could hardly breathe in his stolen uniform? His chest was much thicker and his hips were wider. And he was supposed to stay calm? Yeah, right!

If a guard were to look into his lunch pail, he wouldn't see his lunch. Instead, he'd see two spools of fishing line and an air pistol. The air pistol was COIL's first generation of non-lethal weaponry, the smallest of them all, the NL-1. It was the size of a Beretta 9-millimeter, with a high-compression CO_2 canister. The pistol was semi-automatic, with a maximum effective range of fifteen yards, and had thirty-pellet rounds crammed into the pistol grip.

No one seemed to pay Toad any mind as he slowed his pace to fall in behind a party of four arriving for the night shift.

"Toad is at the gatehouse. Over."

With a casual yawn, Toad pushed through the turnstile. Three guards manned the gatehouse. It wouldn't weather a good storm, but the flimsy building seemed a definite obstacle in reaching Tower Two.

The three in the booth stopped talking to watch the new guard follow the others into the courtyard. Toad kept his head down as he walked out of sight around the corner of the first building.

"Okay, hold up, Toad. You've got a straggler on your left. Over."

Setting his lunch pail on the ground, Toad fiddled with his bootlace. To his left, a guard walked across the courtyard from the three isolation cells on the southern fence line to the group of buildings to the north and west. From the corner of his eye, Toad mentally acknowledged the isolation cells. Helena was in the most eastward one, the one on the end. Memphis had been up on the tower since before dusk and hadn't seen anyone retrieve her for any sort of entertainment.

"You're good, Toad. Beeline to Tower One. Go. Over."

Picking up his pail, Toad changed direction and headed

straight across the yard to the southwest tower. The last shift was gone, and this shift was still getting situated. He tucked his chin down, knowing that both towers could see him clearly now. If they leaned out of their Plexiglas crow's nests, he knew what to say. Fuzzi, Chloe's taxi driver, had given him one general phrase to memorize.

Movement on his right. Toad stiffened as a man exited a building and stood in front of the door.

"It's all right, Toad. He's just lightin' a cig. You're almost to the tower. Over."

He reached out and gripped the handle to the tower's access door. Locked? It wasn't supposed to be locked! Turning it harder, it clicked. Oh, not locked, just rusty. With relief, he opened the door just wide enough to duck inside and pulled it closed behind him.

"Toad is inside Tower One and out of my visual. Over."

Above him, Toad saw a rickety spiral staircase that wound forty feet up to a grated floor where two soldiers were gabbing. He held his breath, but saw no indication that they'd heard him enter far below them.

The team didn't expect him to report his status to them quite yet. They knew he'd need to maintain radio silence for several minutes.

Toad tested his footing on the step to see how much noise it made. It seemed more solid than he originally thought. He tiptoed up, pausing halfway to remove the NL-1 from his lunch pail and tuck it into his waistband.

He'd climbed only ten more steps when the guards above noticed him through the grated floor. Toad knew they were addressing him, but he kept his head down and stomped on the stairs to make noise, as if he couldn't hear them. Just a little closer . . .

One guard demanded something so sternly that Toad finally stopped and grinned up at them. Though he was only six steps from the grate, he'd never get through the floor hatch that opened upward if they didn't want him to. All they had to do was stand on the hatch. But he didn't have to get through the grate; he only had to shoot through it.

"Oh, just another day," Toad said in Malay, the only phrase he knew.

Again, he started up the stairs as the guards shook their heads at one another in confusion. Just as Toad reached for the hatch, one of them put his foot on it. The other guard barked orders and pointed across the yard. Toad could guess what he might be saying: *Your orders are wrong; you're not supposed to be here; you idiot, you're probably not even night shift!*

Taking three steps back, Toad drew his pistol. As fast as he could work the trigger, he pumped three pellets at the nearest man, then the next. Three wasn't nearly enough, since the grate screened out over half the pellets. He aimed at the first again and peppered him on the forehead and cheek as he bent to retrieve the rifle that leaned in the corner. While the second guard fumbled with the safety on his rifle, Toad was able to add a couple more pellets to his chest.

The first guard sagged to the floor an instant before the second one. Toad wiped his sweating brow. He had to do this again at the second tower?

"Tower One, secure," he reported. "Let's do this. Over."

One of the men had fallen on top of the hatch and it took an extra minute to shove the hatch open and climb through it. Using flex-cuffs, Toad tied the wrists and ankles of the unconscious guards and gagged them with pieces of rags.

"Toad! Where are you?"

It was Nathan speaking through Toad's earpiece. Glancing around inside the tower, Toad spotted an ashtray. Perfect. He tied the end of one spool of fishing line to the ashtray and peered down the outside southwest wall. Scooter and Nathan crouched there in black fatigues, just outside the fences, small packs on their backs.

Toad hurled the ashtray over both fences where it bounced on the ground next to Scooter. Scooter tied a cable onto the fishing line, then waved at Toad. Reeling the line in, Toad pulled the cable up to the tower. It was a steep angle, nearly seventy-five degrees. Cutting the line, Toad then fastened the cable to the grated floor.

"Cable secure. Over."

Below, Scooter used a rubber mallet to pound two long stakes into the ground to secure his end of the cable. Then Nathan tested it with a tug. Nobody wanted to fall against the razor wire, or worse yet, between the two fences.

Nathan went up first, his arms doing all the work, his legs limp over the cable to steady his weight. It took him over a minute to scale the forty feet. Toad dragged him in through the gunner's window and motioned for Scooter to climb up. Shouldering his NL-3, Nathan took stock of their new station.

"Eagle Eyes is in position in Tower One. Over."

"Roger that, Eagle Eyes," Memphis replied.

A moment later, Scooter spilled into the tower.

"Scooter in position. Over."

"Roger that, Tower One. Chloe, come in. Over."

"Chloe standing by . . ."

"Cue fog and go to your next station. Over."

"Cuing fog. Moving on. Over."

Chloe was to hustle to her position in the east, a few blocks from the prison, where a miniature fireworks display was hidden against a chicken coup.

"Tower One, this is Memphis. You have company. Do you copy?"

Nathan pushed Toad to the window to check the prison yard. A guard walked across the courtyard.

"He's approaching the isolation cells," Toad reported. "He might be getting Helena!"

They waited breathlessly. If the guard were fetching Helena to take her inside one of the buildings, she'd be tough to find without turning the compound into a war zone. But the guard only peeked into each cell and returned across the yard.

"We're clear," Toad said. "He's gone. He didn't take Helena. She's still there."

Scooter moved to the window.

"I see fog. Look. It's working."

White mist wafted through the holes of several sewer covers. It was a vaporous wisp at first, then became thicker, but not enough to look like smoke.

"Tower One, Memphis here. No one else in sight. Toad

should be on his way to Tower Two. Over."

Toad was nearly ready. He stuffed the fishing line into his lunch pail and reloaded his air pistol. He counted his rounds; he'd used twenty-four out of thirty on only two guards. Now he had to take out twice that many men in the next tower and the gatehouse—with only one clip. Without a farewell, he threw open the hatch and clamored down the stairs.

"Bruno and Milk, this is Memphis. Come in. Over."

"Bruno and Milk here. Over."

"Toad is moving toward you. Stand by. Over."

"Standing by. Over."

As Toad exited the tower, Nathan and Scooter covered him from above and behind, though the NL-3 was only good for one hundred yards. Beyond that, he was on his own.

In front and above him, he could see the glowing butts of two cigarettes in Tower Two. The light was fading quickly, but he could make out the rifles slung over their shoulders. He wouldn't be able to catch these too unawares; they were already in the rhythm of their shift. They could look straight down and see the gatehouse where Toad was to take out two or three guards. But, thankfully, they couldn't see the front or the inside of the booth, as the team had hoped would be the case.

"Chloe, come in. This is Toad," he whispered into his mic.

"This is Chloe. What's up? Over."

"No need for the fireworks. I repeat, no need for a distraction. The front of the booth is hidden from the tower after all. Please confirm. Over."

Chloe groaned. Everyone knew she hoped to do something more than just turn on the fog machine.

"Understood. No Fourth of July for me. Over."

"You sure about that, Toad?" Nathan asked. "It's dark enough for fireworks. Over."

"I'm sure. Out."

Before Toad arrived at the gatehouse, he eyed where he would step near the fence. The brightest lights would be behind him when he faced the booth occupants. They'd be partially blinded by the bright halogens.

He heard the guards talking before he could see them. Taking a deep breath, he tried not to think about the op resting entirely on his shoulders. In Morocco, five months earlier, an op had rested on Bruno's shoulders, since he was the only black man on the team. Now it was the Asian Toad's turn. And ever since Toad had been handed the three phases of this op, he knew phases two and three would be do-or-die.

Moving wide around the corner of the gatehouse, he headed for his spot. Two men stood in front of the gatehouse. A few more steps and Toad would be in place. The men noticed him and stopped talking. Toad glanced up at the tower. He was barely out of their vision. Looking back at the gatehouse, now in full view, he saw two more men sitting on stools inside the shack. Four men, thirty rounds.

Toad had practiced speed-loading the NL-1. He was fast, but not fast enough to reload while the others charged across six yards with live ammo. But he never considered turning back. The two in the gatehouse would have to go first, since they were nearest the radio. Toad set his lunch pail on the ground. Straightening up, he drew his pistol and steadied it with two hands. For a split second, the men didn't realize what he was doing. Maybe it was the lights; maybe it was sheer surprise.

Before anyone flinched, Toad put two rounds into the neck of one of the guards inside the booth. He staggered backwards. The man next to him reacted in slow motion. He gaped at his friend, his eyes searching the body for signs of blood. Then he received three pellets of his own on the right cheek.

The guards outside the gatehouse ducked and scrambled backwards into the chain-link fence. They raised their hands defensively, and one screamed as Toad fired at them in turn.

The tower called out. Toad reloaded his pistol. He'd spent fourteen rounds on the four, but all four were down; he'd done it. But he realized that the hardest part was probably yet to come.

Toad heard the tower call again.

"Oh, just another day!" he yelled back.

He waited. No one from the tower inquired further.

"Gatehouse secure," he reported, cupping his hand over his mouth.

Though Toad wasn't a covert spy, he was trying to think as one. He knew only one master spy—Corban—and he knew the stories of how Corban could get into any place.

It was a long way up to the top of Tower Two. They would never let a stranger into their nest. He didn't even speak their language. And it was too risky for anyone with any common sense to try to attack a tower that had two armed guards. How would Corban get into the tower?

Then, quite suddenly, it came to him—a clown act. He and Bruno were witty and constantly ribbing each other, all in good fun. It kept them sharp. Now his wit was in demand here. *Thank You, Lord.*

Toad moved from behind the gatehouse into the guards' line of vision. Taking a deep breath, he sang a little ditty he remembered from his marching band days.

"Da da-da da da . . ."

With pail in hand and pistol tucked securely at his waist, Toad danced toward the tower access door. One guard noticed him right away and laughed as he leaned out the tower window to see more. He called for his companion to check out the clown, too. But by that time, Toad was inside the tower and starting up the spiral stairs.

The guards stared down through the grate, hands on their hips and grins on their faces, as Toad danced up the stairs to his tune. When he came to the end of the song, he instantly started it over again. He took three steps up . . .

"Da-da-da . . ."

Then he took two Broadway steps down.

"Da-da di-da . . ."

When they tried to interrupt him, he silenced them with a wave of his hand to let him finish. That only made them laugh more. Swinging open the hatch, they clapped him on the back for his little performance as he finished with a few grand-finale notes.

They shook their heads and laughed as Toad backed

away from them to one side of the tower. He drew and shot them each three times in the upper chest before they lost their smiles.

"Tower Two secure. Give me two minutes, Bruno. Over."

"Roger. We're standing by."

Toad tied up the two guards. There was a sturdy ashtray in this tower, also. He attached a line to it and tossed it over the fences. Milk fastened the cable, and Toad dragged it up. Milk was lighter and faster, so he started up first.

"Tower Two, this is Tower One. I can barely see over the fog. Trouble at gatehouse. Over."

Going to the south window, Toad looked down.

"I don't see anything. What is it? Over."

"Either someone didn't inhale deep enough, or he's sleepwalking. Over."

Just then, one of the guards Toad had taken out in the booth staggered into view. His legs were wobbly, as if he were still somewhat intoxicated by the pellets' vapors. Toad aimed his pistol and fired five pellets, but they only bounced harmlessly off the man's back. The distance was too great for his pistol. The guard stopped and turned. He looked up and saw Toad leaning out the window. Realization registered on the Malaysian's face. His senses were returning fast.

"Milk!" Toad called. "I need you!"

"Almost there . . ."

Throwing a leg over the back windowsill, Milk climbed through. He took his NL-3 off his back as the guard below began to back away. The man's mouth gaped as Milk's white face loomed in the window above. Aiming his new generation rifle through the window, Milk put a single burst of five pellets at the guard's chest at thirty yards. The guard turned to run, fell to a crawl, then lay flat.

Fog drifted across the courtyard.

"Toad, get back to Tower One before more wake up," Memphis said. "Visibility is getting bad from here, Eagle Eyes. Don't delay as soon as Toad is there to cover you. Over."

"Roger."

Racing down the stairs, Toad emerged into a cloud of white. It thinned as a light breeze blew, but he couldn't see the other tower at all. He jogged past the guard Milk had silenced.

"Walk, Toad!" Bruno's voice echoed in his ear. "We know you're Flash, but now's not the time. Over."

"Roger."

But the fog was so thick now, he could've run and not been seen by anyone on the ground.

Entering Tower One's access door, Toad nearly collided with Nathan. Nathan handed him his NL-3 in exchange for Toad's NL-1.

"Let's get this over with, huh?" Nathan slapped his Chinese friend on the shoulder. He checked the NL-1's load. "This is your last clip?"

"Yep. Make it last."

"Should be enough. Get up there and cover me, huh?"

...✝...

Nathan waited until Toad was halfway up the tower before he stepped into the courtyard.

"Eagle Eyes is in the soup," he announced.

"Roger, Eagle," Memphis said. "I can't see a thing, so you're on your own. Over."

"Me, either. Scooter here. I'm closest, but I'm blind. Over."

Just as blind, Nathan was about to say as much, when he heard gravel crunch under boots to his left. The first isolation cell was ten yards to his right. The source of the noise moved in front of him. It was a guard with a flashlight.

"Eagle Eyes, this is Memphis. You should be there by now. Over."

Nathan aimed his pistol at the guard's head. The ex-Marine moved behind the man as the guard opened a sliding window on the first cell door and shined his light inside. Then Nathan moved beside him in the fog. The guard barked something crudely at the cell occupant, then moved to cell two, laughing and mumbling to himself.

"Eagle Eyes, do you copy? This is Memphis. Over."

"Maybe his radio malfunctioned," Scooter suggested over the radio. "It's quiet enough out here that we'll hear even the slightest scuffle if he gets into trouble. Over."

Fearful of rustling his fatigues, Nathan couldn't click his radio in response. He kept his muzzle on the guard's head, now only three yards away.

The man shined his light into cell two and taunted the prisoner inside. Nathan expected him to continue on to cell three to check on Helena. Instead, the guard turned and walked straight into Nathan's pistol. With the muzzle pressed against his head, the man gulped and froze. They were close enough now to see each other's facial features. There was no mistaking big Nathan with his handlebar mustache—he was an American cowboy.

"Speak English?" Nathan asked softly, aware of how sound traveled in fog. "Keys? You have keys?"

He understood Nathan's hand motion. Without looking down, the guard produced a ring of keys from his belt loop and set them in Nathan's outstretched hand. Only then did Nathan click his radio three times to give his team a positive response.

"Roger that, Eagle Eyes."

Nathan took half a pace back. The guard eyed the barrel of the gun. Lowering his aim, Nathan shot the man point-blank on the chin. The surprise shocked people more often than any pain they might experience. His head snapped back as if he'd been punched. He tripped backwards and caught his balance, his hand feeling his chin as he realized he hadn't received a fatal wound at all. But then he collapsed. Reaching out in time to catch the man before he fell hard, Nathan lowered him to the ground.

There were four keys on the ring. He fingered through them as he approached the third cell door. The second key he tried slipped into the lock. Hesitating, he cocked his ear. All was quiet, maybe too quiet. Nathan turned around and peered into the fog. Was someone there? It had all been too easy. Traps were easy like that. The cheese was always convenient for the mouse. Toad had done his part. The night had gone better than anyone expected.

And that's why he wasn't too shocked to find the third cell—Helena's cell—empty. That's why the guard hadn't checked it. She wasn't there. He closed the door and scurried to cell two's door.

"Helena!" he whispered loudly in German. "I'm here to get you!"

Then he did the same at cell one . . . and waited. Nothing. He faced the fog again. This was what Corban had been concerned about. They'd already taken Helena somewhere else. Nathan touched his arm where she'd scratched him, but he refused to bow to conspiracy theories. There had to be an explanation. It couldn't be a trap. Helena still needed to be rescued!

†

CHAPTER TWENTY-EIGHT

Nathan wiped perspiration off his brow, or maybe it was dampness from the mist that was completely enveloping the prison now. Before he lost his sense of direction in the fog, he put his back against the isolation building. Calling off the mission was out of the question. He was the leader. All he needed was a new plan.

"Chloe, this is Eagle Eyes. Over."

"This is Chloe. Go."

"Since Helena is not, I repeat, not in her cell, where is the first place I should look? Over."

No one cluttered the radio waves with exclamations or surprised comments. Nathan knew his team would all move with the conflict, adjust, and begin working to find solutions before the problem became overwhelming.

"Eagle Eyes, this is Chloe. Where are you? Over."

"In front of cell one. Over."

"Okay. The building next to Tower One, you know it? Over."

"A little. It's the tallest, with an entrance on the southwest side. Over."

"Right. Skip that entrance. Go to the next entrance west. Do you copy? Over."

"I copy. The second entrance from the right. Over."

"Affirmative."

"So you're talking about the middle building. That's the one I go in? Over."

Nathan headed into the fog.

"Roger. You've got it. Helena told me once that she was in there. There are some offices. It must be a command post of some sort. Over."

"Roger. Anyone see anything up there? Over."

"Negative." Memphis cleared his throat. "Looks like cloud cover."

"I'm still blind," Scooter reported.

Nathan stopped short. He'd come upon the building sooner than expected.

"This is Milk. If he's going in, I'm taking post against the building outside. Over."

Glancing to his right, Nathan saw the corner of the building he was talking about. Milk would be there in sixty seconds. He waited, then heard Milk's heavy breathing as he tromped into place. Milk nodded at Nathan. The Ohio native was wearing a green bandana.

"Milk is in position. South by southeast corner. Eagle Eyes is going in. Over."

With his weapon aimed at the door, Milk nodded assuredly at Nathan once more. Nathan returned the gesture and moved forward, gripping his pistol with both hands.

"This is Memphis. We have roughly four minutes before the guards at the gatehouse are wide-awake. Over."

Nathan tried to block the pressure of that knowledge

out of his mind. Bruno would take care of the gatehouse, if that became an issue. Helena. He had to find Helena. He had to rescue her. That was all that mattered now.

Cracking the door to the building, he peered into a dimly lit foyer. Checking both ways, he slipped inside and let the door click shut behind him. Nathan paused to listen.

"I hear laughter to the left. Eagle going left. Over."

"Roger, Eagle. Careful."

Focusing ahead, Nathan's eyes were leveled over his gun. The laughter had been from a woman. He refused to believe it was Helena or to think what it could mean.

He pushed through a half-open doorway into a commons area where two concession machines stood. Snacks and sodas. On the wall was a blackboard full of memos. Then another crossroads. To the left were dark offices. The sounds were coming from his right. Everything within him told him to follow the noise. Helena needed his help. But he hesitated, his scratched arm burning like an angry reminder.

"Milk, report."

"Nothin's happenin', brother. All's quiet. Over."

"Okay, I'm going deeper. Pretty deserted so far. I can hear voices in the back to my right. Over."

"I'll come in if you need me, Eagle. Over."

"Negative, Milk. Watch that door. No one else can see anything through that fog. You've got my back. Over."

"Roger."

Nathan took two steps right, but something told him to look left, through the office windows. The blood in his veins turned to ice. A computer monitor had been left on in one office, illuminating the wall. He wanted to follow the noise to the right, but he couldn't resist what he saw: his own photograph on the wall.

Sidestepping to the left, he entered a narrow hallway that led to two offices. Their nearest walls were giant windows. Ducking into the first office, he squinted at a tack board filled with pictures and flowcharts, typed and scribbled notes. He turned on a desk lamp and angled it at another wall with even more pictures. Shaking his head, he tried to decipher the writing, but it was in Malay. The pictures said enough.

He kept his gun trained on the door and touched his mic.

"Come in, Scooter. This is Eagle. Over."

"Scooter here. Go."

"Take over Milk's position ASAP. Milk, when you're relieved, come to me. Left through the doors. You'll find me. Copy? Over."

"I copy. Coming pronto. Over."

"Bruno, the gatehouse is coming to life by now. You and Scooter put them back to sleep. Over."

"Roger."

"Chloe, how long till that fog machine turns off? Over."

"The machine'll click off in about five minutes. The fog will dissipate after that. Over."

"Listen closely, Chloe. I'm looking at a wall and a half of our faces. Photos, notes, you, and the whole team. It's not just you and me coming to visit. They got us at the hotel and around the city. Over."

"Explain. Over."

"Pictures of everyone. Leaving the hotel, walking on the street in the market, even in the taxi. Nothing left to explain. Over."

"Do they have Corban?"

He searched the tack board and the wall.

"Negative. But they have a lot of writing. Charts. Like they were trying to figure out what we were up to. And a hierarchy tree. They know I'm in charge. Over."

"Are we expected tonight? Over."

"I don't think so. No welcome committee so far. We weren't supposed to see this. Over."

Nathan tensed as Milk came into sight, then they both relaxed. Milk took up a post in the narrow hallway.

"Milk's with me. I'm taking everything I see, then going for Helena. Over."

Tucking his pistol into his belt, Nathan used both hands to tear everything off the walls, paying no mind to tacks and staples.

"Scooter, this is Bruno. You see what I see? Over."

"Got 'em," Scooter informed. A few seconds passed. "Gatehouse sleeping again. Over."

"Nice shooting."

Moving fast, Nathan had everything from the walls in his hands, roughly stacked. He rolled it all up and found tape to secure it. Then he went to Milk and stuffed the roll of papers down the back of his shirt.

"Why me?" Milk joked.

"In case I don't make it out. I'm going into that section. Hear the voices?"

"Eagle, this is Chloe."

"Go, Chloe."

"I've been thinking. This stinks. Maybe you were right about Helena. She was using you . . . all of us. Call this recon. Let's pull out. Over."

"Chloe, we've come this far. Even you said—"

"Eagle, I understand. I don't like it either. Maybe we cared too much. Remember your arm? Over."

"What's she talkin' about, Eagle?" Scooter asked. "Let's do this!"

Pressing his fingers against his scratched arm, Nathan felt tenderness and swelling he hadn't noticed before. Infection was setting in. He shook his head and prayed for guidance. Nothing made sense. And Chloe had fought the hardest to get Helena out!

"Nathan, what is she talkin' about?" Milk pressed for more information. "Are we pullin' out or not?"

"Chloe, are you at the van? Over."

"Affirmative."

"Memphis, get off the tower. Good thing we packed up already. They would've been waiting for us back at the hotel. Over."

"Roger, Eagle Eyes. Memphis descending. Over."

"I'm going deeper. Milk's my backup. Scooter, you're the standstill. We'll be coming out fast. Let's do this quick. Over."

"Roger. Let's do it!" Scooter cheered.

"Anything goes bad in there, you get those papers out to Chloe," he ordered as he moved around Milk.

"Got it."

Taking a deep breath, Nathan moved out, fast and

smooth. The bad guys knew who they were, so there was little mystery. Now they were the Flash and Bang Team again. Go in, cause a ruckus, and pull out.

Working silently, Nathan followed the sounds through a string of offices to the right of the foyer. Determined and focused, he didn't bump a wastebasket or even brush against a desk. He moved into a game room just as one guard hit a cue ball on the pool table. Another guard was sitting on a bench against the wall. And there was Helena, on his lap, laughing as he played with her hair.

The guard playing pool looked up in time to receive two pellets. He crashed against the wall, the stick clattering to the floor. The other guard pushed Helena off his lap as he rose and scratched for his sidearm buckled low in a holster. Nathan covered his face with pellets. The man managed to clear his pistol, then fell back into his chair, the pistol dangling from his fingers.

Nathan rushed toward Helena, but she moved away from him, keeping the pool table between them. They had dressed her seductively in a low-cut blouse, and her make-up was on so thick, she looked like a clown.

"Helena! Come on! I'm getting you out of here!"

"What're you doing here, Nathan?" she said, her perfect English a shock to him. It was then that he saw the derringer in her hand. The miniature two-barrel was nearly concealed in her palm. All Nathan could do was stare in disbelief as she raised it and shot him in the left thigh.

The small caliber bullet didn't pass through. Like shrapnel, it hit bone and tore tissue. He fell over, not fighting to stand, as Helena screamed orders in Malay.

Boots sounded from a deeper hallway. Nathan heard rifle rounds being chambered. Gritting his teeth, he pulled himself under the pool table for some cover. Never would he surrender.

"This is Nathan. I'm down! Pull out! Get to Corban! It's an ambush! Helena's one of them. Scatter! Pull out!"

"We're not leaving you!" Scooter fumed.

"That's an order! Milk, get out! Bruno, cover—"

Hands grasped his legs and dragged him out from under the table. Helena yelled more orders and pointed outside. Nathan shot two in the head before a rifle stock pounded him in the face, smashing his nose and drowning him in blood. Three were on him, punching, and kicking. By instinct, he fought back, kicking even with his injured leg. Sweeping them off their feet, he wrestled with them until one came to his senses and shot Nathan again.

As Nathan slipped out of consciousness, he heard gunfire in the courtyard. Milk's screams cut through the foggy darkness, and a body thudded to the stoney pavement.

Then Nathan was still.

t

Helena Rauch stepped off her chartered jet into the Mediterranean air that blew in from Egypt's Nile delta. As the Alexandrian airport bustled around her, she breathed a sigh of relief. The flight from Malaysia had been long, but her mission to entrap the COIL operatives had lasted weeks longer than anticipated. They'd finally taken the bait.

The whir of a hydraulic lift drew her attention. She turned and watched the tail of her jet open to unload a shipping container. The airport personnel unstrapped the container and rolled it down a ramp onto a flatbed cart. Her Malaysian bodyguard, a confidant from the prison, was greeted by an Egyptian airport official. They both gestured for her to follow them to the nearest hangar. Helena let them go ahead as she watched her precious cargo ease through the giant hangar door.

The Malaysian mission hadn't gone completely the way she and her cohorts had planned, but Helena hadn't walked away empty-handed. She had expected the COIL operatives to rescue her from the Malaysian prison, but her ambush hadn't been as prepared as she thought. COIL had taken over half the prison with their toy guns before her high-priced Malaysian guards could react. In the end, however, she'd captured Nathan Isaacson, the one he called Milk, and a Chinese operative nicknamed Toad. Helena's initial objective had been to capture Corban Dowler, but he hadn't involved himself in the operation as much as she'd wished.

Still, the Christians who played spy games had been crippled by their efforts to rescue her, which was what Abaddon had wanted. She couldn't help but smile at her good fortune. And the Malaysian government had been so cooperative! Corban Dowler hadn't suspected a thing, and now she had three of his men.

"Helena."

Spinning around, she faced her lover, the beautiful Branden Fairchild. He opened his arms, his eyes warm and inviting. She ran to him and they embraced. They hadn't been together since before the Malaysian operation began.

"You made it!" she cried. "It's been too long! Did you get Corban?"

"No, but the next best thing—his family." He held her at arm's length. "I've left them in Jersey with Velt. How many did you capture?"

"Three. Nathan Isaacson and two others. We wounded the rest who came into the compound, though."

"Is our client here?" Branden gazed toward the hangar. "Washing my hands of these Christians you captured can't happen quickly enough! It was great that you connected with Victor Ivanvolt. He'll find a way to use them against Corban and COIL. Abaddon must be so proud of you!"

"I didn't think we'd find a man who hates COIL as much

as we do! Come. Ivanvolt should be here already. We're to meet in the hangar."

…✝…

The two walked hand in hand to the open door. Branden anticipated meeting the captives that Helena had flown in from the Pacific Rim. Both of their missions had been successful. They hungered for what Abaddon might have for them next.

In the hangar, Branden and Helena approached a black limousine parked behind the storage container. The limo driver stepped from the driver's seat, greeting them with a slight bow. He was a dark-skinned, middle-aged man in a Russian-tailored suit. After opening the limo's rear door, he stood rigidly at attention.

Branden's eyes sparkled with glee as a short, aging Russian climbed out of the luxury car. The man's goatee was perfectly fashioned to a point, a style representing a lost Soviet era, and his gray pinstriped suit was perfectly pressed. Flashy gold cuff links distracted the eye. He glared at them through thick glasses topped by bushy eyebrows.

The stranger didn't greet Branden with a friendly smile, but Branden didn't care. Like dozens of people Branden had used before, the Russian would serve his purpose against COIL.

Helena stepped forward.

"So glad to meet you again, Mr. Ivanvolt. Branden Fairchild, this is Victor Ivanvolt. We can't thank you enough for your support, sir. We've all heard of your success in ridding your region of the Christians."

"It's a pleasure, sir," Branden said. "Helena mentioned

that you met a few days ago, but she talks about you like she's known you for years."

Victor Ivanvolt, the renowned Russian assassin, embraced Branden roughly, each exchanging the traditional kiss on both cheeks.

"I also have waited for such an opportunity," Victor said, his English heavily accented. "Corban Dowler has been an adversary for many years. Show what you have brought me."

"Over here." Helena led the way to the storage container's door. Nearby, her Malaysian bodyguard dismissed the Egyptian official, then walked to the container, awaiting instructions. Helena nodded at him. "Open it."

Standing beside Victor, Branden watched the man out of the corner of his eye. There was something familiar about the Russian—the way he walked, or talked, or . . . something. Branden glanced over his shoulder at Victor's limo, but the driver was nowhere in sight.

"Have we met before, Mr. Ivanvolt?" Branden asked. "Perhaps in Poland? Have you spent time in Warsaw?"

"I visited many years ago. Do you gamble?"

"No, that's not it." Branden frowned and shook his head. "How will you use the captives against Corban Dowler? Just to spite him, I regret not killing them myself, but I'm sure you have a plan."

"Ah, I have a delicious plan." Victor assured him with a sinister chuckle. "Corban Dowler will trade himself for any one of his operatives, yet you have more than one, yes?"

"Yes, three. Helena was quite successful."

The storage container door swung open on squeaky hinges. The Malaysian attendant placed his hand inside his jacket where his firearm was tucked, but the container's occupants were in no shape to resist or attack. Branden's heart skipped a beat in delight as he laid eyes on Nathan and the two others. He recognized them from the photographs Helena had sent him. All three COIL operatives were wounded, their clothes matted with blood and filth. Surprisingly, the past week in the box hadn't killed them. Branden noticed Victor's face was filled with similar pleasure.

The three supported one another, even in their desperate state, as they rose to their knees. They grimaced at the first light they'd seen in a week.

"They have a strong odor," Victor said. "How do I know they are worth anything? You are certain they are COIL agents? They do not appear to be anyone of significance."

"The big one is Nathan Isaacson, Corban Dowler's primary Special Forces leader," Helena said. "The other two are commandos on the same team. All were handpicked by Corban himself. And you are right, he would no doubt trade himself to free even one. If you hate Corban as much as you claim, they are the key to his heart and operation."

"Very well. What is your asking price?" Victor asked. "I have other business to attend."

"Consider them a gift from Abaddon," Branden said.

"Abaddon? This man, I do not know. I do not accept gifts from one I do not know. I have met with you today only because we share this common foe: Corban Dowler."

"Mr. Ivanvolt, if you despise the Christians, you and

Abaddon are already companions, not strangers." Branden cast a worried glance at Helena. "Use these three for your purposes. The sooner we humble Corban and bring his organization to ruin, the sooner our world will be free of his hypocrisy and other warring faiths. We cannot do it alone. Together we can defeat them."

Turning, Victor faced Branden directly.

"I want to meet this Abaddon if we have this much in common. You must set up an appointment."

Branden frowned. Victor's eyes . . . they looked like . . .

"Abaddon doesn't meet with anyone face to face." Helena answered for Branden as she gave him a nudge. "Accept this gesture as our way of saying we would like to work with you more in the future."

Victor and Branden's eyes were locked. One corner of Victor's mouth turned up as Branden's mouth went dry.

"What's going on, Branden?" Helena whispered.

"Helena, how did you make contact with this man?" he asked without looking away from Victor. Branden clenched his teeth to stop his trembling jaw.

"He contacted me, but I spoke to our friend in Syria. What's the matter? Everyone knows Victor Ivanvolt. You know all he's done in Russia for our cause."

"If you touch me," Branden snarled at Victor, "your family dies!"

"Branden! I apologize, Mr. Ivanvolt! He's been under a lot of tension recently."

"Oh, you don't need to apologize, Brandon," Victor said calmly. "It is I who should be apologizing. I continue to ruin your plans, don't I, Branden? You might want to know that

Velt is in custody, and my family is safe."

Taking a step back, Helena's bewildered eyes darted from man to man.

"Branden?"

The Malaysian escort closed the storage container and backed away.

In his blinding anger, Branden didn't think about what Victor was doing as he slipped off his glasses and, while maintaining eye contact with Branden, pulled the glasses apart into three pieces.

"It's a hard lesson to learn," Corban Dowler stated, his voice no longer disguised, "that darkness will be completely defeated by the Light." The frame of his glasses emitted a thin red laser beam, which he aimed at the Malaysian. "He's the only one who's armed, right? I checked with customs."

An instant later, a tiny dart shot out from the earpiece section of the glasses and lodged into the Malaysian's chest muscle. He flinched at the sting, drew his sidearm, and then collapsed. Helena screamed and fought to catch her breath as Egyptian police sirens squealed in the distance.

"No! It can't be!" Helena snarled and pointed at Corban. "This can't be! I checked him out, Branden, just like you taught me! It's not my fault!"

Branden's lower lip trembled in his fury. His fists clenched and unclenched. He needed Abaddon's help, but neither Abaddon nor the voice from his childhood was anywhere near.

"No one has ever beaten me," Branden whispered, "until you."

"It wasn't me," Corban stated. "It was never me. I just stumble around a step at a time. Jesus Christ is who makes my steps worth anything. It's He who is the Unbeaten One."

Three Egyptian police vehicles pulled into the hangar's entrance. Half a dozen officials jogged up to the storage container.

"Sorry we're late, Mr. Ivanvolt," a police sergeant said. "Are these the ones?"

"You can't charge me with anything here," Branden said. "We just arrived in Egypt. I've committed no crimes!"

One officer opened the storage container as the others seized Helena and Branden.

"Human trafficking and kidnapping are crimes, Branden Fairchild," Corban said, "even in Egypt. But you probably won't be here long. As I understand it, the United States has an extradition order already filed for you two. Give my thanks to Chip, won't you?"

A strange calm came over Branden. The Egyptian officials hesitated, handcuffs at the ready, waiting for Corban's word. Instead of surrendering, however, Branden reached out and grabbed Helena by the neck, then hurled her at the Egyptians. Helena screamed as she collided with the police.

Branden kicked at Corban and dashed for the limousine. With a quick look back, he saw the sergeant push Helena aside and draw his sidearm, aiming straight at Branden. But Corban raised his arms and jumped in front of the sergeant.

"Don't shoot! Let him go!"

The Egyptian officer held his fire as Branden tugged the limo door open.

"Let me go, Corban?" Branden laughed and shook his head. "You Christians are so weak."

The passenger door on the other side of the limo opened, and the chauffeur stood there, aiming an NL-2 machine pistol at Branden. Branden shrieked as he realized his plan was foiled. The driver pulled the trigger, peppering Branden with a dozen pellets.

"That should do it, Zvi," Corban said as he approached. Branden slumped to the hangar floor, one leg still inside the limo. "If we are weak, Branden, then what does that make you?" Branden's eyes closed.

...✝...

An officer handcuffed Helena while others picked up her Malaysian bodyguard. Though Branden was unconscious, the look of shock remained on his face as they carried him past Corban to a waiting car.

"You don't know who he is!" Helena yelled at the police as they pulled her away. "He's Corban Dowler! Corban, you may have stopped us, but you cannot stop Abaddon!"

"Right now? Perhaps not, but eventually, he'll fall. Jesus Christ wins it all in the end." Corban nodded at the sergeant. "Take them away. Thanks for your help. I've got it from here."

"It's okay, Zvi!" Corban said as he tugged off his disguise. "Give me a hand."

Zvi Azmaveth stood up from behind the limo as he tucked the NL-2 into his waistband.

"Just don't tell Chloe that you pulled me off a diamond

deal in Cairo to play your chauffeur." The man chuckled and walked over to the storage container. "She likes to think she's the only one who stares danger in the face."

Corban and Zvi stepped into the container. Nathan, Milk, and Toad tried to stand to greet their boss, but they could only look up from their hands and knees.

"Come on, boys. We're going home."

Zvi took Milk by the arm while Corban and Toad supported Nathan. The operatives were wounded and dehydrated, but Nathan looked to be in the worst shape.

"I guess . . . I don't need to tell you . . . Operation Helena was . . . an ambush," Nathan whispered hoarsely to Corban.

"The devil's getting desperate to get rid of us." Corban helped his men into the limo. "We can expect more of the same until Christ returns."

"What about Abaddon?" Milk asked. "Did we flush him out?"

"Not yet, but darkness can't hide forever."

Using binoculars, Corban studied Heathrow Airport nearly a mile away. He stood that morning on the roof of a five-story apartment building in London, England, the damp air penetrating his blue blazer.

Just twelve hours ago, he'd posed as Victor Ivanvolt and taken back his three COIL agents from Branden Fairchild. After leaving Egypt, they'd flown to England to make sure Nathan received prompt medical attention for his two gunshot wounds. It had already been a week since the Malaysian incident. Nathan was quite weak and his condition was quickly deteriorating.

But Nathan's next round of treatment would have to wait. Even now, he and the other two agents were downstairs in a friend's apartment, the foreign hospital too dangerous with Abaddon still on the prowl. Nathan would have to hold on until America—if they even made it to America.

Still peering through the binoculars, Corban could see their chartered jet parked halfway in the hangar. A mechanic on the tarmac had called it luck when he'd noticed a mechanical problem on the jet during refueling. Definitely sabotage. The jet would've never made the flight over the Atlantic.

Luck? Corban thought not. It was God's continued watch-care over His servants. It was grace—until their loving Lord called them out of this evil world.

Corban felt a chill and looked over his shoulder. He was still alone on the roof. Perhaps the thought of Abaddon made him tense. Though the COIL office was running unhindered again, there still were no leads on the demonic mastermind. They couldn't be too careful; Abaddon would surely try something again. COIL was too effective against darkness to be ignored.

His satellite phone rang. It was Chloe. He paused in thought before answering.

Chloe had returned to the States a week earlier with the rest of the Flash and Bang Team. No doubt she felt responsible for the Malaysian ambush during Operation Helena. Even though Chloe had misread the situation, Corban wasn't angry. She would be a better agent now because she'd been targeted. They would all be wiser next time. God helped His people to grow through adversity.

And the world would continue to turn, Corban decided with a calming resolve. COIL would continue to stand and seek other like-minded servants to be lights in the darkness. If not Abaddon, there would be another foe, but in the end, Jesus Christ would destroy the darkness entirely.

"Lord God," Corban prayed, "please help my faith."

Corban answered his phone. Another crisis needed his attention.

…✝…

Luigi Putelli stood in the moon shadows of the elm tree across the street from the new Dowler residence. He'd not fully healed from the bullet wounds, but that hadn't stopped him from finding the family.

The Italian ex-assassin pushed two more sticks of gum between his teeth as he watched the house—for only one reason now. Men like Corban who stood firm would always have enemies. He'd failed Corban in the past. When Corban needed help again, Luigi would be ready.

And by watching Corban, Luigi hoped to learn and understand more about Corban's God. Anyone who had escaped death as often as Corban and his family must have Someone besides Luigi watching over them.

Just maybe that Someone had been watching over Luigi as well . . .

According to **Prisoneralert.com**, a ministry of Voice of the Martyrs, Christians are being persecuted for their faith in more than forty nations around the world today. "In some of these nations, it is illegal to own a Bible, to share your faith in Christ, change your faith, or teach your children about Jesus. Those who boldly follow Christ—in spite of government edict or radical opposition—can face harassment, arrest, torture, and even death. Yet Christians continue to meet for worship and to witness for Christ, and the church in restricted nations is growing."

Today, several relief organizations come to the aid of Christians in oppressed countries, as did the fictitious organization, COIL, in this book, *Dark Liaison*. Sometimes these groups work in the light of day to raise funds to help the persecuted or needy. Some print Bibles to ship or smuggle across closed borders. Other ministries help maintain hidden safe houses or secret printing presses in spiritually oppressed countries. Still others are called to work in the shadows, but no less in the Light of the Gospel.

One such ministry invaluable to suffering Christians today is **Voice of the Martyrs (VOM)** (persecution.com). They're a powerful tool used by God, not only bringing relief and the Word of God to the needy, but also bringing souls to Him.

VOM serves as a voice to the world to make sure those who are suffering for Christ are not forgotten. They also spread the gospel to restricted nations. As VOM shares on their **Bibles Unbound Covert Operations** website

(biblesunbound.com), it "provides New Testaments into closed or hostile areas where mailing Bibles is not possible.

In these dangerous, hostile, or closed areas, Bibles are delivered by faithful, courageous believers willing to risk all in order to ensure Bibles get into the hands of those who desire them."

For decades, VOM has been active in North Korea, launching tens of thousands of "Scripture Balloons," helium-filled balloons printed with Scriptures and other gospel messages. And in recent years, VOM worked to collect as many fax numbers as possible inside North Korea and has sent weekly faxes containing Christian messages and Scripture verses on love and forgiveness.

The Voice of the Martyrs is currently sending Action Packs to Pakistan, Iraq, and Sudan. "They distribute your Action Pack along with a Bible or Gospel storybook to the country that currently needs Action Packs the most." Visit **persecution.com/actionpacks/** for info and a list of suggested items to encourage suffering believers.

VOM actively supports Christians in China through Christmas Care Packs and Christian literature. They also have the Blanket and a Bible ministry outreach to the Sudanese. The ministry has even partnered with a pilot who flies over FARC-controlled areas of Colombia, dropping small packages attached to parachutes. The packages float into FARC camps and villages, each containing Christian books and a solar-powered radio pre-tuned to a Christian station. Before the parachute is dropped, the radio is turned on so even if the chute catches in a tree, someone will hear the radio and climb to retrieve it. Visit the VOM website at **www.persecution.com** to learn more about ministry opportunities in many countries.

The following can be found on the FAQ page on the **Prisoner Alert** website:

VOM's five main purposes are based on Hebrews 13:3:

1. To encourage and empower Christians to fulfill the Great Commission in areas of the world where they are persecuted for their involvement in propagating the gospel of Jesus Christ. We accomplish this by providing Bibles, literature, radio broadcasts, and other forms of aid.

2. To give relief to the families of Christian martyrs in these areas of the world.

3. To equip local Christians to love and win to Christ their enemies who are opposed to the gospel in countries where believers are actively persecuted for their Christian witness.

4. To undertake projects of encouragement, helping believers rebuild their lives and Christian witness in countries that have formerly suffered Communist oppression.

5. To emphasize the fellowship of all believers by informing the world of atrocities committed against Christians and by remembering their courage and faith.

~

To sign up for a **free monthly newsletter**, or the **free book**, ***Tortured for Christ***, by VOM founder Richard Wurmbrand, visit **persecution.com**.

~~

Be-A-Voice Network

Become an advocate voice for the persecuted church in your church and community by becoming a member of VOM's Be-A-Voice Network. This network offers volunteer opportunities to people like you and me to help our persecuted brothers and sisters around the world. If you are willing to PRAY, WRITE, or SHARE with others, then the Be-A-Voice Network is for you! See the **beavoice.com** website for ways you can help persecuted Christians.

~

Note from Author D.I. Telbat:

I'm so thankful for Voice of the Martyrs and many other like-minded organizations, and countless individuals who reach out to our suffering brothers and sisters. If we can't participate in these activities firsthand, we can take part through prayer and giving when and where we can.

Pray for the many believers who face persecution. They need God's protection, provision, and strength. And pray that God will use these afflicted believers to reach even their tormentors with the Gospel of Christ.
–D.I. Telbat

ACKNOWLEDGEMENTS

Without the generous and extensive help
and input of many people, this book
would have remained in the file cabinet.
I especially thank my parents,
whose encouraging support
through the years is unequaled;
Jamie and Marilyn, for their editing insights;
Susan Hughes of MyIndependentEditor.com,
whose professional vision was exceptional;
Connie, whose instruction
I'm still soaking in after so many years;
Kim, for her contributions regarding Braille;
and Dee, my assistant and manager, whose
valuable knowledge and dependable attention
has left me choking from exhaustion,
yet yearning for more.

COIL – Commission of International Laborers – Christian Relief Organization.

      --Location: Manhattan, New York City. Other offices: Moscow, Nanjing, Berlin, Guatemala City

      --Founder: Corban James Dowler

      --Funding: Author A.B. Leever (11%), Contributions (14%), Unknown (75%)

      --Directives: Further the Gospel of Christ; Provide early warning and extraction for Christians in jeopardy; Screen and train COIL caseworkers and operatives.

DGSE – French Secret Service (Directorate-General for External Security)

Mossad – Israeli Secret Service (Institute for Intelligence and Special Operations)

NL-1 – COIL's non-lethal air pistol, single shot firing capacity; 30 rounds, CO2 cartridge; Maximum effective range: 15 yards; Pellets: water soluble, tranquillizer effective time: 20 minutes.

NL-2 – COIL's non-lethal machine pistol; fully automatic or single shot firing capacity; 250 rounds, CO2 cartridge; Cycle rate: 600 rounds per minute; Maximum effective range: 50 yards; Pellets: see NL-1 specs.

NL-3 – COIL's non-lethal assault rifle; fully automatic, 5 round burst, or single shot firing capacity; Cycle rate: 600 rounds per minute; Maximum effective range: 100 yards; Pellets: see NL-1 specs.

ABOUT THE AUTHOR

D.I. (David) Telbat is a Christian author best known for his clean Suspenseful Fiction with a Faith Focus. This includes his bestselling and award-winning *COIL Series*, *Steadfast Series*, *Last Dawn Series,* and other Christian Suspense and End Times novels.

David studied writing in school and worked for a time in the newspaper field. Getting into serious trouble with the law as a young man became a turning point in his life. The Lord used that experience to draw David into a personal relationship with Him. Re-focusing his life for Christ, he now seeks to honor God with his life and writing by doing what he loves most—writing and Christian ministry. At this time, D.I. Telbat lives on the West Coast, but keeps his home base in the Northwest US. You can find his complete list of books and bio at:

https://books2read.com/DITelbat/.

Through the bi-weekly D.I. Telbat Newsletter, David offers his free Christian short stories, Author Reflection articles, or his Novel Update News. Many D.I. Telbat stories and books are about persecuted Christians—their sacrifices and their rescues. To subscribe to his bi-weekly newsletter, as well as receive exclusive subscriber gifts, visit his author site underlined above, or at https://ditelbat.com. Also, he has other items of interest for readers on his Book Funnel page found at https://books.bookfunnel.com/for-all-readers.

Please leave your comments wherever you bought this book. Reviews greatly help authors, and David Telbat would love to hear your thoughts on his works. He takes reader reviews into consideration as he makes future publishing plans.

There is no redemption without sacrifice.